THE
MOTHER'S
RECOMPENSE

EDITH WHARTON

Desolation is a delicate thing.
—Shelley

INTRODUCTION BY
LOUIS AUCHINCLOSS

Scribner Paperback Fiction
Published by Simon & Schuster

SCRIBNER PAPERBACK FICTION
Simon & Schuster Inc.
Rockefeller Center
1230 Avenue of the Americas
New York, NY 10020

First Scribner Paperback Fiction edition 1996
SCRIBNER PAPERBACK FICTION and design are trademarks of Macmillan Library Reference USA, Inc. under license by Simon & Schuster, the publisher of this work.

7 9 10 8 6

Library of Congress Cataloging-in-Publication Data
Wharton, Edith, 1862–1937.
The mother's recompence / Edith Wharton. —1st Scribner
pbk. fiction ed.
p. cm.
I. Title.
[PS3545.H16M6   1996]
813'.52—dc20   96-24304
CIP

ISBN 978-0-684-82531-1

My excuses are due to the decorous shade of Grace Aguilar, loved of our grandmothers, for deliberately appropriating, and applying to uses so different, the title of one of the most admired of her tales.

E.W.

Introduction

In 1925, the year in which *The Mother's Recompense* was published, Edith Wharton was sixty-three, and the *oeuvre* for which she is famous was almost complete. She had made what was to be her last trip to her native land two years before, and although she always had a steady stream of American visitors to her two houses in France, she was beginning to lose touch with the United States of the prohibition era. Her mood of nostalgia for the brownstone Manhattan of her childhood, in which she now espied virtues that had been less apparent to her younger eyes, had produced some of her finest fiction: *The Age of Innocence* (1920) and *Old New York* (1924). Now she was ready again to try her hand at the contemporary American scene; it was to be the last time that she did so successfully.

The Mother's Recompense opens on the Riviera, where Edith Wharton lived in winter, and never were her descriptive powers more brilliantly used than in establishing the small, petty, socially stained, expatriate community of gamblers, alcoholics and women with a past, in which Kate Clephane, outlawed by respectable New York for her desertion of her husband and infant daughter, has sought a precarious refuge. The sudden translation of the heroine back to Manhattan and prosperity when her unforgiving mother-in-law dies and her now wealthy grown-up daughter sends for her is done with superb dramatic effect. For Kate, expecting difficulty, is at first enraptured, then simply relieved and at last disillusioned by the bland atmosphere of forgiveness, or rather oblivion, in which her old fault seems to have been lost. Are there *no* standards left, she muses, looking about her at the casual manners, the rackety parties. She almost misses the iron which had branded her. After all, at least in those old cruel days, some people had cared about something.

In an earlier story *Autres Temps* . . . (1916), set before the war, Edith Wharton had treated the same theme with a difference. Mrs. Lidcote, who has, like Kate Clephane, deserted a spouse and daughter, returns to New York from the Florence of her exile to give her now adult child moral support in what she supposes to be a repetition of her own sad story. Leila has left her husband to marry her lover. But Mrs. Lidcote discovers that Leila can do so with impunity and that her social position, if anything, is actually enhanced by the more popular second spouse. The bewildered mother fancies for a brief moment that her own case will now be included in the general amnesty, but here she is wrong, and she finds, when one of her own contemporaries comes to dine with Leila, that her own dinner is served upstairs on a tray. She learns the grim rule that society does not revise its judgments for those already condemned. That Leila can do what was not allowed her mother cannot alter the record or suspend the latter's sentence.

Kate Clephane, of course, finds just the opposite: the record has now been wiped clean. Her trial will be of a very different sort, with the moral judgment supplied not by a condemnatory society but by a condemnatory Kate. It is a neat twist. Kate discovers that the radiant, brilliant daughter, whom she immediately adores and idolizes, is irretrievably in love with a former lover of Kate's, Chris Fenno, a war hero but a bit of a drifter and dilettante, who, if not actually mercenary, will find Anne Clephane's wealth extremely handy. Yet Chris's flaws would be as nothing to Kate had she never met him and if she did not love him still. Nor are they anything to the rest of the Clephane world, ignorant as it is of the old affair. Chris is considered quite good enough for Anne. If the match is to be broken off, it must be done by Kate alone.

The central problem for the reader of today—and it may well also have been the same for a reader in 1925—is that Kate is making too much of the circumstance. Her horror approaches the horror of Oedipus when he learns that he has married his mother. Kate, like Hamlet in T. S. Eliot's essay, "is dominated by an emotion which is inexpressible because it is in excess of the facts as they appear." Hamlet's mother is not an adequate equivalent for the disgust that she occasions in her son, nor is the prospect of a sexual union between Anne and Chris Fenno sufficiently revolting to cause Kate such trauma.

To begin with, Anne does not know of her mother's love affair, nor need she ever discover it. And Chris, who has not been aware that Anne is Kate's daughter when they meet and fall in love, shows every proper emotion of shock and dismay when he learns the truth. Under the circumstances—and considering the years that have passed—what truly loving mother would deliberately destroy her daughter's happiness over such a scruple? In the film *The Graduate*, where the same situation is presented in our times, the mother's frantic efforts to prevent her daughter's marriage are shown as motivated by jealousy. But with Kate, Edith Wharton does not consider such motivations as necessarily evil. Jealousy is simply part and parcel of a situation that is so inherently vile that it must be aborted at any price:

> A dark fermentation boiled up into her brain; every thought and feeling was clogged with thick entangling memories . . . Jealous? Was she jealous of her daughter? Was she physically jealous? Was that the real secret of her repugnance, her instinctive revulsion? Was that why she had felt from the first as if some incestuous horror hung between them?
>
> She did not know—it was impossible to analyze her anguish. She knew only that she must fly from it, fly as far as she could from the setting of these last indelible impressions. How had she ever imagined that she could keep her place at Anne's side—that she could either outstay Chris, or continue to live under the same roof with them?

Kate goes at last to a minister and tells him her problem, pretending it is that of a friend. The cleric is candid about what he thinks of a marriage between the daughter and lover under such circumstances: he calls it an "abomination." But after a brief reflection he counsels against what he calls "sterile pain," the pain that would be caused by the revelation of old facts that cannot now be changed and need never be known. Kate, however, is still not convinced and continues to hope that, even if she does not adopt the extreme remedy of telling her daughter all, Chris will ultimately not have the gall—or the nerve—to go through with the marriage. When he shows no disposition to back out, the question is squarely put up to her: will she speak out and ruin her daughter's life?

Edith Wharton pulled herself out of the difficulty that was beginning to engulf her plot with an excellent stratagem. Kate is suddenly faced with her daughter's proposal that they continue to live together even after the marriage. Agitated by the sight of Anne's and Chris's embraces, Kate betrays too much emotion and is unable to furnish a credible excuse for her refusal. At this, a horrible suspicion enters Anne's mind. She cries out:

"You don't hate him? But then you're in love with him—you're in love with him, and I've known it all along!"

Faced with an accusation that is to her so much less terrible than the full truth, Kate regains her powers of dissimulation and treats her daughter's outburst as simply nerves. She then gives the totally acceptable reason that she herself is planning to marry. Fred Landers, an old and faithful beau, has indeed proposed to her. The situation is saved, and Kate knows now that she has been saved from a graver error.

Yet having got out of the Eliot–Hamlet trap, what does Edith Wharton do but plunge right back into it? For when Fred Landers repeats the proposal that Kate, contrary to what she has told Anne, had not accepted, she turns it down. Why? Because she has felt obliged first to tell him about Chris, and he has been visibly shocked, though not so much so as to rescind his offer. What he has minded, moreover, is not the triangular aspect of Kate's problem but the fact that she should ever have been the mistress of such a man as Fenno. This puts his agitation on the simple ground of jealousy of her past, which any woman should be able to cope with.

What then is Kate's real reason for refusing him? That he *ought* to disapprove of her! "He had overcome his strongest feelings, his most deep-rooted repugnance; he had held out his hand to her, in the extremity of her need, across the whole width of his traditions and his convictions; and she had blest him for it and stood fast on her own side." She had shut away "in a little space of peace and light the best thing that had ever happened to her."

But if that isn't sterile pain, I should like to know what is.

Edith Wharton took this conclusion of her tale very seriously indeed, and was indignant with critics who wrote that her novel should have ended happily. "*Should* have!" she echoed in derision. She insisted that the clue was in the quotation from Shelley on the title page: "Desolation is a delicate thing." But I impenitently fail to see why Fred Landers and Kate Clephane would not have happier and better lives married to each other. He would have had occasional twinges at the thought of her in Chris's arms, and their visits to the Fennos would have uneasy moments, but what of that? Had Edith Wharton herself wished to marry her old bachelor friend, Walter Berry, would his disgust at her long past affair with the philandering, bisexual blackmailed Morton Fullerton (and Berry *would* have been disgusted) have stopped her for a minute? I doubt it. What she was really bringing out in Kate was the latter's belated stand against the tolerances of post-World War I American society which in her view had reached a pitch of blandness that threatened to destroy all the old standards of taste and morality. This anger at the shape that Edith Wharton thought she saw her country taking was to make her shrill and flaw her later work. *The Mother's Recompense* is really the last of her major fictions.

Louis Auchincloss

THE
MOTHER'S
RECOMPENSE

BOOK ONE

I

Kate Clephane was wakened, as usual, by the slant of Riviera sun across her bed. It was the thing she liked best about her shabby cramped room in the third-rate Hôtel de Minorque et de l'Univers: that the morning sun came in at her window, and yet that it didn't come too early.

No more sunrises for Kate Clephane. They were associated with too many lost joys—coming home from balls where one had danced one's self to tatters, or from suppers where one had lingered, counting one's winnings (it was wonderful, in the old days, how often she had won, or friends had won for her, staking a *louis* just for fun, and cramming her hands with thousand franc bills); associated, too, with the scramble up hill through the whitening gray of the garden, flicked by scented shrubs, caught on perfidious prickles, up to the shuttered villa askew on its heat-soaked rock—and then, at the door, in the laurustinus-shade that smelt of honey, that unexpected kiss (well honestly, yes, unexpected, since it had long been settled that one was to remain "just friends"); and the pulling away from an insistent arm, and the one more pressure on hers of lips young enough to be fresh after a night of drinking and play and more drinking. And she had never let Chris come in with her at that hour, no, not once, though at the time there was only Julie the cook in the house, and goodness knew . . . Oh, but she had always had her pride—people ought to remember *that* when they said such things about her . . .

That was what the sunrise reminded Kate Clephane of—as she supposed it did most women of forty-two or so (or was it really forty-four last week?). For nearly twenty years now she had lived chiefly with women of her own kind, and she no longer very sincerely believed there were any others, that is to say among women properly so called. Her female world was made up of three categories: frumps, hypocrites and the "good sort"—like herself. After all, the last was the one she preferred to be in.

Not that she could not picture another life—if only one had met the right man at the right hour. She remembered her one week—that tiny little week of seven days, just six years ago—when she and Chris had gone together to a lost place in Normandy where there wasn't a railway within ten miles, and you had to drive in the farmer's cart to the farm-house smothered in apple-blossoms; and Chris and she had gone off every morning for the whole day, while he sketched by willowy river-banks, and under the flank of mossy village churches; and every day for seven days she had watched the farmyard life waking at dawn under their windows, while she dashed herself with cold water and did her hair and touched up her face before he was awake, because the early light is so pitiless after thirty. She remembered it all, and how sure she had been then that she was meant to live on a farm and keep chickens; just as sure as he was that he was meant to be a painter, and would already have made a name if his parents hadn't called him back to Baltimore and shoved him into a broker's office after Harvard—to have him off their minds, as he said.

Yes, she could still picture that kind of life: every fibre in her kept its glow. But she didn't believe in it; she knew now that "things didn't happen like that" for long, that reality and durability were attributes of the humdrum, the prosaic and the dreary. And it was to escape from reality and durability that one plunged into cards, gossip, flirtation, and all the artificial excitements which society so lavishly provides for people who want to forget.

She and Chris had never repeated that week. He had never suggested doing so, and had let her hints fall unheeded, or turned them off with a laugh, whenever she tried, with shy tentative allusions, to coax him back to the idea; for she had found out early that one could never ask him anything point-blank—it just put his back up, as he said himself. One had to manœuvre and wait; but when didn't a woman have to manœuvre and wait? Ever since she had left her husband, eighteen years ago, what else had she ever done? Sometimes, nowadays, waking alone and unrefreshed in her dreary hotel room, she shivered at the memory of all the scheming, planning, ignoring, enduring, accepting, which had led her in the end to—this.

Ah, well—

"Aline!"

After all, there was the sun in her window, there was the triangular glimpse of blue wind-bitten sea between the roofs, and a new day beginning, and hot chocolate coming, and a new hat to try on at the milliner's, and—

"*Aline!*"

She had come to this cheap hotel just in order to keep her maid. One couldn't afford everything, especially since the war, and she preferred veal for dinner every night to having to do her own mending and dress her hair: the unmanageable abundant hair which had so uncannily survived her youth, and sometimes, in her happier moods, made her feel that perhaps, after all, in the eyes of her friends, other of its attributes survived also. And besides, it looked better for a lone woman who, after having been thirty-nine for a number of years, had suddenly become forty-four, to have a respectable-looking servant in the background; to be able, for instance, when one arrived in new places, to say to supercilious hotel-clerks: "My maid is following with the luggage."

"Aline!"

Aline, ugly, neat and enigmatic, appeared with the breakfast-tray. A delicious scent preceded her.

Mrs. Clephane raised herself on a pink elbow, shook her hair over her shoulders, and exclaimed: "Violets?"

Aline permitted herself her dry smile. "From a gentleman."

Colour flooded her mistress's face. Hadn't she known that something good was going to happen to her that morning— hadn't she felt it in every touch of the sunshine, as its golden finger-tips pressed her lids open and wound their way through her hair? She supposed she was superstitious. She laughed expectantly.

"A gentleman?"

"The little lame boy with the newspapers that Madame was kind to," the maid continued, arranging the tray with her spare Taylorized gestures.

"Oh, poor child!" Mrs. Clephane's voice had a quaver which she tried to deflect to the lame boy, though she knew how impossible it was to deceive Aline. Of course Aline knew everything—well, yes, that was the other side of the medal. She often said to her mistress: "Madame is too much alone—Madame ought to make some new friends—" and what did that mean, except that Aline knew she had lost the old ones?

But it was characteristic of Kate that, after a moment, the quaver in her voice did instinctively tilt in the direction of the lame boy who sold newspapers; and when the tears reached her eyes it was over his wistful image, and not her own, that they flowed. She had a way of getting desperately fond of people she had been kind to, and exaggeratedly touched by the least sign of their appreciation. It was her weakness—or her strength: she wondered which?

"Poor, poor little chap. But his mother'll beat him if she finds out. Aline, you must hunt him up this very day and pay back what the flowers must have cost him." She lifted the violets and pressed them to her face. As she did so she caught sight of a telegram beneath them.

A telegram—for her? It didn't often happen nowadays. But after all there was no reason why it shouldn't happen once again—at least once. There was no reason why, this very day, this day on which the sunshine had waked her with such a promise, there shouldn't be a message at last, the message for which she had waited for two years, three years; yes, exactly three years and one month—just a word from him to say: *"Take me back."*

She snatched up the telegram, and then turned her head toward the wall, seeking, while she read, to hide her face from Aline. The maid, on whom such hints were never lost, immediately transferred her attention to the dressing-table, skilfully deploying the glittering troops on that last battlefield where the daily struggle still renewed itself.

Aline's eyes averted, her mistress tore open the blue fold and read: "Mrs. Clephane dead—"

A shiver ran over her. *Mrs. Clephane dead?* Not if Mrs.

Clephane knew it! Never more alive than today, with the sun crisping her hair, the violet scent enveloping her, and that jolly north-west gale rioting out there on the Mediterranean. What was the meaning of this grim joke?

The first shock over, she read on more calmly and understood. It was the other Mrs. Clephane who was dead: the one who used to be her mother-in-law. Her first thought was: "Well, serve her right"— since, if it was so desirable to be alive on such a morning it must be correspondingly undesirable to be dead, and she could draw the agreeable conclusion that the other Mrs. Clephane had at last been come up with—oh, but thoroughly.

She lingered awhile on this pleasing fancy, and then began to reach out to wider inferences. "But if—but if—but little Anne—"

At the murmur of the name her eyes filled again. For years now she had barricaded her heart against her daughter's presence; and here it was, suddenly in possession again, crowding out everything else, yes, effacing even Chris as though he were the thinnest of ghosts, and the cable in her hand a cockcrow. "But perhaps now they'll let me see her," the mother thought.

She didn't even know who "they" were, now that their formidable chieftain, her mother-in-law, was dead. Lawyers, judges, trustees, guardians, she supposed—all the natural enemies of woman. She wrinkled her brows, trying to remember who, at the death of the child's father, had been appointed the child's other guardian—old Mrs. Clephane's overpowering assumption of the office having so completely effaced her associate that it took a few minutes to fish him up out of the far-off past.

"Why, poor old Fred Landers, of course!" She smiled retrospectively. "I don't believe he'd prevent my seeing the child if he were left to himself. Besides, isn't she nearly grown up? Why, I do believe she must be."

The telegram fell from her hands, both of which she now impressed into a complicated finger-reckoning of how old little Anne must be, if Chris were thirty-three, as he certainly was—no, thirty-one, he couldn't be more than thirty-one, because *she*, Kate, was only forty-two . . . yes, forty-two . . . and she'd always acknowledged to herself that there were nine years between them; no, eleven years, if she were really forty-two; yes, but was she? Or, goodness, was she actually forty-five? Well, then, if she was forty-five—just supposing it for a minute—and had married John Clephane at twenty-one, as she knew she had, and little Anne had been born the second summer afterward, then little Anne must be nearly twenty . . . why, quite twenty, wasn't it? But then, how old would *that* make Chris? Oh, well, he *must* be older than he looked . . . she'd always thought he was. That boyish way of his, she had sometimes fancied, was put on to make her imagine there was a greater difference of age between them than there really was—a device he was perfectly capable of making use of for ulterior purposes. And of course she'd never been that dreadful kind of woman they called a "baby-snatcher". . . But if Chris were thirty-one, and she forty-five, then how old *was* Anne?

With impatient fingers she began all over again.

The maid's voice, seeming to come from a long way off, respectfully reminded her that the chocolate would be getting cold. Mrs. Clephane roused herself, looked about the room, and exclaimed: "My looking-glass, please." She wanted to settle that question of ages.

As Aline approached with the glass there was a knock at the door. The maid went to it, and came back with her small inward smile.

"Another telegram."

Another? This time Mrs. Clephane sat bolt upright. What could it be, now, but a word from him, a message at last? Oh, but she was ashamed of herself for thinking of such a thing at such a moment. Solitude had demoralized her, she supposed. And then her child was so far away, so invisible, so un-known—and Chris of a sudden had become so near and real again, though it was three whole years and one month since he had left her. And at her age— She opened the second message, trembling. Since Armistice Day her heart had not beat so hard.

"New York. Dearest mother," it ran, "I want you to come home at once. I want you to come and live with me. Your daughter Anne."

"You asked for the looking-glass, Madame," Aline pa-tiently reminded her.

Mrs. Clephane took the proffered glass, stared into it with eyes at first unseeing, and then gradually made out the reflection of her radiant irrepressible hair, a new smile on her lips, the first streak of gray on her temples, and the first tears—oh, she couldn't remember for how long—running down over her transfigured face.

"Aline—" The maid was watching her with narrowed eyes. "The Rachel powder, please—"

Suddenly she dropped the glass and the powderpuff, buried her face in her hands, and sobbed.

II

She went out an hour later, her thoughts waltzing and eddying like the sunlit dust which the wind kept whirling round the corners in spasmodic gusts. Everything in her mind was hot and cold, and beating and blowing about, like the weather on that dancing draughty day; the very pavement of the familiar streets, and the angles of the buildings, seemed to be spinning with the rest, as if the heaviest substances had suddenly grown imponderable.

"It must," she thought, "be a little like the way the gravestones will behave on the Day of Judgment."

To make sure of where she was she had to turn down one of the white streets leading to the sea, and fix her eyes on that wedge of blue between the houses, as if it were the only ballast to her brain, the only substantial thing left. "I'm glad it's one of the days when the sea is firm," she thought. The glittering expanse, flattened by the gale and solidified by the light, rose up to meet her as she walked toward it, the pavement lifting her and flying under her like wings till it dropped her down in the glare of the Promenade, where the top-knots of the struggling palms swam on the wind like chained and long-finned sea-things against that sapphire wall climbing half-way up the sky.

She sat down on a bench, clinging sideways as if lashed to a boat's deck, and continued to steady her eyes on the Mediterranean. To collect her thoughts she tried to imagine that nothing had happened, that neither of the two cables had come, and that she was preparing to lead her usual life, as mapped out in the miniature engagement-book in her handbag. She had her "set" now in the big Riviera town where she had taken refuge in 1916, after the final break with Chris, and where, after two years of war-work and a "Reconnaissance Française" medal, she could carry her head fairly high, and even condescend a little to certain newcomers.

She drew forth the engagement-book, smiling at her childish game of "pretending." At eleven, a hat to try on; eleven-thirty, a dress; from then to two o'clock, nothing; at two, a slow solemn drive with poor old Mrs. Minity (in the last-surviving private victoria in the town); tea and bridge at Countess Lanska's from four to six; a look in at the Rectory of the American church, where there was a Ladies' Guild meeting about the Devastated Regions' Fancy Fair; lastly a little dinner at the Casino, with the Horace Betterlys and a few other pals. Yes—a rather-better-than-the-average day. And now— Why, now she could kick over the whole apple-cart if she chose; chuck it all (except the new dress and hat!): the tedious drive with the prosy patronizing old woman; the bridge, which was costing her more than it ought, with that third-rate cosmopolitan set of Laura Lanska's; the long discussion at the Rectory as to whether it would "do" to ask Mrs. Schlachtberger to take a stall at the Fair in spite of her unfortunate name; and the little dinner with the Horace Betterlys and their dull noisy friends, who wanted to "see life" and didn't know that you can't see it unless you've first had the brains to imagine it . . . Yes, she could drop it all now, and never never see one of them again . . .

"My daughter . . . my daughter Anne . . . Oh, you don't know my little girl? She *has* changed, hasn't she? Growing up is a way the children have . . . Yes, it is ageing for a poor mother to trot about such a young giantess . . . Oh, I'm going gray already, you know—here, on the temples. *Fred Landers?* It is you, really? Dear old Fred! No, of course I've never forgotten you . . . Known me anywhere? You would? Oh, nonsense! Look at my gray hair. But *men* don't change—lucky men! Why, I remember even that Egyptian seal-ring of yours . . . My daughter . . . my daughter Anne . . . let me introduce you to this big girl of mine . . . my little Anne . . ."

It was curious: for the first time she realized that, in thinking back over the years since she had been parted from Anne, she seldom, nowadays, went farther than the episode with Chris. Yet it was long before—it was eighteen years ago—that she had "lost" Anne: "lost" was the euphemism she had invented (as people called the Furies The Amiable Ones), because a mother couldn't confess, even to her most secret self, that she had willingly deserted her child. Yet that was what she had done; and now her thoughts, shrinking and shivering, were being forced back upon the fact. She had left Anne when Anne was a baby of three; left her with a dreadful pang, a rending of the inmost fibres, and yet a sense of unutterable relief, because to do so was to escape from the oppression of her married life, the thick atmosphere of self-approval and unperceivingness which emanated from John Clephane like coal-gas from a leaking furnace. So she had put it at the time—so, in her closest soul-scrutiny, she had to put it still. "I couldn't breathe—" that was all she had to say in her own defence. She had said it first—more's the pity—to Hylton Davies; with the result that two months later she was on his yacht, headed for the West Indies . . . And even then she couldn't breathe any better; not after the first week or two. The asphyxiation was of a different kind, that was all.

It was a year later that she wrote to her husband. There was no answer: she wrote again. "At any rate, let me see Anne . . . I can't live without Anne . . . I'll go and live with her anywhere you decide . . ." Again no answer . . . She wrote to her mother-in-law, and Mrs. Clephane's lawyer sent the letter back unopened. She wrote, in her madness, to the child's nurse, and got a reply from the same legal firm, requesting her to cease to annoy her husband's family. She ceased.

Of all this she recalled now only the parting from Anne, and the subsequent vain efforts to recover her. Of the agent of her release, of Hylton Davies, she remembered, in the deep sense of remembering, nothing. He had become to her, with his flourish and his yachting-clothes, and the big shining yacht, and the cocoa-palms and general setting of cool drinks and tropical luxury, as unreal as somebody in a novel, the highly coloured hero (or villain) on the "jacket". From her inmost life he had vanished into a sort of remote pictorial perspective, where a woman of her name figured with him, in muslin dresses and white sunshades, herself as unreal as a lady on a "jacket" . . . Dim also had grown the years that followed: lonely humdrum years at St.-Jean-de-Luz, at Bordighera, at Dinard. She would settle in a cheap place where there were a circulating library, a mild climate, a few quiet bridge-playing couples whom one got to know through the doctor or the clergyman; then would grow tired and drift away again. Once she went back to America, at the time of her mother's death . . . It was in midsummer, and Anne (now ten years old) was in Canada with her father and grandmother. Kate Clephane, not herself a New Yorker, and with only two or three elderly and disapproving relatives left in the small southern city of her origin, stood alone before the elaborately organized defences of a vast New York clan, and knew herself helpless. But in her madness she dreamed of a dash to Canada, an abduction—schemes requiring money, friends, support, all the power and ruse she was so lacking in. She gave that up in favour of a midnight visit (inspired by *Anna Karénine*) to the child's nursery; but on the way to Quebec she heard that the family had left in a private car for the Rocky Mountains. She turned about and took the first steamer to France.

All this, too, had become dim to her since she had known Chris. For the first time, when she met him, her soul's lungs seemed full of air. Life still dated for her from that day—in spite of the way he had hurt her, of his having inflicted on her the bitterest pain she had ever suffered, he had yet given her more than he could take away. At thirty-nine her real self had been born; without him she would never have had a self . . . And yet, at what a cost she had bought it! All the secluded penitential years that had gone before wiped out at a stroke—stained, defiled by follies she could not bear to think of, among people from whom her soul recoiled. Poor Chris! It was not that he was what is called "vicious"—but he was never happy without what he regarded as excitement; he was always telling her that an artist had to have excitement. She could not reconcile his idea of what this stimulus consisted in with his other tastes and ideas—with that flashing play of intelligence which had caught her up into an air she had never breathed before. To be capable of that thought-play, of those flights, and yet to need gambling, casinos, rowdy crowds, and all the pursuits devised to kill time for the uninventive and lethargic! He said he saw things in that kind

15

of life that she couldn't see—but since he also saw this unseeable (and she knew he did) in nature, in poetry and painting, in their shared sunsets and moonrises, in their first long dreaming days, far from jazz-bands and baccarat tables, why wasn't that enough, and how could the other rubbishy things excite the same kind of emotions in him? It had been the torment of her torments, the inmost pang of her misery, that she had never understood; and that when she thought of him now it was through that blur of noise and glare and popping corks and screaming bands that she had to grope back to the first fleeting Chris who had loved her and waked her.

At eleven o'clock she found herself, she didn't know how, at the milliner's. Other women, envious or undecided, were already flattening their noses against the panes. "That bird of Paradise . . . what they cost nowadays!" But she went in, cool and confident, and asked gaily to try on her new hat. She must have been smiling, for the saleswoman received her with a smile.

"What a complexion, ma'am! One sees you're not afraid of the wind."

But when the hat was produced, though it was the copy of one she had already tried on, it struck Mrs. Clephane as absurdly youthful, even ridiculous. Had she really been dressing all this time like a girl in her teens?

"You forget that I've a grown-up daughter, Madame Berthe."

"*Allons, Madame plaisante!*"

She drew herself up with dignity. "A daughter of twenty-one; I'm joining her in New York next week. What would she think of me if I arrived in a hat more youthful than hers? Show me something darker, please: yes, the one with the autumn leaves. See, I'm growing gray on the temples—don't try to make me look like a flapper. What's the price of that blue fox over there? I like a gray fur with gray hair."

In the end she stalked out, offended by the milliner's refusal to take her gray hair seriously, and reflecting, with a retrospective shiver, that her way of dressing and her demeanour must have thoroughly fixed in all these people's minds the idea that she was one of the silly vain fools who imagine they look like their own daughters.

At the dress-maker's, the scene repeated itself. The dashing little frock prepared for her—an orange silk handkerchief peeping from the breast-pocket on which an anchor was embroidered—made her actually blush; and reflecting that money wouldn't "matter" now (the thought of the money had really not come to her before) she persuaded the dressmaker to take the inappropriate garment back, and ordered, instead, something sober but elaborate, and ever so much more expensive. It seemed a part of the general unreal rapture that even the money-worry should have vanished.

Where should she lunch? She inclined to a quiet restaurant in a back street; then the old habit of following the throng, the need of rubbing shoulders with a crowd of unknown people, swept her automatically toward the Casino, and sat her down, in a blare of brass instruments and hard sunshine, at the only table left. After all, as she had often heard Chris say, one could feel more alone in a crowd . . . But gradually it came over her that to feel alone was not in the least what she wanted. She had never, for years at any rate, been able to bear it for long; the crowd, formerly a solace and an escape, had become a habit, and being face to face with her own thoughts was like facing a stranger. Oppressed and embarrassed, she tried to "make conversation" with herself; but the soundless words died unuttered, and she sought distraction in staring about her at the unknown faces.

Their number became oppressive: it made her feel small and insignificant to think that, of all this vulgar feasting throng, not one knew the amazing thing which had befallen her, knew that she was awaited by an only daughter in a big house in New York, a house she would re-enter in a few days—yes, actually in a few days—with the ease of a long-absent mistress, a mistress returning from an immense journey, but to whom it seems perfectly natural and familiar to be once again smiling on old friends from the head of her table.

The longing to be with people to whom she could tell her news made her decide, after all, to live out her day as she had originally planned it. Before leaving the hotel she had announced her departure to the astonished Aline (it was agreeable, for once, to astonish Aline) and despatched her to the post office with a cable for New York and a telegram for a Paris steamship company. In the cable she had said simply: "Coming darling." They were the words with which she used to answer little Anne's calls from the nursery: that impatient reiterated "Mummy—Mummy—I want my *Mummy!*" which had kept on echoing in her ears through so many sleepless nights. The phrase had flashed into her head the moment she sat down to write the cable, and she had kept murmuring to herself ever since: "Mummy—Mummy—I want my *Mummy!*" She would have liked to quote the words to Mrs. Minity, whose door she was now approaching; but how could she explain to the old lady, who was deaf and self-absorbed, and thought it a privilege for any one to go driving with her, why little Anne's cry had echoed so long in the void? No; she could not speak of that to any one: she must stick to her old "take-it-for-granted" attitude, the attitude which had carried her successfully over so many slippery places.

Mrs. Minity was very much pre-occupied about her foot-warmer. She spent the first quarter of an hour in telling Mrs. Clephane that the Rector's wife, whom she had taken out the day before, had possessed herself of the object without so much as a "may I," and kept her big feet on it till Mrs. Minity had had to stop the carriage and ask the coachman in a loud voice how it was that *The Foot-warmer* had not been put in as usual. Whereupon, if you please, Mrs. Merriman had simply said: "Oh, I have it, thanks, dear Mrs. Minity—such a comfort, on these windy days!" "Though why a woman who keeps no carriage, and has to tramp the streets at all hours, should have cold feet I can't imagine—nor, in fact, wholly believe her when she says so," said Mrs. Minity, in the tone of one to whom a defective circulation is the recognized prerogative of carriage-owners. "I notice, my dear, that *you* never complain of being cold," she added approvingly, relegating Kate, as an enforced pedestrian, to Mrs. Merriman's class, but acknowledging in her a superior sense of propriety. "I'm always glad," she added, "to take you out on windy days, for battling with the *mistral* on foot must be so very exhausting, and in the carriage, of course, it is so easy to reach a sheltered place."

Mrs. Minity was still persuaded that to sit in her hired victoria, behind its somnolent old pair, was one of the most rapid modes of progression devised by modern science. She talked as if her carriage were an aeroplane, and was as particular in avoiding narrow streets, and waiting at the corner when she called for friends who lived in them, as if she had to choose a safe alighting-ground.

Mrs. Minity had come to the Riviera thirty years before, after an attack of bronchitis, and finding the climate milder and the life easier than in Brooklyn, had not gone back. Mrs. Clephane never knew what roots she had broken in the upheaval, for everything immediately surrounding her assumed such colossal proportions that remoter facts, even concerning herself, soon faded to the vanishing-point. Only now and then, when a niece from Bridgeport sent her a bottle of brandy-peaches, or a nephew from Brooklyn wrote to say that her income had been reduced by the foreclosure of a mortgage, did the family emerge from its transatlantic mists, and Mrs. Minity become, for a moment, gratified or irate at the intrusion. But such emotions, at their acutest, were but faint shadows of those aroused by the absence of her foot-warmer, or the Salvation Army's having called twice in the same month for her subscription, or one of the horses having a stiff shoulder, and being replaced, for a long hazardous week, by another, known to the same stable for twenty years, and whom the *patron* himself undertook to drive, so that Mrs. Minity should not miss her airing. She *had* thought of staying in till her *own* horse recovered; but the doctor had absolutely forbidden it, so she had taken her courage in both hands, and gone out with the substitute, who was not even of the same colour as the horse she was used to. "But I took valerian every night," she added, "and doubled my digitalis."

Kate Clephane, as she listened (for the hundredth time), remembered that she had once thought Mrs. Minity a rather impressive old lady, somewhat arrogant and very prosy, but with a distinct "atmosphere," and a charming half-obsolete vocabulary, suggesting "Signers" and Colonial generals, which was a refreshing change from the over-refinement of Mrs. Merriman and the Betterlys' monotonous slang. Now, compared to certain long-vanished figures of the Clephane background—compared even to the hated figure of old Mrs. Clephane—Mrs. Minity shrank to the semblance of a vulgar fussy old woman.

"Old Mrs. Clephane never bragged, whatever she did,"

Kate thought: "how ridiculous all that fuss about driving behind a strange horse would have seemed to her. After all, good breeding, even in the odious, implies a certain courage . . ." Her mother-in-law, as she mused, assumed the commanding yet not unamiable shape of a Roman matron of heroic mould, a kind of "It-hurts-not-O-my-Pætus," falling first upon the sword.

The bridge-players in Countess Lanska's pastille-scented and smoke-blurred drawing-room seemed to have undergone the same change as Mrs. Minity. The very room, as Kate entered, on fire from the wind, seemed stuffier, untidier and, yes—vulgarer—than she had remembered. The empty glasses with drowned lemon-peel, the perpetually unemptied ash-trays, the sketches by the Countess's latest protégé— splashy flower markets, rococo churches, white balustrades, umbrella-pines and cobalt seas—the musical instruments tossed about on threadbare cashmere shawls covering still more threadbare sofas, even the heart-rending gaze of the outspread white bear with the torn-off ear which, ever since Kate had known him, had clung to his flattened head by the same greasy thread: all this disorder was now, for the first time, reflected in the faces about the card-tables. Not one of them, men or women, if asked where they had come from, where they were going, or why they had done such and such things, or refrained from doing such other, would have answered truthfully; not, as Kate knew, from any particular, or at any rate permanent, need of concealment, but because they lived in a chronic state of mental inaccuracy, excitement and inertia, which made it vaguely exhilarating to lie and definitely fatiguing to be truthful.

She had not meant to stay long, for her first glance at their new faces told her that to them also she would not be able to speak of what had happened. But, to subdue her own

21

agitation and divert their heavy eyes, the easiest thing was to take her usual hand at bridge; and once she had dropped into her place, the familiar murmur of "No trumps . . . yes . . . diamonds . . . Who dealt? . . . No bid . . . No . . . yes . . . no . . .", held her to her seat, soothed by the mesmeric touch of habit.

At the Rectory Mrs. Merriman exclaimed: "Oh, *there* she is!" in a tone implying that she had had to stand between Mrs. Clephane and the assembled committee.

Kate remembered that she was secretary, and expected to read the minutes.

"Have I kept you all waiting? So sorry," she beamed, in a voice that sang hallelujahs. Mrs. Merriman pushed the book toward her with a protecting smile; and Mrs. Parley Plush of the Villa Mimosa (she always told you it had been quite her own idea, calling it that) visibly wondered that Mrs. Merriman should be so tolerant.

They were all there: the American Consul's wife, mild, plump and irreproachable; the lovely Mrs. Prentiss of San Francisco, who "took things" and had been involved in a drug scandal; the Comtesse de Sainte Maxime, who had been a Loach of Philadelphia, and had figured briefly on the operatic stage; the Consul's sister, who dressed like a flapper, and had been engaged during the war to a series of American officers, all of whom seemed to have given her celluloid bangles; and a pale Mrs. Marsh, who used to be seen about with a tall tired man called "the Colonel", whose family-name was not Marsh, but for whom she wore mourning when he died, explaining—somewhat belatedly—that he was a cousin. Lastly, there was Mrs. Fred Langly of Albany, whose husband was "wanted" at home for misappropriation of funds, and who, emerging from the long seclusion consequent on this unfortunate episode, had now blossomed into a "prominent war-worker", while Mr. Langly devoted himself to the composition of patriotic poems, which he read (flanked by the civil and military authorities) at all the allied Inaugurations and Commemorations; so that by the close of the war he had become its recognized bard, and his "Lafayette, can we forget?" was quoted with tears by the very widows and orphans he had defrauded. Facing Mrs. Merriman sat the Rector, in clerical pepper-and-salt clothes and a secular pepper-and-salt moustache, talking cheerful slang in a pulpit voice.

Mrs. Clephane looked about her with new eyes. Save for their hostess, the Consul's wife and Mrs. Langly, "things" had been said of all the women; even concerning Mrs. Parley Plush, the older inhabitants (though they all went to her teas at the Villa Mimosa) smiled and hinted. And they all knew each other's stories, or at least the current versions, and affected to disapprove of each other and yet be tolerant; thus following the example of Mrs. Merriman, who simply wouldn't *listen* to any of those horrors, and of Mr. Merriman, whose principle it was to "believe the best" till the worst stared him in the face, and then to say: "I understand it all happened a long while ago."

To all of them the Rectory was a social nucleus. One after another they had found their way there, subscribed to parochial charities, sent Mrs. Merriman fruit and flowers, and suppressed their yawns at Mothers' Meetings and Sewing Circles. It was part of the long long toll they had to pay to the outraged goddess of Respectability. And at the Rectory they had made each other's acquaintance, and thus gradually widened their circle, and saved more hours from solitude, their most dreaded enemy. Kate Clephane knew it all by heart: for eighteen years she had trodden that round. The

Rector knew too; if ever a still youngish and still prettyish woman, in quiet but perfect clothes with a scent of violets, asked to see him after service, he knew she was one more recruit. In all the fashionable Riviera colonies these ladies were among the staunchest supporters of their respective churches. Even the oldest, stoutest, grimmest of his flock had had her day; Mr. Merriman remembered what his predecessor had hinted of old Mrs. Orbitt's past, and how he had smiled at the idea, seeing Mrs. Orbitt, that first Sunday, planted in her front pew like a very Deborah.

Some of the prettiest—or who had been, at least— exchanged parishes, as it were; like that sweet Lady de Tracey, who joined the American fold, while Miss Julia Jettridge, from New York, attended the Anglican services. They both said it was because they preferred "the nearest church"; but the Rector knew better than that.

Then the war came; the war which, in those bland southern places and to those uprooted drifting women, was chiefly a healing and amalgamating influence. It was awful, of course, to admit even to one's self that it could be that; but, in the light of her own deliverance, Kate Clephane knew that she and all the others had so viewed it. They had shuddered and wept, toiled hard, and made their sacrifices; of clothes and bridge, of butter and sweets and carriage-hire—but all the while they were creeping slowly back into the once impregnable stronghold of Social Position, getting to know people who used to cut them, being invited to the Préfecture and the Consulate, and lots of houses of which they used to say with feigned indifference: "Go to *those* dreary people? Not for the world!" because they knew they had no chance of getting there.

Yes: the war had brought them peace, strange and horrible as it was to think it. Kate's eyes filled as she looked about the table at those haggard powdered masks which had once glittered with youth and insolence and pleasure. All they wanted now was what she herself wanted only a few short hours ago: to be bowed to when they caught certain people's eyes; to be invited to one more dull house; to be put on the Rector's Executive Committees, and pour tea at the Consuless's "afternoons".

"May I?" a man's voice fluted; and a noble silver-thatched head with a beak-like nose and soft double chin was thrust into the doorway.

"Oh, Mr. Paly!" cried Mrs. Merriman; and murmured to the nearest ladies: "For the music—I thought he'd better come today."

Every one greeted Mr. Paly with enthusiasm. It *was* poky, being only women and the Rector. And Mr. Paly had the dearest little flat in one of the old houses of the "Vieux Port", such a tiny flat that one wondered how any one so large, manly and yet full of quick womanish movements, managed to fit in between the bric-a-brac. Mr. Paly clasped his hostess's hand in a soft palm. "I've brought my young friend Lion Carstairs; you won't mind? He's going to help me with the programme."

But one glance at Mr. Carstairs made it clear that he did not mean to help any one with anything. He held out two lax fingers to Mrs. Merriman, sank into an armchair, and let his Antinous-lids droop over his sullen deep gray eyes. "He's awfully good on Sicilian music . . . noted down folk-songs at Taormina . . ." Mr. Paly whispered, his leonine head with its bushy eye-brows and silver crown bending confidentially to his neighbour.

"Order!" rapped the Rector; and the meeting began.

At the Casino that night Kate Clephane, on the whole, was

more bored than at the Rectory. After all, at the Merrimans'
there was a rather anxious atmosphere of kindliness, of a
desire to help, and a retrospective piety about the war which
had served them such a good turn, and of which they were
still trying, in their tiny measure, to alleviate the ravages.

Whereas the Betterlys—

"What? Another begging-list? No, my dear Kate; you
don't! Stony-broke; that's what I am, and so's Harry—ain't
you, Harry?" Marcia Betterly would scream, clanking her
jewelled bangles, twisting one heavy hand through her
pearls, and clutching with the other the platinum-
and-diamond wrist-bag on which she always jokingly pre-
tended that Kate Clephane had her eye. "Look out, Sid,
she's a regular train-robber; hold you up at your own door. I
believe she's squared the police: if she hadn't she'd 'a been
run in long ago . . . Oh, the *war? What war?* Is there another
war on? What, that old one? Why, I thought *that* one was over
long ago . . . You can't get anybody I know to talk about it
even!"

"Guess we've got our work cut out paying for it," added
Horace Betterly, stretching a begemmed and bloated hand
toward the wine-list.

"Well, I should *say!*" his wife agreed with him.

"Sid, what form of liquid refreshment?" And "Sid", a
puffy Chicago business man, grew pink in his effort to look
knowing and not name the wrong champagne . . .

It was odd: during her drive with Mrs. Minity, at Madame
Lanska's, and again at the Rectory, Kate Clephane had
meant to proclaim her great news—and she had not yet
breathed a word of it. The fact was, it was too great; too
precious to waste on Mrs. Minity's inattention, too sacred to
reveal to Madame Lanska's bridge players, and too glorious
to overwhelm those poor women at the Rectory with. And

now, in the glare and clatter of the Casino, with the Sids and Harrys exchanging winks, and the Mrs. Sids and Harrys craning fat necks to see the last new cocotte, or the young Prince about whom there were such awful stories—here, of all places, to unbare her secret, name her daughter: how could she ever have thought it possible?

Only toward the end of the long deafening dinner, when Marcia and Mrs. Sid began to make plans for a week at Monte Carlo, and she found herself being impressed into the party (as she had, so often and so willingly, before) did Mrs. Clephane suddenly find herself assuming the defensive.

"You can't? Or you *won't?* Now, you Kate-cat you," Marcia threatened her with a scented cigarette, "own up now—what's doing? What you onto this time? Ain't she naughty? *We* ain't grand enough for her, girls!" And then, suddenly, at a sign from Horace, and lowering her voice, but not quite enough to make the communication private: "See here, Kate darling—of course, you know, *as our guest:* why, of course, naturally." While, on the other side, Mrs. Sid drawled: "What I want to know is: where else *can* anybody go at this season?"

Mrs. Clephane surveyed her calmly. "To New York—at least I can."

They all screamed it at her at once: "N'York?" and again she dropped the two syllables slowly from disdainful lips.

"Well, I never! Whaffor, though?" questioned Horace from the depths of a fresh bumper.

Mrs. Clephane swept the table with a cool eye. "Business—family business," she said.

"*Criky!*" burst from Horace. And: "Say, Sid, a drop of *fine*, just to help us over the shock? Well, here's to the success of the lady's Family Business!" he concluded with a just perceptible wink, emptying his champagne goblet and replacing it by the big bubble-shaped liqueur glass into which a thoughtful waiter had already measured out the proper quantity of the most expensive *fine*.

III

As Kate Clephane stood on deck, straining her eyes at the Babylonian New York which seemed to sway and totter toward her menacingly, she felt a light hand on her arm.

"Anne!"

She barely suppressed the questioning lift of her voice; for the length of a heart-beat she had not been absolutely certain. Then . . . yes, there was her whole youth, her whole married past, in that small pale oval—her own hair, but duskier, stronger; something of her smile too, she fancied; and John Clephane's straight rather heavy nose, beneath old Mrs. Clephane's awful brows.

"But the eyes—you chose your own eyes, my darling!" She had the girl at arms'-length, her own head thrown back a little: Anne was slightly the taller, and her pale face hung over her mother's like a young moon seen through mist.

"So wise of you! Such an improvement on anything we had in stock . . ." How absurd! When she thought of the things she had meant to say! What would her child think her? Incurably frivolous, of course. Well, if she stopped to consider *that* she was lost . . . She flung both arms about Anne and laid a long kiss on her fresh cheek.

"My Anne . . . little Anne . . ."

She thirsted to have the girl to herself, where she could touch her hair, stroke her face, draw the gloves from her hands, kiss her over and over again, and little by little, from that tall black-swathed figure, disengage the round child's body she had so long continued to feel against her own, like a warmth and an ache, as the amputated feel the life in a lost limb.

"Come, mother: this way. And here's Mr. Landers," the girl said. Her voice was not unkind; it was not cold; it was only muffled in fold on fold of shyness, embarrassment and constraint. After all, Kate thought, it was just as well that the crowd, the confusion and Fred Landers were there to help them over those first moments.

"Fred Landers! Dear old Fred! Is it you, really? Known me anywhere? Oh, nonsense! Look at my gray hair. But you—" She had said the words over so often in enacting this imagined scene that they were on her lips in a rush; but some contradictory impulse checked them there, and let her just murmur "Fred" as her hand dropped into that of the heavy grizzled man with a red-and-yellow complexion and screwed-up blue eyes whom Time had substituted for the thin loose-jointed friend of her youth.

Landers beamed on her, silent also; a common instinct seemed to have told all three that for the moment there was nothing to say—that they must just let propinquity do its mysterious work without trying to hasten the process.

In the motor Mrs. Clephane's agony began. "What do they think of *me?*" she wondered. She felt so sure, so safe, so enfolded, with them; or she would have, if only she could have guessed what impression she was making. She put it in the plural, because, though at that moment all she cared for was what Anne thought, she had guessed instantly that, for a time at least, Anne's view would be influenced by her guardian's.

The very tone in which he had said, facing them from his seat between the piled-up bags: "You'll find this young woman a handful—I'm not sorry to resign my trust—" showed the terms the two were on. And so did Anne's rejoinder: "I'm not a handful now to any one but myself—I'm in my own hands, Uncle Fred."

He laughed, and the girl smiled. Kate wished her daughter and she had been facing each other, so that she could have seen the whole stretch of the smile, instead of only the tip dimpling away into a half-turned cheek. So much depended, for the mother, on that smile—on the smile, and the motion of those grave brows. The whole point was, how far did the one offset the other?

"Yes," Mr. Landers assented, "you're a free agent now—been one for just three weeks, haven't you? So far you've made fairly good use of your liberty."

Guardian and ward exchanged another smile, in which Kate felt herself generously included; then Landers's eye turned to hers. "You're not a bit changed, you know."

"Oh, come! Nonsense." Again she checked that silly "look at my gray hair." "I hope one never is, to old friends—after the first shock, at any rate."

"There wasn't any first shock. I spotted you at once, from the pier."

Anne intervened in her calm voice. "I recognized mother too—from such a funny old photograph, in a dress with puffed sleeves."

Mrs. Clephane tried to smile. "I don't know, darling, if I recognized you . . . You were just there . . . in me . . . where you've always been . . ." She felt her voice breaking, and was glad to have Mr. Landers burst in with: "And what do you say to our new Fifth Avenue?"

She stood surveying its upper reaches, that afternoon, from the window of the sitting-room Anne had assigned to her. Yes; Fred Landers was right, it was a new, an absolutely new, Fifth Avenue; but there was nothing new about Anne's house. Incongruously enough—in that fluid city, where the stoutest buildings seemed like atoms forever shaken into new patterns by the rumble of Undergrounds and Elevateds—the house was the very one which had once been Kate's, the home to which, four-and-twenty years earlier, she had been brought as a bride.

Her house, since she had been its mistress; but never hers in the sense of her having helped to make it. John Clephane lived by proverbs. One was that fools built houses for wise men to live in; so he had bought a fool's house, furniture and all, and moved into it on his marriage. But if it had been built by a fool, Kate sometimes used to wonder, how was it that her husband found it to be planned and furnished so exactly as he would have chosen? He never tired of boasting of the fact, seemingly unconscious of the unflattering inference to be drawn; perhaps, if pressed, he would have said there was no contradiction, since the house had cost the fool a great deal to build, and him, the wise man, very little to buy. It had been, he was never tired of repeating, a bargain, the biggest kind of a bargain; and that, somehow, seemed a reason (again Kate didn't see why) for leaving everything in it unchanged, even to the heraldic stained glass on the stairs and the Jacobean mantel in a drawing-room that ran to Aubusson . . . And here it all was again, untouched, unworn—the only difference being that she, Kate, was installed in the visitor's suite on the third floor (swung up to it in a little jewel-box of a lift), instead of occupying the rooms below which had once been "Papa's and Mamma's". The change struck her at once—and the fact that Anne, taking her up, had first pressed the wrong button, the one for the floor below, and then reddened in correcting her mistake. The girl evidently guessed that her mother would prefer not to go back to those other rooms; her having done so gave Kate a quick thrill.

"You don't mind being so high up, mother?"

"I like it ever so much better, dear."

"I'm so glad!" Anne was making an evident effort at expansiveness. "That's jolly of you—like this we shall be on the same floor."

"Ah, you've kept the rooms you had—?" Kate didn't know how to put it.

"Yes: the old nursery. First it was turned into a school-room, then into my den. One gets attached to places. I never should have felt at home anywhere else. Come and see."

Ah, here, at last, in the grim middle-aged house, were youth and renovation! The nursery, having changed its use, had perforce had to change its appearance. Japanese walls of reddish gold; a few modern pictures; books; a budding wistaria in a vase of Corean pottery; big tables, capacious armchairs, an ungirlish absence of photographs and personal trifles. Not particularly original; but a sober handsome room, and comfortable, though so far from "cosy." Kate wondered: "Is it her own idea, or is this what the new girl likes?" She recalled the pink and white trifles congesting her maiden bower, and felt as if a rather serious-minded son were showing her his study. An Airedale terrier, stretched before the fire, reinforced the impression. She didn't believe many of the new girls had rooms like this.

"It's all your own idea, isn't it?" she asked, almost shyly.

"I don't know—yes. Uncle Fred helped me, of course. He knows a lot about Oriental pottery. I called him 'Uncle' after father died," Anne explained, "because there's nothing else to call a guardian, is there?"

On the wall Kate noticed a rough but vivid oil-sketch of a branch of magnolias. She went up to it, attracted by its purity of colour. "I like that," she said.

Anne's eyes deepened. "Do you? I did it."

"You, dear? I didn't know you painted." Kate felt herself suddenly blushing; the abyss of all she didn't know about her daughter had once more opened before her, and she just managed to murmur: "I mean, not like *this*. It's very broad— very sure. You must have worked . . ."

The girl laughed, caught in the contagion of her mother's embarrassment. "Yes, I've worked hard— I care for it a great deal."

Kate sighed and turned from the picture. The few words they had exchanged—the technical phrases she had used— had called up a time when the vocabulary of the studio was forever in her ears, and she wanted, at that moment, to escape from it as quickly as she could.

Against the opposite wall was a deep sofa, books and a reading-lamp beside it. Kate paused. "That's just where your crib used to stand!" She turned to the fireplace with an unsteady laugh. "I can see you by the hearth, in your little chair, with the fire shining through your bush of hair, and your toys on the shelf in front of you. You thought the sparks were red birds in a cage, and you used to try to coax them through the fender with bits of sugar."

"Oh, did I? You darling, to remember!" The girl put an arm about Kate. It seemed to the mother, as the young warmth flowed through her, that everything else had vanished, and that together they were watching the little girl with the bush of hair coaxing the sparks through the fender.

Anne had left her, and Mrs. Clephane, alone in her window, looked down on the new Fifth Avenue. As it surged past, a huge lava-flow of interlaced traffic, her tired bewildered eyes seemed to see the buildings move with the vehicles, as a stationary train appears to move to travellers on another line. She fancied that presently even the little Washington Square Arch would trot by, heading the tide of sky-scrapers from the lower reaches of the city . . . Oppressed and confused, she rejected the restless vision and called up in its place the old Fifth Avenue, the Fifth Avenue still intact at her marriage, a thoroughfare of monotonously ugly brown houses divided by a thin trickle of horse-drawn carriages; and she saw her mother-in-law, in just such a richly-curtained window, looking down, with dry mental comments, on old Mrs. Chivers's C-spring barouche and Mrs. Beaufort's new chestnut steppers, and knowing how long ago the barouche had been imported from Paris, and how much had been paid for the steppers—for Mrs. Clephane senior belonged to the generation which still surveyed its world from an upper window, like the Dutch ancestresses to whom the doings of the street were reported by a little mirror.

The contrast was too great; Kate Clephane felt herself too much a part of that earlier day. The overwhelming changes had all happened, in a whirl, during the years of her absence; and meanwhile she had been living in quiet backwaters, or in the steady European capitals where renewals make so little mark on the unyielding surface of the past. She turned back into the room, seeking refuge in its familiar big-patterned chintz, the tufted lounge, the woolly architecture of the carpet. It was thoughtful of Anne to have left her . . . They were both beginning to be oppressed again by a sense of obstruction: the packed memories of their so different pasts had jammed the passages between them. Anne had visibly felt that, and with a light kiss slipped out. "She's perfect," her mother thought, a little frightened . . .

She said to herself: "I'm dead tired—" put on a dressing-gown, dismissed the hovering Aline, and lay down by the fire. Then, in the silence, when the door had shut, she understood how excited she was, and how impossible it would be to rest.

Her eyes wandered about the unchanged scene, and into the equally familiar bedroom beyond—the "best spare-room" of old days. There hung the same red-eyed Beatrice Cenci above the double bed. John Clephane's parents had travelled in the days when people still brought home copies of the Old Masters; and a mixture of thrift and filial piety had caused John Clephane to preserve their collection in the obscurer corners of his house. Kate smiled at the presiding genius selected to guard the slumbers of married visitors (as Ribera monks and Caravaggio gamblers darkened the digestive processes in the dining-room); she smiled, as she so often had—but now without bitterness—at the naïve incongruities of that innocent and inquisitorial past. Then her eye lit on the one novelty in the room: the telephone at her elbow. Oh, to talk to some one—to talk to Fred Landers, instantly! "There are too many things I don't know . . . I'm too utterly in the dark," she murmured. She rushed through the directory, found his number, and assailed his parlour-maid with questions. But Mr. Landers was not at home; the parlour-maid's inflexion signified: "At this hour?" and a glance at the clock showed Kate that the endless day had barely reached mid-afternoon. Of course he would not be at home. But the parlour-maid added: "He's always at his office till five."

His office! Fred Landers had an office—had one still! Kate remembered that two-and-twenty years ago, after lunching with them, he used always to glance at his watch and say: "Time to get back to the office." And he was well-off—always had been. He needn't—needn't! What on earth did he do there, she wondered? What results, pecuniary or other, had he to show for his quarter-century of "regular hours"? She remembered that his profession had been legal—most of one's men friends, in those remote days, were lawyers. But she didn't fancy he had ever appeared in court; people consulted him about investments, he looked after estates. For the last years, very likely, his chief business had been to look after Anne's; no doubt he was one of John Clephane's executors, and also old Mrs. Clephane's. One pictured him as deeply versed in will-making and will-interpreting: he had always, in his dry mumbling way, rather enjoyed a quibble over words. Kate thought, by the way, that he mumbled less, spoke more "straight from the shoulder," than he used to. Perhaps it was experience, authority, the fact of being consulted and looked up to, that had changed the gaunt shambling Fred Landers of old days into the four-square sort of man who had met her on the pier and disentangled her luggage with so little fuss. Oh, yes, she was sure the new Fred Landers could help her—advice was just what she wanted, and what, she suspected, he liked to give.

She called up his office, and in less than a minute there was his calm voice asking what he could do.

"Come at once—oh, Fred, you must!"

She heard: "Is there anything wrong?" and sent him a reassuring laugh.

"Nothing—except *me*. I don't yet know how to fit in. There are so many things I ought to be told. Remember, I'm so unprepared—"

She fancied she felt a tremor of disapproval along the wire. Ought she not to have gone even as far as that on the telephone?

"Anne's out," she added hastily. "I was tired, and she told me to rest. But I can't. How can I? Can't you come?"

He returned, without the least acceleration of the syllables: "I never leave the office until—"

"Five. I know. But just today—"

There was a pause. "Yes; I'll come, of course. But you know there's nothing in the world to bother about," he added patiently. ("He's saying to himself," she thought, " 'that's the sort of fuss that used to drive poor Clephane out of his wits'.")

But when he came he did not strike her as having probably said anything of the sort. There was no trace of "the office", or of any other preoccupation, in the friendly voice in which he asked her if she wouldn't please stay lying down, and let him do the talking.

"Yes, I want you to. I want you to tell me everything. And first of all—" She paused to gather up her courage. "What does Anne know?" she flung at him.

Her visitor had seated himself in the armchair facing her. The late afternoon light fell on his thick ruddy face, in which the small eyes, between white lids, looked startlingly blue. At her question the blood rose from his cheeks to his forehead, and invaded the thin pepper-and-salt hair carefully brushed over his solidly moulded head.

"Don't—don't try to find out, I beg of you; I haven't," he stammered.

She felt his blush reflected on her own pale cheek, and the

tears rose to her eyes. How was he to help her if he took that tone? He did not give her time to answer, but went on, in a voice laboriously cheerful: "Look forward, not back: that's the thing to do. Living with young people, isn't it the natural attitude? And Anne is not the kind to dig and brood: thank goodness, she's health itself, body and soul. She asks no questions; never has. Why should I have put it into her head that there were any to ask? Her grandmother didn't. It was her policy . . . as it's been mine. If we didn't always agree, the old lady and I, we did on *that*." He stood up and leaned against the mantel, his gaze embracing the pyramidal bronze clock on which a heavily-draped Muse with an Etruscan necklace rested her lyre. "Anne was simply given to understand that you and her father didn't agree; that's all. A girl," he went on in an embarrassed tone, "can't grow up nowadays without seeing a good many cases of the kind about her; Lord forgive me, they're getting to be the rule rather than the exception. Lots of things that you, at her age, might have puzzled over and thought mysterious, she probably takes for granted. At any rate she behaves as if she did.

"Things didn't always go smoothly between her and her grandmother. The child has talents, you know; developed 'em early. She paints cleverly, and the old lady had her taught; but when she wanted a studio of her own there was a row—I was sent for. Mrs. Clephane had never heard of anybody in the family having a studio; that settled it. Well, Anne's going to have one now. And so it was with everything. In the end Anne invariably gets what she wants. She knew of course that you and her grandmother were not the best of friends—my idea is that she tried to see you not long after her father died, and was told by the old lady that she must wait till she was of age. They neither of them told me so—but, well, it was in the air. And Anne waited. But now she's doubly free—and you see the first use she's made of her freedom." He had recovered his ease, and sat down again, his hands on his knees, his trouser-hem rather too high above wrinkled socks and solemn square-toed boots. "I may say," he added smiling, "that she cabled to you without consulting me—without consulting anybody. I heard about it only when she showed me your answer. That ought to tell you," he concluded gaily, "as much as anything can, about Anne. Only take her for granted, as she will you, and you've got your happiest days ahead of you—see if you haven't."

As he blinked at her with kindly brotherly eyes she saw in their ingenuous depths the terror of the man who has tried to buy off fate by one optimistic evasion after another, till it has become second nature to hand out his watch and pocket-book whenever reality waylays him.

She exchanged one glance with that lurking fear; then she said: "Yes; you're right, I suppose. But there's not only Anne. What do other people know? I ought to be told."

His face clouded again, though not with irritation. He seemed to understand that the appeal was reasonable, and to want to help her, yet to feel that with every word she was making it more difficult.

"What they know? Why . . . why . . . what they *had* to . . . merely that . . ." ("What you yourself forced on them," his tone seemed to imply.)

"That I went away . . ."

He nodded.

"With another man . . ."

Reluctantly he brought the words out after her: "With another man."

"With Hylton Davies . . ."

"Hylton Davies . . ."

"And travelled with him—for nearly two years."

He frowned, but immediately fetched a sigh of relief. "Oh, well—abroad. And he's dead." He glanced at her cautiously, and then added: "He's not a man that many people remember."

But she insisted: "After that . . ."

Mr. Landers lifted his hand in a gesture of reassurance; the cloud was lifted from his brow. "After that, we all know what your life was. You'll forgive my putting it bluntly: but your living in that quiet way—all these years—gradually produced a change of opinion . . . told immensely in your favour. Even among the Clephane relations . . . especially those who had glimpses of you abroad . . . or heard of you when they were there. Some of the family distinctly disapproved of—of John's attitude; his persistent refusal . . . yes, the Tresseltons even, and the Drovers— I know they all did what they could—especially Enid Drover—"

Her blood rushed up and the pulses drummed in her temples. "If I cry," she thought "it will upset him—" but the tears rose in a warm gush about her heart.

"Enid Drover? I never knew—"

"Oh, yes; so that for a long time I hoped . . . we all hoped . . ."

She began to tremble. Even her husband's sister Enid Drover! She had remembered the Hendrik Drovers, both husband and wife, as among the narrowest, the most inexorable of the Clephane tribe. But then, it suddenly flashed across her, if it hadn't been for the episode with Chris perhaps she might have come back years before. What mocking twists fate gave to one's poor little life-pattern!

"Well—?" she questioned, breathless.

He met her gaze now without a shadow of constraint. "Oh, well, you know what John was—always the slave of anything he'd once said. Once he'd found a phrase for a thing, the phrase ruled him. He never could be got beyond that first vision of you . . . you and Davies . . ."

"Never—?"

"No. All the years after made no difference to him. He wouldn't listen. 'Burnt child dreads the fire' was all he would say. And after he died his mother kept it up. She seemed to regard it as a duty to his memory . . . She might have had your life spread out before her eyes, day by day, hour by hour . . . it wouldn't have changed her." He reddened again. "Some of your friends kept on trying . . . but nothing made any difference."

Kate Clephane lay silent, staring at the fire. Tentatively, fearfully, she was building up out of her visitor's tones, his words, his reticences, the incredible fact that, for him and all her husband's family—that huge imperious clan—her life, after she had left them, had been divided into two sharply differentiated parts: the brief lapse with Hylton Davies, the long expiation alone. Of that third episode, which for her was the central fact of her experience, apparently not a hint had reached them. She was the woman who had once "stooped to folly", and then, regaining her natural uprightness, had retained it inflexibly through all the succeeding years. As the truth penetrated her mind she was more frightened than relieved. Was she not returning on false pretences to these kindly forgiving relations? Was it not possible, indeed almost certain, that a man like Frederick Landers, had he known about Chris, would have used all his influence to dissuade Anne from sending for her, instead of exerting it in the opposite sense, as he avowedly had? And, that being so, was she not taking them all unawares, actually abusing their good faith, in passing herself off as the penitential figure whom the passage of blameless years had gradually changed from the offending into the offended? Yet was it, after all, possible that the affair with Chris, and the life she had led with him, could so completely have escaped their notice? Rumour has a million eyes, and though she had preserved appearances in certain, almost superstitious, ways, she had braved them recklessly in others, especially toward the end, when the fear of losing Chris had swept away all her precautions. Then suddenly the explanation dawned on her. She had met Chris for the first time less than a year before the outbreak of the war, and the last of their months together, the most reckless and fervid, had been overshadowed, blotted out of everybody's sight, in that universal eclipse.

She had never before thought of it in that way: for her the war had begun only when Chris left her. During its first months she and he had been in Spain and Italy, shut off by the safe Alps or the neutral indifference; and the devouring need to keep Chris amused, and herself amusing, had made her fall into the easy life of the Italian watering-places, and the careless animation of Rome, without any real sense of being in an altered world. Around them they found only the like-minded; the cheerful, who refused to be "worried", or the argumentative and paradoxical, like Chris himself, who thought it their duty as "artists" or "thinkers" to ignore the barbarian commotion. It was only in 1915, when Chris's own attitude was mysteriously altered, and she found him muttering that after all a fellow couldn't stand aside when all his friends and the chaps of his own age were getting killed—only then did the artificial defences fall, and the reality stream in on her. Was his change of mind genuine? He often said that his opinions hadn't altered, but that there were times when opinions didn't count . . . when a fellow just had to *act*. It was her own secret thought (had been, perhaps, for longer than she knew); but with Chris—could one ever tell? Whatever he was doing, he was sure, after a given time, to want to be doing something else, and to find plausible reasons for it: even the war might be serving merely as a pretext for his unrest. Unless . . . unless he used it as an excuse for leaving her? Unless being with *her* was what it offered an escape from? If only she could have judged him more clearly, known him better! But between herself and any clear understanding of him there had hung, from the first, the obscuring mist of her passion, muffling his face, touch, speech (so that now, at times, she could not even rebuild his features or recall his voice), obscuring every fold and cranny of his character, every trick of phrase, every doubling and dodging of his restless mind and capricious fancy. Sometimes, in looking back, she thought there was only one sign she had ever read clearly in him, and that was the first sign of his growing tired of her. Disguise that as she would, avert her eyes from it, argue it away, there the menace always was again, faint but persistent, like the tiny intermittent pang which first announces a mortal malady.

And of all this none of the people watching her from across the sea had had a suspicion. The war had swallowed her up, her and all her little concerns, as it had engulfed so many million others. It seemed written that, till the end, she should have to be thankful for the war.

Her eyes travelled back to Fred Landers, whose sturdy bulk, planted opposite her, seemed to have grown so far off and immaterial. Did he really guess nothing of that rainbow world she had sent her memory back to? And what would he think or say if she lifted the veil and let him into it?

"He'll hate me for it—but I must," she murmured. She raised herself on her elbow: "Fred—"

The door opened softly to admit Anne, with the Airedale at her heels. They brought in a glow of winter air and the strange cold perfume of the dusk.

"Uncle Fred? How jolly of you to have come! I was afraid I'd left mother alone too long," the girl said, bending to her mother's cheek. At the caress the blood flowed back into Kate's heart. She looked up and her eyes drank in her daughter's image.

Anne hung above her for a moment, tall, black-cloaked, remote in the faint light; then she dropped on her knees beside the couch.

"But you're *tired* . . . you're utterly done up and worn out!" she exclaimed, slipping an arm protectingly behind her mother. There was a note of reproach and indignation in her voice. "You must never be tired or worried about things any more; I won't have it; we won't any of us have it. Remember, I'm here to look after you now—and so is Uncle Fred," she added gaily.

"That's what I tell her—nothing on earth to worry about *now*," Mr. Landers corroborated, getting up from his chair and making for the door with muffled steps.

"Nothing, nothing—ever again! You'll promise me that, mother, won't you?"

Kate Clephane let her hand droop against the strong young shoulder. She felt herself sinking down into a very Bethesda-pool of forgetfulness and peace. From its depths she raised herself just far enough to say: "I promise."

IV

Anne, withdrawing from her mother's embrace, had decreed, in a decisive tone: "And now I'm going to ring for Aline to tuck you up in bed. And presently your dinner will be brought; consommé and chicken and champagne. Is that what you'll like?"

"Exactly what I shall like. But why not share it with you downstairs?"

But the girl had been firm, in a sweet yet almost obstinate way. "No, dearest—you're really tired out. You don't know it yet; but you will presently. I want you just to lie here, and enjoy the fire and the paper; and go to sleep as soon as you can."

Where did her fresh flexible voice get its note of finality? It was—yes, without doubt—an echo of old Mrs. Clephane's way of saying: "We'll consider that *settled*, I think."

Kate shivered a little; but it was only a passing chill. The use the girl made of her authority was so different—as if the old Mrs. Clephane in her spoke from a milder sphere—and it was so sweet to be compelled, to have things decided for one, to be told what one wanted and what was best for one.

For years Kate Clephane had had to order herself about: to tell herself to rest and not to worry, to eat when she wasn't hungry, to sleep when she felt staring wide-awake. She would have preferred, on the whole, that evening, to slip into a tea-gown and go down to a quiet dinner, alone with her daughter and perhaps Fred Landers; she shrank from the hurricane that would start up in her head as soon as she was alone; yet she liked better still to be "mothered" in that fond blundering way the young have of mothering their elders. And besides, Anne perhaps felt—not unwisely—that again, for the moment, she and her mother had nothing more to say to each other; that to close on that soft note was better, just then, than farther effort.

At any rate, Anne evidently did not expect to have her decision questioned. It was that hint of finality in her solicitude that made Kate, as she sank into the lavender-scented pillows, feel—perhaps evoked by the familiar scent of cared-for linen—the closing-in on her of all the old bounds.

The next morning banished the sensation. She felt only, now, the novelty, the strangeness. Anne, entering in the wake of a perfect breakfast tray, announced that Uncle Hendrik and Aunt Enid Drover were coming to dine, with their eldest son, Alan, with Lilla Gates (Lilla Gates, Kate recalled, their married daughter) and Uncle Fred Landers. "No one else, dear, on account of this—" the girl touched her mourning dress—"but you'll like to begin quietly, I know—after the fatigue of the crossing, I mean," she added hastily, lest her words should seem to imply that her mother might have other reasons for shrinking from people. "No one else," she continued, "but Joe and Nollie. Joe Tresselton, you know, married Nollie Shriner—yes, one of the Four-teenth Street Shriners, the one who was first married to Frank Haverford. She was divorced two years ago, and married Joe immediately afterward." The words dropped from her as indifferently as if she had said: "She came out two years ago, and married Joe at the end of her first season."

"Nollie Tresselton's everything to me," Anne began after a pause. "You'll see—she's transformed Joe. Everybody in the family adores her. She's waked them all up. Even Aunt Enid, you know—. And when Lilla came to grief—"

"Lilla? Lilla Gates?"

"Yes. Didn't you know? It was really dreadful for Aunt Enid—especially with her ideas. Lilla behaved really badly; even Nollie thinks she did. But Nollie arranged it as well as she could . . . Oh, but I'm boring you with all this family gossip." The girl paused, suddenly embarrassed; then, glancing out of the window: "It's a lovely morning, and not too cold. What do you say to my running you up to Bronx Park and back before lunch, just to give you a glimpse of what Nollie calls our *New* York? Or would you rather take another day to rest?"

The rush through the vivid air; the spectacle of the new sumptuous city; of the long reaches above the Hudson with their showy architecture and towering "Institutions"; of the smooth Boulevards flowing out to cared-for prosperous suburbs; the vista of Fifth Avenue, as they returned, stretching southward, interminably, between monumental façades and resplendent shop-fronts—all this and the tone of Anne's talk, her unconscious allusions, revelations of herself and her surroundings, acted like champagne on Kate Clephane's brain, making the world reel about her in a headlong dance that challenged her to join it. The way they all took their mourning, for instance! She, Anne, being her grandmother's heiress (she explained) would of course not wear colours till Easter, or go to the Opera (except to matinées) for at least another month. Didn't her mother think she was right? "Nollie thinks it awfully archaic of me to mix up music and mourning; what have they got to do with each other, as she says? But I know Aunt Enid wouldn't like it . . . and she's been so kind to me. Don't you agree that I'd better not?"

"But of course, dear; and I think your aunt's right."

Inwardly, Kate was recalling the inexorable laws which had governed family affliction in the New York to which she had come as a bride: three crape-walled years for a parent, two for sister or brother, at least twelve solid months of black for grandparent or aunt, and half a year (to the full) for cousins, even if you counted them by dozens, as the Clephanes did. As for the weeds of widowhood, they were supposed to be measured only by the extent of the survivor's affliction, and *that* was expected to last as long, and proclaim itself as unmistakably in crape and seclusion, as the most intolerant censor in the family decreed—unless you were prepared to flout the whole clan, and could bear to be severely reminded that your veil was a quarter of a yard shorter than cousin Julia's, though her bereavement antedated yours by six months. Much as Kate Clephane had suffered under the old dispensation, she felt a slight recoil from the indifference that had succeeded it. She herself, just before sailing, had re-placed the coloured finery hastily bought on the Riviera by a few dresses of unnoticeable black, which, without suggesting the hypocrisy of her wearing mourning for old Mrs. Clephane, yet kept her appearance in harmony with her daughter's; and Anne's question made her glad that she had done so.

The new tolerance, she soon began to see, applied to everything; or, if it didn't, she had not yet discovered the new prohibitions, and during all that first glittering day seemed to move through a millennium where the lamb of pleasure lay down with the lion of propriety . . . After all, this New York into which she was being reinducted had never, in any of its stages, been hers; and the fact, which had facilitated her flight from it, leaving fewer broken ties and uprooted habits, would now, she saw, in an equal measure simplify her return. Her absence, during all those years, had counted, for the Clephanes, only in terms of her husband's humiliation; there had been no family of her own to lament her fall, take up her defence, quarrel with the clan over the rights and wrongs of the case, force people to take sides, and leave a ramification of vague rancours to which her return would give new life. The old aunts and indifferent cousins at Meridia—her remote inland town—had bowed their heads before the scandal, thanking fortune that the people they visited would probably never hear of it. And now she came back free of everything and every one, and rather like a politician resuming office than a prodigal returning to his own.

The sense of it was so rejuvenating that she was almost sure she was looking her best (and with less help than usual from Aline) when she went down to dinner to meet the clan. Enid Drover's appearance gave a momentary check to her illusion: Enid, after eighteen years, seemed alarmingly the same—pursed-up lips, pure vocabulary and all. She had even kept, to an astonishing degree, the physical air of her always middle-aged youth, the smooth complexion, symmetrically-waved hair and empty eyes that made her plump small-nosed face like a statue's. Yet the mere fact of her daughter Lilla profoundly altered her—the fact that she could sit beaming maternally across the table at that impudent stripped version of herself, with dyed hair, dyed lashes, drugged eyes and unintelligible dialect. And her husband, Hendrik Drover— the typical old New Yorker—that he too should accept this outlawed daughter, laugh at her slang, and greet her belated entrance with the remark: "Top-notch get-up tonight, Lil!"

"Oh, Lilla's going on," laughed Mrs. Joe Tresselton, slipping her thin brown arm through her cousin's heavy white one.

Lilla laughed indolently. "Ain't *you?*"

"No—I mean to stay and bore Aunt Kate till the small hours, if she'll let me."

Aunt Kate! How sweet it sounded, in that endearing young voice! No wonder Anne had spoken as she did of Nollie. Whatever Mrs. Joe Tresselton's past had been, it had left on her no traces like those which had smirched and deadened Lilla. Kate smiled back at Nollie and loved her. She was prepared to love Joe Tresselton too, if only for having brought this live thing into the family. Personally, Joe didn't at first offer many points of contact: he was so hopelessly like his cousin Alan Drover, and like all the young American officers Kate had seen on leave on the Riviera, and all the young men who showed off collars or fountain-pens or golf-clubs in the backs of American magazines. But then Kate had been away so long that, as yet, the few people she had seen were always on the point of being merged into a collective American Face. She wondered if Anne would marry an American Face, and hoped, before that, to learn to differentiate them; meanwhile, she would begin by practising on Joe, who, seating himself beside her with the collective smile, seemed about to remark: "See that Arrow?"

Instead he said: "Anne's great, isn't she, Aunt Kate?" and thereby acquired an immediate individuality for Anne's mother.

Dinner was announced, and at the dining-room door Kate wavered, startled by the discovery that it was still exactly the same room—black and gold, with imitation tapestries and a

staring white bust niched in a red marble over-mantel—and
feeling once more uncertain as to what was expected of her.
But already Anne was guiding her to her old seat at the head
of the table, and waiting for her to assign their places to the
others. The girl did it without a word; just a glance and the
least touch. If this were indeed a mannerless age, how
miraculously Anne's manners had been preserved!

And now the dinner was progressing, John Clephane's
champagne bubbling in their glasses (it seemed oddest of all
to be drinking her husband's Veuve Clicquot), Lilla steadily
smoking, both elbows on the table, and Nollie Tresselton
leading an exchange of chaff between the younger cousins,
with the object, as Kate Clephane guessed, of giving her, the
newcomer, time to take breath and get her bearings. It was
wonderful, sitting there, to recall the old "family dinners",
when Enid's small censorious smile (Enid, then in her
twenties!) seemed as inaccessible to pity as the forbidding
line of old Mrs. Clephane's lips; when even Joe Tresselton's
mother (that lazy fat Alethea Tresselton) had taken her cue
from the others, and echoed their severities with a mouth
made for kissing and forgiving; and John Clephane, at the
foot of the table, proud of his house, proud of his wine, proud
of his cook, still half-proud of his wife, was visibly saying to
himself, as he looked about on his healthy handsome relatives: "After all, blood is thicker than water."

The contrast was the more curious because nothing, after
all, could really alter people like the Drovers. Enid was still
gently censorious, though with her range of criticism so
deflected by the huge exception to be made for her daughter
that her fault-finding had an odd remoteness: and Hendrik
Drover, Kate guessed, would be as easily shocked as of old
by allusions to the "kind of thing they did in Europe",
though what they did at home was so vividly present to him

in Lilla's person, and in the fact of Joe Tresselton's having married a Fourteenth Street Shriner, and a divorced one at that.

It was all too bewildering for a poor exile to come to terms with—Mrs. Clephane could only smile and listen, and be thankful that her own case was so evidently included in the new range of their indulgence.

But the young people—what did they think? That would be the interesting thing to know. They had all, she gathered, far more interests and ideas than had scantily furnished her own youth, but all so broken up, scattered, and perpetually interrupted by the strenuous labour of their endless forms of sport, that they reminded her of a band of young entomologists, equipped with the newest thing in nets, but in far too great a hurry ever to catch anything. Yet perhaps it seemed so only to the slower motions of middle-age.

Kate's glance wandered from Lilla Gates, the most obvious and least interesting of the group, to Nollie Shriner (one of the "awful" Fourteenth Street Shriners); Nollie Shriner first, then Nollie Haverford, wife of a strait-laced Albany Haverford, and now Nollie Tresselton, though she still looked, with her brown squirrel-face and slim little body, like a girl in the schoolroom. Yes, even Nollie seemed to be in a great hurry; one felt her perpetually ordering and sorting and marshalling things in her mind, and the fact, Kate presently perceived, now and then gave an odd worn look of fixity to her uncannily youthful face. Kate wondered when there was ever time to enjoy anything, with that perpetual alarm-clock in one's breast.

Her glance travelled on to her own daughter. Anne seemed eager too, but not at such a pace, or about such a multiplicity of unrelated things. Perhaps, though, it was only the fact of being taller, statelier—old-fashioned words still fitted Anne—which gave her that air of boyish aloofness. But no; it was the mystery of her eyes—those eyes which, as Kate had told her, she had chosen for herself from some forgotten ancestral treasury into which none of the others had dipped. Between olive and brown, but flecked with golden lights, a little too deep-set, the lower lid flowing up smooth and flat from the cheek, and the black lashes as evenly set as the microscopic plumes in a Peruvian feather-ornament; and above them, too prominent, even threatening, yet melting at times to curves of maiden wonder, the obstinate brows of old Mrs. Clephane. What did those eyes portend?

Kate Clephane glanced away, frightened at the riddle, and absorbed herself in the preoccupying fact that the only way to tell the Drovers from the Tresseltons was to remember that the Drovers' noses were even smaller than the Tresseltons' (but would that help, if one met one of either tribe alone?). She was roused by hearing Enid Drover question plaintively, as the ladies regained the drawing-room: "But after all, why *shouldn't* Anne go too?"

The women formed an interrogative group around Mrs. Clephane, who found herself suddenly being scrutinized as if for a verdict. She cast a puzzled glance at Anne, and her daughter slipped an arm through hers but addressed Mrs. Drover.

"Go to Madge Glenver's cabaret-party with Lilla? But there's no real reason at all why I shouldn't—except that my preference, like Nollie's, happens to be for staying at home this evening."

Mrs. Drover heaved a faint sigh of relief, but her daughter, shrugging impatient shoulders out of her too-willing shoulder-straps, grumbled: "Then why doesn't Aunt Kate come too? You'll talk her to death if you all stay here all the evening."

Nollie Tresselton smiled. "So much for what Lilla thinks of the charm of our conversation!"

Lilla shrugged again. "Not your conversation particularly. I hate talking. I only like noises that don't mean anything."

"Does that rule out talking—*quite?*"

"Well, I hate cleverness, then; you and Anne are always being clever. You'll tire Aunt Kate a lot more than Madge's party would." She stood there, large and fair, the features of her small inexpressive face so like her mother's, the lines of her relaxed inviting body so different from Mrs. Drover's righteous curves. Her painted eyes rested curiously on Mrs. Clephane. "You don't suppose she spent her time in Europe sitting at home like this, do you?" she asked the company with simplicity.

There was a stricken pause. Kate filled it by saying with a laugh: "You'll think I might as well have, when I tell you I've never in my life been to a cabaret-party."

Lilla's stare deepened; she seemed hardly able to take the statement in. "What did you do with your evenings, then?" she questioned, after an apparently hopeless search for alternatives.

Mrs. Drover had grown pink and pursed-up; even Nollie Tresselton's quick smile seemed congealed. But Kate felt herself carrying it off on wings. "Very often I just sat at home alone, and thought of you all here, and of our first evening together—this very evening."

She saw Anne colour a little, and felt the quick pressure of her arm. That they should have found each other again, she and Anne!

The butler threw open the drawing-room door with solemnity. "A gentleman has called in his motor for Mrs. Gates; he sends word that he's in a hurry, madam, please."

"Oh," said Lilla, leaping upon her fan and vanity bag. She

was out of the room before the butler had rounded off his sentence.

Mrs. Drover, her complacency restored, sank down on a plump Clephane sofa that corresponded in richness and ponderosity with her own person. "Lilla's such a baby!" she sighed; then, with a freer breath, addressed herself to sympathetic enquiries as to Mrs. Clephane's voyage. It was evident that, as far as the family were concerned, Anne's mother had been born again, seven days earlier, on the gang-plank of the liner that had brought her home. On these terms they were all delighted to have her back; and Mrs. Drover declared herself particularly thankful that the voyage had been so smooth.

V

Smoothness, Kate Clephane could see, was going to mark the first stage of her re-embarkation on the waters of life. The truth came to her, after that first evening, with the surprised discovery that the family had refrained from touching on her past not so much from prudery, or discretion even, as because such retrogressions were jolting uncomfortable affairs, and the line of least resistance flowed forward, not back. She had been right in guessing that her questions as to what people thought of her past were embarrassing to Landers, but wrong in the interpretation of his embarrassment. Like every one else about her, he was caught up in the irresistible flow of existence, which somehow reminded her less of a mighty river tending seaward than of a moving stairway revolving on itself. "Only they all think it's a river . . ." she mused.

But such thoughts barely lit on her tired mind and were gone. In the first days, after she had grasped (without seeking its explanation) the fact that she need no longer be on her guard, that henceforth there would be nothing to conjure away, or explain, or disguise, her chief feeling was one of illimitable relief. The rapture with which she let herself sink into the sensation showed her for the first time how tired she was, and for how long she had been tired. It was almost as if this sense of relaxation were totally new to her, so far back did her memory have to travel to recover a time when she had not waked to apprehension, and fallen asleep rehearsing fresh precautions for the morrow. In the first years of her marriage there had been the continual vain effort to adapt herself to her husband's point of view, to her mother-in-law's standards, to all the unintelligible ritual with which they barricaded themselves against the alarming business of living. After that had come the bitterness of her first disenchantment, and the insatiable longing to be back on the nursery floor with Anne; then, through all the ensuing years, the many austere and lonely years, and the few consumed with her last passion, the ever-recurring need of one form of vigilance or another, the effort to keep hold of something that might at any moment slip from her, whether it were her painfully-regained "respectability" or the lover for whom she had forgone it. Yes; as she looked back, she saw herself always with taut muscles and the grimace of ease; always pretending that she felt herself free, and secretly knowing that the prison of her marriage had been liberty compared with what she had exchanged it for.

That was as far as her thoughts travelled in the first days. She abandoned herself with the others to the flood of material ease, the torrent of facilities on which they were all embarked. She had been scornful of luxury when it had symbolized the lack of everything else; now that it was an adjunct of her recovered peace she began to enjoy it with the rest, and to feel that the daily perfection of her breakfast-tray, the punctual renewal of the flowers in her sitting-room, the inexhaustible hot water in her bath, the swift gliding of

Anne's motor, and the attentions of her household of servants, were essential elements of this new life.

At last she was at rest. Even the nature of her sleep was changed. Waking one morning—not with a jerk, but slowly, voluntarily, as it were—out of a soundless, dreamless night, a miraculous draught of sleep, she understood that for years even her rest had been unrestful. She recalled the uncertainty and apprehension always woven through her dreams, the sudden nocturnal wakings to a blinding, inextinguishable sense of her fate, her future, her past; and the shallow turbid half-consciousness of her morning sleep, which would leave her, when she finally woke from it, emptied of all power of action, all hope and joy. Then every sound that broke the night-hush had been irritating, had pierced her rest like an insect's nagging hum; now the noises that accompanied her falling asleep and awakening seemed to issue harmoniously out of the silence, and the late and early roar of Fifth Avenue to rock her like the great reiterations of the sea.

"This is peace . . . this *must* be peace," she repeated to herself, like a botanist arrested by an unknown flower, and at once guessing it to be the rare exquisite thing he has spent half his life in seeking.

Of course she would not have felt any of these things if Anne had not been the Anne she was. It was from Anne's presence, her smile, her voice, the mystery of her eyes even, that the healing flowed. If Kate Clephane had an apprehension left, it was her awe—almost—of that completeness of Anne's. Was it possible, humanly possible, that one could cast away one's best treasure, and come back after nearly twenty years to find it there, not only as rare as one had remembered it, but ripened, enriched, as only beautiful things are enriched and ripened by time? It was as if one had set out some delicate plant under one's window, so that it might be an object of constant vigilance, and then gone away, leaving it unwatched, unpruned, unwatered—how could one hope to find more than a dead stick in the dust when one returned? But Anne was real; she was not a mirage or a mockery; as the days passed, and her mother's life and hers became adjusted to each other, Kate felt as if they were two parts of some delicate instrument which fitted together as perfectly as if they had never been disjoined—as if Anne were that other half of her life, the half she had dreamed of and never lived. To see Anne living it would be almost the same as if it were her own; would be better, almost; since she would be there, with her experience, and tenderness, to hold out a guiding hand, to help shape the perfection she had sought and missed.

These thoughts came back to her with particular force on the evening of Anne's reappearance at the Opera. During the weeks since old Mrs. Clephane's death the Clephane box had stood severely empty; even when the Opera House was hired for some charity entertainment, Anne sent a cheque but refused to give the box. It was awfully "archaic", as Nollie Tresselton said; but somehow it suited Anne, was as much in her "style" as the close braids folded about her temples. "After all, it's not so easy to be statuesque, and I like Anne's memorial manner," Nollie concluded.

Tonight the period of formal mourning for old Mrs. Clephane was over, and Anne was to go to the Opera with her mother. She had asked the Joe Tresseltons and her guardian to join them first at a little dinner, and Kate Clephane had gone up to dress rather earlier than usual. It was her first public appearance, also, and—as on each occasion of her new life when she came on some unexpected survival of her youth, a face, a voice, a point of view, a room in which the furniture had not been changed—she was astonished, and curiously agitated, at setting out from the very same house for the very same Opera box. The only difference would be in the mode of progression; she remembered the Parisian landau and sixteen-hand chestnuts with glittering plated harness that had waited at the door in her early married days. Then she had a vision of her own toilet, of the elaborate business it used to be: Aline's predecessor, with cunning fingers, dividing and coiling the generous ripples of her hair, and building nests of curls about the temples and in the nape; then the dash up in her dressing-gown to Anne's nursery for a last kiss, and the hurrying back to get into her splendid brocade, to fasten the diamond coronet, the ruby "sunburst", the triple pearls. John Clephane was fond of jewels, and particularly proud of his wife's, first because he had chosen them, and secondly because he had given them to her. She sometimes thought he really admired her only when she had them all on, and she often reflected ironically on Esther's wifely guile in donning her regal finery before she ventured to importune Ahasuerus. It certainly increased Kate Clephane's importance in her husband's eyes to know that, when she entered her box, no pearls could hold their own against hers except Mrs. Beaufort's and old Mrs. Goldmere's.

It was years since Kate Clephane had thought of those jewels. She smiled at the memory, and at the contrast between the unobtrusive dress Aline had just prepared for her, and all those earlier splendours. The jewels, she supposed, were Anne's now; since modern young girls dressed as richly as their elders, Anne had no doubt had them reset for her own use. Mrs. Clephane closed her eyes with a smile of pleasure, picturing Anne (as she had not yet seen her) with bare arms and shoulders, and the orient of the pearls merging in that of her young skin. It was lucky that Anne was tall enough to look her best in jewels. Thence the mother's fancy wandered to the effect Anne must produce on other imaginations; on those, particularly, of young men. Was she already, as they used to say, "interested"? Among the young men Mrs. Clephane had seen, either calling at the house, or in the course of informal dinners at the Tresseltons', the Drovers', and other cousins or "in-laws", she had remarked none who seemed to fix her daughter's attention. But there had been, as yet, few opportunities: the mitigated mourning for old Mrs. Clephane did at least seclude them from general society, and when a girl as aloof as Anne was attracted, the law of contrasts might draw her to some one unfamiliar and undulled by propinquity.

"Or an older man, perhaps?" Kate considered. She thought of Anne's half-daughterly, half-feminine ways with her former guardian, and then shrugged away the possibility that her old stolid Fred could exercise a sentimental charm. Yet the young men of Anne's generation, those her mother had hitherto met, seemed curiously undifferentiated and immature, as if they had been kept too long in some pure and enlightened school, eternally preparing for a life into which their parents and professors could never decide to let them plunge . . . It struck Mrs. Clephane that Chris, when she first met him, must have been about the age of these beautiful inarticulate athletes . . . and Heaven knew how many lives he had already run through! As he said himself, he felt every morning when he woke as if he had come into a new fortune, and had somehow got to "blow it all in" before night.

Kate Clephane sat up and brushed her hand over her eyes. It was the first time Chris had been present to her, in that insistent immediate way, since her return to New York. She had thought of him, of course—how could she cast even a glance over her own past without seeing him there, woven into its very texture? But he seemed to have receded to the plane of that past: from his torturing actual presence her new life had delivered her . . . She pressed both hands against her eyes, as if to crush and disperse the image stealthily forming; then she rose and went into her bedroom, where, a moment before, she had heard Aline laying out her dress.

The maid had finished and gone; the bedroom was empty. The change of scene, the mere passage from one room to another, the sight of the evening dress and opera-cloak on the bed, and of Beatrice Cenci looking down on them through her perpetual sniffle, sufficed to recall Kate to the present. She turned to the dressing-table, and noticed a box which had been placed before her mirror. It was of ebony and citron-wood, embossed with agates and cornelians, and heavily clasped with chiselled silver; and from the summit of the lid a silver Cupid bent his shaft at her.

Kate broke into a faint laugh. How well she remembered that box! She did not have to lift the lid to see its padded trays and tufted sky-blue satin lining! It was old Mrs. Clephane's jewel-box, and on Kate's marriage the dowager had solemnly handed it over to her daughter-in-law with all that it contained.

"I wonder where Anne found it?" Kate conjectured, amused by the sight of one more odd survival in that museum of the past which John Clephane's house had become. A little key hung on one of the handles, and she put it in the lock, and saw all her jewels lying before her. On a slip of paper Anne had written: "Darling, these belong to you. Please wear some of them tonight . . ."

As she entered the opera-box Kate Clephane felt as if the great central chandelier were raying all its shafts upon her, as if she were somehow caught up into and bound on the wheel of its devouring blaze. But only for a moment—after that it seemed perfectly natural to be sitting there with her daughter and Nollie Tresselton, backed by the usual cluster of white waistcoats. After all, in this new existence it was Anne who mattered, not Anne's mother; instantly, after the first plunge, Mrs. Clephane felt herself merged in the blessed anonymity of motherhood. She had never before understood how exposed and defenceless her poor unsupported personality had been through all the lonely years. Her eyes rested on Anne with a new tenderness; the glance crossed Nollie Tresselton's, and the two triumphed in their shared admiration. "Oh, there's no one like Anne," their four eyes told each other.

Anne looked round and intercepted the exchange. Her eyes smiled too, and turned with a childish pleasure to the pearls hanging down over her mother's black dress.

"Isn't she beautiful, Nollie?"

Young Mrs. Tresselton laughed. "You two were made for each other," she said.

Mrs. Clephane closed her lids for an instant; she wanted to drop a curtain between herself and the stir and brightness, and to keep in her eyes the look of Anne's as they fell on the pearls. The episode of the jewels had moved the mother strangely. It had brought Anne closer than a hundred confidences or endearments. As Kate sat there in the dark, she saw, detached against the blackness of her closed lids, a child stumbling with unsteady steps across a windy beach, a funny flushed child with sand in her hair and in the creases of her fat legs, who clutched to her breast something she was bringing to her mother. "It's for mummy," she said solemnly, opening her pink palms on a dead star-fish. Kate saw again the child's rapturous look, and felt the throb of catching her up, star-fish and all, and devouring with kisses the rosy body and tousled head.

In themselves the jewels were nothing. If Anne had handed her a bit of coal—or another dead star-fish—with that look and that intention, the gift would have seemed as priceless. Probably it would have been impossible to convey to Anne how indifferent her mother had grown to the Clephane jewels. In her other life—that confused intermediate life which now seemed so much more remote than the day when the little girl had given her the star-fish— jewels, she supposed, might have pleased her, as pretty clothes had, or flowers, or anything that flattered the eye. Yet she could never remember having regretted John Clephane's jewels; and now they would have filled her with disgust, with abhorrence almost, had they not, in the interval, become Anne's . . . It was the girl who gave them their beauty, made them exquisite to the mother's sight and touch, as though they had been a part of her daughter's loveliness, the expression of something she could not speak.

Mrs. Clephane suddenly exclaimed to herself: "I am rewarded!" It was a queer, almost blasphemous, fancy—but it came to her so. She was rewarded for having given up her daughter; if she had not, could she ever have known such a moment as this? She had been too careless and impetuous in her own youth to be worthy to form and guide this rare creature; and while she seemed to be rushing blindly to her destruction, Providence had saved the best part of her in saving Anne. All these scrupulous self-controlled people— Enid and Hendrik Drover, Fred Landers, even the arch enemy, old Mrs. Clephane—had taken up the task she had flung aside, and carried it out as she could never have done. And she had somehow run the mad course allotted to her, and come out of it sane and sound, to find them all waiting there to give her back her daughter. It was incredible, but there it was. She bowed her head in self-abasement.

The box door was opening and shutting softly, on the stage voices and instruments soared and fell. She did not know how long she sat there in a kind of brooding rapture. But presently she was roused by hearing a different voice at her elbow. She half opened her eyes, and saw a newcomer sitting by Anne. It was one of the young men who came to the house; his fresh blunt face was as inexpressive as a foot-ball; he might have been made by a manufacturer of sporting-goods.

"—in the box over there; but he's gone now; bolted. Said he was too shy to come over and speak to you. Give you my word, he's got it bad; we couldn't get him off the subject."

"*Shy?*" Anne murmured ironically.

"That's what he said. Said he's never had the microbe before. Anyhow, he's bolted off home. Says he don't know when he'll come back to New York."

Kate Clephane, watching her daughter through narrowed lids, perceived a subtle change in her face. Anne did not blush—that close-textured skin of hers seldom revealed the motions of her blood. Her delicate profile remained shut, immovable; she merely lowered her lids as if to keep in a vision. It was Kate's own gesture, and the mother recognized it with a start. She had been right, then; there *was* some one—some one whom Anne had to close her eyes to see! But who was he? Why had he been too shy to come to the box? Where did he come from, and whither had he fled?

Kate glanced at Nollie Tresselton, wondering if she had overheard; but Nollie, in the far corner of the box, leaned forward, deep in the music. Joe Tresselton had vanished, Landers slumbered in the rear. With a little tremor of satisfaction, Kate saw that she had her daughter's secret to herself: if there was no one to enlighten her about it at least there was no one to share it with her, and she was glad. For the first time she felt a little nearer to Anne than all the others.

"It's odd," she thought, "I always knew it would be some one from a distance." But there are no real distances nowadays, and she reflected with an inward smile that the fugitive would doubtless soon reappear, and her curiosity be satisfied.

That evening, when Anne followed her into her bedroom, Mrs. Clephane opened the wardrobe in which she had placed the jewel-box. "Here, my dear; you shall choose one thing for me to wear. But I want you to take back all the rest."

The girl's face clouded. "You won't keep them, then? But they're all yours!"

"Even if they were, I shouldn't want them any longer. But they're not, they're only a trust—" she paused, half smiling—"a trust till your wedding."

She had tried to say the word lightly, but it echoed on through the silence like a peal of silver bells.

"Oh, my wedding! But I shall never marry," said Anne, laughing joyously, and catching her mother in her arms. It was the first time she had made so impulsive a movement; Kate Clephane, trembling a little, held her close.

It brought the girl nearer, made her less aloof, to hear that familiar old denial. "Some day before long," the mother thought, "she'll tell me who he is."

VI

Kate Clephane lay awake all night thinking of the man who had been too shy to come into the box.

Her sense of security, of permanence, was gone. She understood now that it had been based on the idea that her life would henceforth go on just as it had for the two months since her return; that she and Anne would always remain side by side. The idea was absurd, of course; if she followed it up, her mind recoiled from it. To keep Anne for the rest of her life unchanged, and undesirous of change—the aspiration was inconceivable. She wanted for her daughter the common human round, no more, but certainly no less. Only she did not want her to marry yet—not till they two had grown to know each other better, till Kate had had time to establish herself in her new life.

So she put it to herself; but she knew that what she felt was just an abject fear of change, more change—of being uprooted again, cast once more upon her own resources.

No! She could not picture herself living alone in a little house in New York, dependent on Drovers and Tresseltons, and on the good Fred Landers, for her moral sustenance. To be with Anne, to play the part of Anne's mother—the one part, she now saw, that fate had meant her for—that was what she wanted with all her starved and world-worn soul. To be the background, the atmosphere, of her daughter's life; to depend on Anne, to feel that Anne depended on her; it was the one perfect companionship she had ever known, the only close tie unmarred by dissimulation and distrust. The mere restfulness of it had made her contracted soul expand as if it were sinking into a deep warm bath.

Now the sense of restfulness was gone. From the moment when she had seen Anne's lids drop on that secret vision, the mother had known that her days of quietude were over. Anne's choice might be perfect; she, Kate Clephane, might live out the rest of her days in peace between Anne and Anne's husband. But the mere possibility of a husband made everything incalculable again.

The morning brought better counsel. There was Anne herself, in her riding-habit, aglow from an early canter, and bringing in her mother's breakfast, without a trace of mystery in her clear eyes. There was the day's pleasant routine, easy and insidious, the planning and adjusting of engagements, notes to be answered, invitations to be sent out; the habitual took Mrs. Clephane into its soothing hold. "After all," she reflected, "young men don't run away nowadays from falling in love." Probably the whole thing had been some cryptic chaff of the youth with the football face; Nollie, indirectly, might enlighten her.

Indirectly; for it was clear to Kate that whatever she learned about her daughter must be learned through observing her, and not through questioning others. The mother could not picture herself as having any rights over the girl, as being, under that roof, anything more than a privileged guest. Anne's very insistence on treating her as the mistress of the house only emphasized her sense of not being so by right: it was the verbal courtesy of the Spaniard who puts all his possessions at the disposal of a casual visitor.

Not that there was anything in Anne's manner to suggest this; but that to Kate it seemed inherent in the situation. It was absurd to assume that her mere return to John Clephane's house could invest her, in any one else's eyes, and much less in her own, with the authority she had lost in leaving it; she would never have dreamed of behaving as if she thought so. Her task, she knew, was gradually, patiently, to win back, of all she had forfeited, the one thing she really valued: her daughter's love and confidence. The love, in a measure, was hers already; could the confidence fail to follow?

Meanwhile, at any rate, she could be no more than the fondest of lookers-on, the discreetest of listeners; and for the moment she neither saw nor heard anything to explain that secret tremor of Anne's eyelids.

At the Joe Tresseltons', a few nights later, she had hoped for a glimpse, a hint. Nollie had invited mother and daughter (with affectionate insistence on the mother's presence) to a little evening party at which some one who was not Russian was to sing—for Nollie was original in everything. The Joe Tresseltons had managed to lend a freshly picturesque air to a dull old Tresselton house near Washington Square, of which the stable had become a studio, and other apartments suffered like transformations, without too much loss of character. It was typical of Nollie that she could give an appearance of stability to her modern furnishings, just as her modern manner kept its repose.

The party was easy and amusing, but even Lilla Gates (whom Nollie always included) took her tone from the mistress of the house, and, dressed with a kind of savage soberness, sat there in her heavy lustreless beauty, bored but triumphant. It was evident that, though at Nollie's she was not in her element, she would not for the world have been left out.

Kate Clephane, while the music immobilized the groups scattered about the great shadowy room, found herself scanning them with a fresh intensity of attention. She no longer thought of herself as an object of curiosity to any of these careless self-engrossed young people; she had learned that a woman of her age, however conspicuous her past, and whatever her present claims to notice, is fated to pass unremarked in a society where youth so undisputedly rules. The discovery had come with a slight shock; then she blessed the anonymity which made observation so much easier.

Only—what was there to observe? Again the sameness of the American Face encompassed her with its innocent uniformity. How many of them it seemed to take to make up a single individuality! Most of them were like the miles and miles between two railway stations. She saw again, with gathering wonder, that one may be young and handsome and healthy and eager, and yet unable, out of such rich elements, to evolve a personality.

Her thoughts wandered back to the shabby faces peopling her former life. She knew every seam of their shabbiness, but now for the first time she seemed to see that they had been worn down by emotions and passions, however selfish, however sordid, and not merely by ice-water and dyspepsia.

"Since the Americans have ceased to have dyspepsia," she reflected, "they have lost the only thing that gave them any expression."

Landers came up as the thought flashed through her mind, and apparently caught its reflection in her smile.

"You look at me as if you'd never seen me before; is it because my tie's crooked?" he asked, sitting down beside her.

"No; your tie is absolutely straight. So is everything else about you. That's the reason I was looking at you in that way. I can't get used to it!"

He reddened a little, as if unaccustomed to such insistent scrutiny. "Used to what?"

"The universal straightness. You're all so young and—and so regular! I feel as if I were in a gallery of marble master-pieces."

"As that can hardly apply to our features, I suppose it's intended to describe our morals," he said with a faint grimace.

"I don't know— I wish I did! What I'm trying to do, of course," she added abruptly and unguardedly, "is to guess how I should feel about all these young men—if I were Anne."

She was vexed with herself that the words should have slipped out, and yet not altogether sorry. After all, one could always trust Landers to hold his tongue—and almost always to understand. His smile showed that he understood now.

"Of course you're trying; we all are. But, as far as I know, Sister Anne hasn't yet seen any one from her tower."

A breath of relief expanded the mother's heart.

"Ah, well, you'd be sure to know—especially as, when she does, it ought to be some one visible a long way off!"

"It ought to be, yes. The more so as she seems to be in no hurry." He looked away. "But don't build too much on that," he added. "I learned long ago, in such matters, to expect only the unexpected."

Kate Clephane glanced at him quickly; his ingenuous countenance wore an unaccustomed shadow. She remembered that, in old days, John Clephane had always jokingly declared—in a tone proclaiming the matter to be one mentionable only as a joke—that Fred Landers was in love with her; and she said to herself that the lesson her old friend referred to was perhaps the one she had unwittingly given him when she went away with another man.

It was on the tip of her tongue to exclaim: "Oh, but I didn't know anything then— I wasn't anybody! My real life, my only life, began years later—" but she checked herself with a start. Why, in the very act of thinking of her daughter, had she suddenly strayed away into thinking of Chris? It was the first time it had happened to her to confront the two images, and she felt as if she had committed a sort of profanation.

She took refuge in another thought that Landers's last words had suggested—the thought that if she herself had matured late, why so might Anne. The idea was faintly reassuring.

"No; I won't build on any theory," she said, answering him. "But one can't help hoping she'll wait till some one turns up good enough for what she's going to be."

"Oh, these mothers!" he laughed, his face smoothing out into its usual guileless lines.

The music was over. The groups flowed past them toward the little tables in another picturesque room, and Lilla Gates swept by in a cluster of guffawing youths. She seemed to have attracted all the kindred spirits in the room, and her sluggish stare was shot with provocation. Ah, there was another mystery! No one explained Lilla—every one seemed to take her for granted. Not that it really mattered; Kate had seen enough of Anne to feel sure she would never be in danger of falling under Lilla's influence. The perils in wait for her would wear a subtler form. But, as a matter of curiosity, and a possible light on the new America, Kate would have liked to know why her husband's niece—surprising offshoot of the prudent Clephanes and stolid Drovers—had been singled out, in this new easy-going society, to be at once reproved and countenanced. Lilla in herself was too uninteresting to stimulate curiosity; but as a symptom she might prove enlightening. Only, here again, Kate had the sense that she, of all the world, was least in a position to ask questions. What if people should turn around and ask them about *her?* Since she had been living under her old roof, and at her daughter's side, the mere suggestion made her tremble. It was curious—and she herself was aware of it—how quickly, unconsciously almost, she had slipped at last into the very attitude the Clephanes had so long tried to force upon her: the attitude of caution and conservatism.

Her glance, in following Lilla, caught Fred Landers's, and he smiled again, but with a slight constraint. Instantly she thought: "He'd like to tell me her whole story, but he doesn't dare, because very likely it began like my own. And it will always go on being like that: whatever I'm afraid to ask they'll be equally afraid to tell." Well, that was what people called "starting with a clean slate", she supposed; would no one ever again scribble anything unguardedly on hers? She felt indescribably alone.

On the way home the mere feeling of Anne's arm against hers drew her out of her solitariness. After all, she had only to wait. The new life was but a few weeks old; and already Anne's nearness seemed to fill it. If only she could keep Anne near enough!

"Did you like it, mother? How do we all strike you, I wonder?" the girl asked suddenly.

"As kinder than anything I ever dreamed."

She thought she felt Anne's surprised glance in the darkness. "Oh, *that!* But why not? It's you who must try to be kind to us. I feel as if we must be so hard to tell apart. In Europe there are more contrasts, I suppose. I saw Uncle Fred helping you to sort us out this evening."

"You mean you caught me staring? I dare say I do. I want so much not to miss anything . . . anything that's a part of your life . . ." Her voice shook with the avowal.

She was answered by a closer pressure. "You wonderful mother! I don't believe you ever will." She was conscious in Anne, mysteriously, of a tension answering her own. "Isn't it splendid to be two to talk things over?" the girl said joyously.

"What things?" Kate Clephane thought; but dared not speak. Her hand on Anne's, she sat silent, feeling her child's heart tremble nearer.

VII

Every one noticed how beautifully it worked; the way, as Fred Landers said, she and Anne had hit it off from their first look at each other on the deck of the steamer.

Enid Drover was almost emotional about it, one evening when she and Kate sat alone in the Clephane drawing-room. It was after one of Anne's "young" dinners, and the other guests, with Anne herself, had been whirled off to some form of midnight entertainment.

"It's wonderful, my dear, how you've done it. Poor mother didn't always find Anne easy, you know. But she's taken a tremendous fancy to you."

Kate felt herself redden with pride. "I suppose it's the novelty, partly," Mrs. Drover continued, with her heavy-stepping simplicity. "Perhaps that's an advantage, in a way." But she pulled up, apparently feeling that, in some obscure manner, she might be offending where she sought to please. "Anne admires your looks so much, you know; and your slightness." A sigh came from her adipose depths. "I do believe it gives one more hold over one's girls to have kept one's figure. One can at least go on wearing the kind of clothes they like."

Kate felt an inward glow of satisfaction. The irony of the situation hardly touched her: the fact that the youth and elasticity she had clung to so desperately should prove one of the chief assets of her new venture. It was beginning to seem natural that everything should lead up to Anne.

"This business of setting up a studio, now; Anne's so pleased that you approve. She had a struggle with her grandmother about it; but poor mother wouldn't give in. She was too horrified. She thought paint so messy—and then how could she have got up all those stairs?"

"Ah, well"—it was so easy to be generous!— "that sort of thing did seem horrifying to Mrs. Clephane's generation. After all, it was not so long before her day that Dr. Johnson said portrait-painting was indelicate in a female."

Mrs. Drover gave her sister-in-law a puzzled look. Her mind seldom retained more than one word in any sentence, and her answer was based on the reaction that particular word provoked. *"Female—"* she murmured—"is that word being used again? I never thought it very nice to apply it to women, did you? I suppose I'm old-fashioned. Nothing shocks the young people nowadays—not even the Bible."

Nothing could have given Kate Clephane greater confidence in her own success than this little talk with Enid Drover. She had been feeling her way so patiently, so stealthily almost, among the outworks and defences of her daughter's character; and here she was actually instated in the citadel.

Anne's "studio-warming" strengthened the conviction. Mrs. Clephane had not been allowed to see the studio; Anne and Nollie and Joe Tresselton, for a breathless week, had locked themselves in with nails and hammers and pots of paint, sealing their ears against all questioning. Then one afternoon the doors were opened, and Kate, coming out of the winter twilight, found herself in a great half-lit room with a single wide window overlooking the reaches of the Sound all jewelled and netted with lights, the fairy span of the Brooklyn Bridge, and the dark roof-forest of the intervening city. It all seemed strangely significant and mysterious in that disguising dusk—full of shadows, distances, invitations. Kate leaned in the window, surprised at this brush of the wings of poetry.

In the room, Anne had had the good taste to let the sense of space prolong itself. It looked more like a great library waiting for its books than a modern studio; as though the girl had measured the distance between that mighty nocturne and her own timid attempts, and wanted the implements of her art to pass unnoticed.

They were sitting—Mrs. Clephane, the Joe Tresseltons and one or two others—about the tea-cups set out at one end of a long oak table, when the door opened and Lilla Gates appeared, tawny and staring, in white furs and big pendulous earrings. She brought with her a mingled smell of cigarettes and Houbigant, and as she stood there, circling the room with her sulky contemptuous gaze, Kate felt a movement of annoyance.

"Why must one forever go on being sorry for Lilla?" she wondered, wincing a little as Anne's lips touched her cousin's mauve cheek.

"It was nice of you to come, Lilla."

"Well—I chucked something bang-up for you," said Lilla coolly. It was evidently her pride to be perpetually invited, perpetually swamped in a multiplicity of boring engagements. She looked about her again, and then dropped into an armchair. "Mercy—you *have* cleared the decks!" she remarked. "Ain't there going to be any more furniture than this?"

"Oh, the furniture's all outside—and the pictures too," Anne said, pointing to the great window.

"What—Brooklyn Bridge ? Lord!—Oh, but I see: you've kept the place clear for dancing. Good girl, Anne! Can I bring in some of my little boys sometimes? Is that a pianola?" she added, with a pounce toward the grand piano in a shadowy corner. "I like this kindergarten," she pronounced.

Nollie Tresselton laughed. "If you come, Anne won't let you dance. You'll all have to sit for her— for hours and hours."

"Well, we'll sit between the dances then. Ain't I going to have a latch-key, Anne?"

She stood leaning against the piano, sipping the cock-tail some one had handed her, her head thrown back, and the light from a shaded lamp striking up at her columnar throat and the green glitter of her earrings, which suggested to Kate Clephane the poisonous antennæ of some giant insect. Anne stood close to her, slender, erect, her small head clasped in close braids, her hands hanging at her sides, dead-white against the straight dark folds of her dress. There was something distinctly unpleasant to Kate Clephane in the proximity of the two, and she rose and moved toward the piano.

As she sat down before it, letting her hands drift into the opening bars of a half-remembered melody, she saw Lilla, in her vague lounging way, draw nearer to Anne, who held out a hand for the empty cock-tail glass. The gesture brought them so close that Lilla, slightly drooping her head, could let fall, hardly above her breath, but audibly to Kate: "He's back again. He bothered the life out of me to bring him here today."

Again Kate saw that quick drop of her daughter's lids; this time it was accompanied by a just-perceptible tremor of the hand that received the glass.

"Nonsense, Lilla!"

"Well, what on earth am I to do about it? I can't get the police to run him in, can I?"

Anne laughed—the faintest half-pleased laugh of impatience and dismissal. "You may have to," she said.

Nollie Tresselton, in the interval, had glided up and slipped an arm through Lilla's.

"Come along, my dear. There's to be no dancing here today." Her little brown face had the worn sharp look it often took on when she was mothering Lilla. But Lilla's feet were firmly planted. "I don't budge till I get another cock-tail."

One of the young men hastened to supply her, and Anne turned to her other guests. A few minutes later the Tresseltons and Lilla went away, and one by one the remaining visitors followed, leaving mother and daughter alone in the recovered serenity of the empty room.

But there was no serenity in Kate. That half-whispered exchange between Lilla Gates and Anne had stirred all her old apprehensions and awakened new ones. The idea that her daughter was one of Lilla's confidants was inexpressibly disturbing. Yet the more she considered, the less she knew how to convey her anxiety to her daughter.

"If I only knew how intimate they really are—what she really thinks of Lilla!"

For the first time she understood on what unknown foundations her fellowship with Anne was built. Were they solid? Would they hold? Was Anne's feeling for her more than a sudden girlish enthusiasm for an agreeable older woman, the kind of sympathy based on things one can enumerate, and may change one's mind about, rather than the blind warmth of habit?

She stood musing while Anne moved about the studio, putting away the music, straightening a picture here and there.

"And this is where you're going to work——"

Anne nodded joyously.

"Lilla apparently expects you to turn it into a dance-hall for her benefit."

"Poor Lilla! She can't see a new room without wanting to fox-trot in it. Life, for her, wherever she is, consists in going somewhere else in order to do exactly the same thing."

Kate was relieved: there was no mistaking the half-disdainful pity of the tone.

"Well—don't give her that latch-key!" she laughed, gathering up her furs.

Anne echoed the laugh. "There are to be only two latch-keys—yours and mine," she said; and mother and daughter went gaily down the steep stairs.

The days, after that, moved on with the undefinable reassurance of habit. Kate Clephane was beginning to feel herself part of an old-established routine. She had tried to organize her life in such a way that it should fit into Anne's without awkward overlapping. Anne, nowadays, after her early canter, went daily to the studio and painted till lunch; sometimes, as the days lengthened, she went back for another two hours' work in the afternoon. When the going was too bad for her morning ride she usually walked to the studio, and Kate sometimes walked with her, or went through the Park to meet her on her return. When she painted in the afternoon, Kate would occasionally drop in for tea, and they would return home together on foot in the dusk. But Mrs. Clephane was scrupulously careful not to intrude on her daughter's working-hours; she held back, not with any tiresome display of discretion, but with the air of caring for her own independence too much not to respect Anne's.

Sometimes, now that she had settled down into this new way of life, she was secretly aware of feeling a little lonely; there were hours when the sense of being only a visitor in the house where her life ought to have been lived gave her the same drifting uprooted feeling which had been the curse of her other existence. It was not Anne's fault; nor that, in this new life, every moment was not interesting and even purposeful, since each might give her the chance of serving Anne, pleasing Anne, in some way or another getting closer to Anne. But this very feeling took a morbid intensity from the fact of having no common memories, no shared associations, to feed on. Kate was frightened, sometimes, by its likeness to that other isolated and devouring emotion which her love for Chris had been. Everything might have been different, she thought, if she had had more to do, or more friends of her own to occupy her. But Anne's establishment, which had been her grandmother's, still travelled smoothly enough on its own momentum, and though the girl insisted that her mother was now the head of the house, the headship involved little more than ordering dinner, and talking over linen and carpets and curtains with old Mrs. Clephane's housekeeper.

Then, as to friends—was it because she was too much engrossed in her daughter to make any? Or because her life had been too incommunicably different from that of her bustling middle-aged contemporaries, absorbed by local and domestic questions she had no part in? Or had she been too suddenly changed from a self-centred woman, insatiable for personal excitements, into that new being, a mother, her centre of gravity in a life not hers?

She did not know; she felt only that she no longer had time for anything but motherhood, and must be content to bridge over, as best she could, the unoccupied intervals. And, after all, the intervals were not many. Her daughter never appeared without instantly filling up every crevice of the present, and overflowing into the past and the future, so that, even in the mother's rare lapses into despondency, life without Anne, like life before Anne, had become unthinkable.

She was revolving this for the thousandth time as she turned into the Park one afternoon to meet Anne on the latter's way homeward. The days were already much longer; the difference in the light, and that premature languor of the air which comes, in America, before the sleeping earth seems to expect it, made Mrs. Clephane feel that the year had turned, that a new season was opening in her new life. She walked on with the vague sense of confidence in the future which the first touch of spring gives. The worst of the way was past—how easily, how smoothly to the feet! Where misunderstanding and failure had been so probable, she was increasingly sure of having understood and succeeded. And already she and Anne were making delightful plans for the spring . . .

Ahead of her, in a transverse alley, she was disagreeably surprised by the sight of Lilla Gates. There was no mistaking that tall lounging figure, though it was moving slowly away from her. Lilla at that hour in the Park? It seemed curious and improbable. Yet Lilla it was; and Mrs. Clephane's conclusion was drawn immediately. "Who is she waiting for?"

Whoever it was had not come; the perspective beyond

Lilla was empty. After a moment she hastened her step, and vanished behind a clump of evergreens at the crossing of the paths. Kate did not linger to watch for her reappearance. The incident was too trifling to fix the attention; after all, what had one ever expected of Lilla but that she might be found loitering in unlikely places, in quest of objectionable people? There was nothing new in that—nor did Kate even regret not having a glimpse of the objectionable person. In her growing reassurance about Anne, Lilla's affairs had lost whatever slight interest they once offered.

She walked on—but her mood was altered. The sight of Lilla lingering in that deserted path had called up old associations. She remembered meetings of the same kind— but was it her own young figure she saw fading down those far-off perspectives? Well—if it were, let it go! She owned no kinship with that unhappy ghost. Serene, middle-aged, respected and respectable, she walked on again out of that vanishing past into the warm tangible present. And at any moment now she might meet Anne.

She had turned down a wide walk leading to one of the Fifth Avenue entrances of the Park. One could see a long way ahead; there were people coming and going. Two women passed, with some noisy children racing before them, a milliner's boy, whistling, his boxes slung over his shoulder, a paralytic pushing himself along in a wheeled chair; then, coming toward her from the direction of Fifth Avenue, a man who half-stopped, recognized her, and raised his hat.

BOOK TWO

VIII

"**C**hris!" she said.

She felt herself trembling all over; then, abruptly, mysteriously, and in the very act of uttering his name, she ceased to tremble, and it came flooding in on her with a shock of wonder that the worst was already over—that at last she was going to be free.

"Well, well," she heard him saying, in that round full voice which always became fuller and more melodious when it had any inner uncertainty to mask; and "If only," she thought, "it doesn't all come back when he laughs!"

He laughed. "I'm so glad . . . *glad*," he reiterated, as if explaining; and with the laugh in her ears she still felt herself as lucidly, as incredibly remote from him.

"Glad?" she echoed, a little less sure of her speech than of her thoughts, and remembering how sometimes the smile in his eyes used to break up her words into little meaningless splinters that she could never put together again till he was gone.

"Of your good luck, I mean . . . I've heard, of course." And now she had him, for the first time, actually reddening and stammering as she herself used to do, and catching at the splinters of his own words! Ah, the trick was done—she could even see, as they continued to face each other in the searching spring light, that he had reddened, thickened, hardened—as if the old Chris had been walled into this new one, and were not even looking at her out of the windows of his prison.

"My good luck?" she echoed again, while the truth still danced in her ears: the truth that she was free, free, free—away from him at last, far enough off to see him and judge him!

It must have been his bad taste—the bad taste that could lead him into such an opening as that—which, from the very first, she had felt in him, and tried not to feel, even when she was worshipping him most blindly.

But, after all, if she felt so free, why be so cruel? Ah, because the terror was still there—it had only shifted its ground. What frightened her now was not the thought of their past but of their future. And she must not let him see that it frightened her. What had his last words been? Ah, yes—. She answered: "Of course I'm very happy to be at home again."

He lowered his voice to murmur: "And I'm happy *for* you."

Yes; she remembered now; it was always in emotional moments that his tact failed him, his subtlety vanished, and he seemed to be reciting speeches learned by heart out of some sentimental novel—the very kind he was so clever at ridiculing.

They continued to stand facing each other, their inspiration spent, as if waiting for the accident that had swept them together to whirl them apart again.

Suddenly she risked (since it was better to know): "So you're living now in New York?"

He shook his head with an air of melancholy. "No such luck. I'm back in Baltimore again. Come full circle. For a time, after the war, I was on a newspaper there; interviewing film-stars and base-ball fans and female prohibitionists. Then I tried to run a Country Club—awful job! All book-keeping, and rows between members. Now Horace Maclew has taken pity on me; I'm what I suppose you'd call his private secretary. No eight-hour day: he keeps me pretty close. It's only once in a blue moon I can get away."

She felt her tightened heart dilating. Baltimore wasn't very far away; but it was far enough as long as he had anything to keep him there. She knew about Horace Maclew, an elderly wealthy bibliophile and philanthropist, with countless municipal and social interests in his own town, and a big country-place just outside it. No; Mr. Maclew's private secretary was not likely to have many holidays. But how long would Chris resign himself to such drudgery? She wanted to be kind and say: "And your painting? Your writing?" but she didn't dare. Besides, he had probably left both phases far behind him, and there was no need, really, for her to concern herself with his new hobbies, whatever they might be. Of course she knew that he and she would have to stand there staring at one another till she made a gesture of dismissal; but on what note was she to make it? The natural thing (since she felt so safe and easy with him) would have been to say: "The next time you're in town you must be sure to look me up—". But, with him, how could one be certain of not having such a suggestion taken literally? Now that he had seen she was not afraid of him he would probably not be afraid of *her;* if he wanted a good dinner, or an evening at the

Opera, he'd be as likely as not to call her up and ask for it.

And suddenly, as they hung there, she caught, over his shoulder, a glimpse of another figure just turning into the Park from the same direction; Anne, with her quick step, her intent inward air, as she always moved and looked when she had just left her easel. In another moment Anne would be upon them.

Mrs. Clephane held out her hand: for a fraction of a second it lay in his. "Well, goodbye; I'm glad to know you've got a job that must be so interesting."

"Oh—interesting!" He dismissed it with a gesture. "But I'm glad to see you," he added; "just to *see* you," with a clever shifting of the emphasis. He paused a moment, and then risked a smile. "You don't look a day older, you know."

She threw her head back with an answering smile. "Why should I, when I feel years younger?"

Thank heaven, an approaching group of people must have obstructed her daughter's view! Mrs. Clephane hurried on, wanting to put as much distance as she could between herself and Chris's retreating figure before she came up with her daughter. When she did, she plunged straight into the girl's eyes, and saw that they were still turned on her inward vision. "Dearest," she cried gaily, "I can see by your look that you've been doing a good day's work."

Anne's soul rose slowly to the surface, shining out between deep lashes. "How do you know, I wonder? I suppose you must have been a great deal with somebody who painted. For a long time afterward one carries the thing about with one wherever one goes." She slipped her arm in Kate's, and turned unresistingly as the latter guided her back toward Fifth Avenue.

"It's dusty in the Park, and I feel as if I wanted a quick

walk home. I like Fifth Avenue when the lights are just coming out," Mrs. Clephane explained.

All night long she lay awake in the great bed of the Clephane spare-room, and stared at Chris. While they still faced each other—and after her first confused impression of his having thickened and reddened—she had seen him only through the blur of her fears and tremors. Even after they had parted, and she was walking home with Anne, the shock of the encounter still tingling in her, he remained far off, almost imponderable, less close and importunate than her memories of him. It was as if his actual presence had exorcised his ghost. But now—

He had not vanished; he had only been waiting. Waiting till she was alone in her room in the sleeping house, in the unheeding city. How alone, she had never more acutely felt. Who on earth was there to intervene between them, when there was not a soul to whom she could even breathe that she had met him? She lay in the darkness with terrified staring eyes, and there he stood, his smile deriding her— a strange composite figure, made equally of the old Chris and the new . . .

It was of no use to shut her eyes; he was between lid and ball. It was of no use to murmur disjointed phrases to herself, conjure him away with the language of her new life, with allusions and incantations unknown to him; he just stood there and waited. Well, then—she would face it out now, would deal with him! But how? What was he to her, and what did he want of her?

Yes: it all came to the question of what he wanted; it always had. When had there ever been a question of what *she* wanted? He took what he chose from life, gathered and let drop and went on: it was the artist's way, he told her. But what could he possibly want of her now, and why did she imagine that he wanted anything, when by his own showing he was so busy and so provided for?

She pulled herself together, suddenly ashamed of her own thoughts. In pity for herself she would have liked to draw the old tattered glamour over him; but there must always have been rents and cracks in it, and now it couldn't by any tugging be made to cover him. No; she didn't love him any longer; she was sure of that. Like a traveller who has just skirted an abyss, she could lean over without dizziness and measure the depth into which she had not fallen. But if that were so, why was she so afraid of him? If it were a mere question of her own social safety, a mean dread of having her past suspected, why, she was more ashamed of that than of having loved him. She would almost rather have endured the misery of still loving him than of seeing what he and she looked like, now that the tide had ebbed from them. She had been a coward; she had been stiff and frightened and conventional, when, from the vantage-ground of her new security, she could so easily have been friendly and generous; she felt like rushing out into the streets to find him, to speak to him as she ought to have spoken, to tell she felt like rushing out into the streets to find him,

And yet she *was!* She supposed it was the old incalculable element in him, that profound fundamental difference in their natures which used to make their closest nearness seem more like a spell than a reality. She understood now that if she had always been afraid of him it was just because she could never tell what she was afraid of . . .

If only there had been some one to whom she could confess herself, some one who would laugh away her terrors! Fred Landers? But she would frighten him more than he reassured her. And the others—the kindly approving family?

What would they do but avert their eyes and beg her to be reasonable and remember her daughter? Well—and her daughter, then? And Anne? Was there any one on earth but Anne who would understand her?

The oppression of the night and the silence, and the rumour of her own fears, were becoming intolerable. She could not endure them any longer. She jumped up, flung on her dressing-gown, and stole out of her room. The corridor was empty and obscure; only a faint light from the lower hall cast its reflection upward on the ceiling of the stairs. From below came the pompous tick of the hall clock, as loud as a knocking in the silence.

She stole to her daughter's door, and kneeling down laid her ear against the crack. Presently, through the hush, she caught the soft rhythmic breath of youthful sleep, and pictured Anne, slim and motionless, her dark hair in orderly braids along the pillow. The vision startled the mother back to sanity. She got up stiffly and stood looking about her with dazed eyes.

Suddenly the light on the stairs, the nocturnal ticking, swept another vision through her throbbing brain. In just such a silence, before the first cold sounds of the winter daylight, she had crept down those very stairs, unchained the front door, slipped back one after another of John Clephane's patent bolts, and let herself out of his house for the last time. Ah, what business had she in it now, her hand on her daughter's door? She dragged herself back to her own room, switched on the light, and sat hunched up in the great bed, mechanically turning over the pages of a fashion-paper she had picked up on her sitting-room table. Skirts were certainly going to be narrower that spring . . .

IX

"Lilla—but of course he comes for Lilla!" she exclaimed.

She raised herself on her elbow, saw the bed-lamp still burning and the fashion paper on the floor beside the bed. The night was not over; there was no grayness yet between the curtains. She must have dropped into a short uneasy sleep, from which Lilla's loitering expectant figure, floating away from her down an alley of the Park, had detached itself with such emphasis that the shock awoke her.

Lilla and Chris . . . but of course they had gone to the Park to meet each other! Why should he have happened to turn in at that particular gate, at that particular hour, unless to find some one who, a few yards off, careless and unconcerned, was so obviously lingering there to be found?

The discovery gave Kate Clephane a sensation of actual physical nausea. She sat up in bed, pushed her hair back from her damp forehead, and repeated the two names slowly, as if trying from those conjoined syllables to disentangle the clue to the mystery. For mystery there was; she was sure of it now! People like Lilla Gates and Chris did not wander aimlessly through Central Park at the secret hour when the winter dusk begins to blur its paths. Every moment of such purposeless lives was portioned out, packed with futilities. Kate had seen enough of that in her enforced association with the idlers of a dozen watering-places, her dreary participation in their idling.

And how the clue, now she held it, explained everything! Explained, first of all, why Chris, the ready, the resourceful, had been so tongue-tied and halting when they met. Why had she not been struck by that before? She saw now that, if she was afraid of him, he was a thousand times more afraid of her! And how could she have imagined that, to a man like Chris, the mere fact of running across a discarded mistress would be disconcerting, or even wholly unpleasant? Who better than he should know how to deal with such emergencies? His past must be strewn with precedents. As her memory travelled back over their life together she recalled their having met, one day at Hadrian's Villa, a little woman, a Mrs. Guy So-and-so—she had even forgotten the name! She and Chris had been wandering, close-linked—for the tourist season was over, and besides, they cared so little who saw them—through the rich garlanded ruins, all perfume and enchantment; and there, in their path, had stood a solitary figure, the figure of a young woman, pretty, well-dressed, with a hungry melancholy face. A little way behind her, a heavy elderly gentleman in blue goggles and an overcoat was having archæological explanations shouted to his deaf ear and curved hand by a guide with a rasping German accent—and Chris, exclaiming: "By Jove, there are the So-and-sos!" had advanced with outstretched hand, introduced the two women, and poured out upon the melancholy newcomer a flood of laughing allusive talk, half chaff, half sentiment, and all as easily, as unconcernedly as if her great eyes had not, all the while, been pleading, pleading with him to remember.

And then, afterward, when Kate had said to him: "But wasn't that the woman you told me about once, who was so desperately unhappy! and wanted to run away with you?" he had merely answered: "Oh, not particularly with *me,* as far as I remember—" and she had hugged his arm closer, and thought how funny he was, and luxuriously pitied the other woman.

Yes; that was the real Chris; always on the spot, easy-going and gay. The stammering evasive apparition in the Park had no resemblance to that Chris; Kate knew instinctively that it was not the fact of meeting her that had so disturbed him, but the fact that, for some reason, the meeting might interfere with his plans. But what plans? Why, his plans with Lilla—which would necessarily bring him in contact with the clan, since they so resolutely backed Lilla up, and thus expose him to—to what? To Kate's betraying him? For a moment she half-laughed at the idea.

For what could she do to injure him, after all? And, whatever his plans were, how could he ever imagine her interfering with them, when to do so would be to betray her own secret? She lay there in the dreary dawn and tried to work her way through the labyrinth. And then, all at once, it came to her: what if he wanted to marry Lilla? And what more probable than that he did? It was evident that living with his people and administering Mr. Maclew's philanthropies was not a life that he would have called "fit for a dog". He liked money, she knew, for all his careless way; he wanted to have it, but he hated to earn it. And if he married Lilla there would be plenty of money. The Drovers would see to that—Kate could imagine nothing more likely to unloose their purse-strings than the possibility of "settling" Lilla, and getting rid of the perpetual menace that her roving fancies hung over her mother's neatly-waved head. Chris, of course, was far too clever not to have seen that, and worked out the consequences in his own mind. If Lilla had been plain and dowdy he wouldn't even have considered it—Kate did him that justice. If he liked money he liked it in a large lordly way, and only as one among several things which it was convenient but not essential to have. He would never do a base thing for money; but, after all, there was nothing base in marrying Lilla if he liked her looks and was amused by her talk, as he probably was. There was one side of Chris, the side Kate Clephane had least explored, and was least capable of understanding, which might very well find its complement in Lilla . . .

Kate's aching eyes continued to strain into the future. If that were really his plan, of course he would be afraid of her! For he knew her too, knew her ever so much better than she did him, and would be sure to guess that, much as she would want to cover up their past, she would not hesitate a moment between revealing it and doing what she called her duty. Her duty—how he used to laugh at the phrase! He told her she had run away from her real duties only for the pleasure of inventing new ones, and that to her they were none the less duties because she imagined them to be defiances. It was one of the paradoxes that most amused him: the picture of her flying from her conscience and always meeting it again in her path, barely disguised by the audacities she had dressed it up in.

Yes; evidently he had asked himself, on the instant, what she would do about Lilla; and the mere fact made her feel, with a fierce desperation, that she must do something. Not that she cared a straw about Lilla, or felt the least "call" to save her—but to have Chris in the family, in the group, to have to smile at him across the Clephane dinner-table, the

Drover dinner-table, all the family dinner-tables, to have to keep up, for all the rest of her life, the double pretence of never having liked him too much, and of now liking him enough to gratify the pride and allay the suspicions of the family—no, she could not imagine herself doing it! She was right to be afraid of him; he was right to be afraid of her.

The return to daylight made her nocturnal logic seem absurd; but several days passed before her agitation subsided. It was only when she found life continuing undisturbed about her, Anne painting for long rapturous hours, Lilla following her same bored round of pleasure, the others placidly engaged in their usual pursuits, and no one mentioning Chris's name, or apparently aware of his existence, that the shadow of her midnight imaginings was lifted.

Once or twice, as the sense of security returned, she thought of letting Chris's name fall, ever so casually, in Fred Landers's hearing. She never got as far as that; but one day she contrived, in speaking of some famous collection of books just coming into the market, to mention Horace Maclew.

Landers's eye kindled. "Ah, what books! His Italian antiphonals are probably the best in the world."

"You know him, then? How—is it long since you last saw his library?" she stammered.

He considered. "Oh, years; not since before the war."

Her heart rose on the mounting hope. "Oh, not since then? . . . I suppose he must have a very good librarian?"

"Used to have; the poor chap was killed in the war, I believe. That reminds me that I heard the other day he was looking for some one."

"Looking for a librarian?" She heard her voice shake. "Not for a private secretary?"

She thought he looked surprised. "I don't think so; but I really don't remember. I know he always has a lot of scribes about him; naturally, with so many irons in the fire. Did you happen to hear of any one who was looking for that sort of job? It might be a kindness to let Maclew know."

She drew her brows together, affecting to consider. "Where did I hear of some one? I can't remember either. One is always hearing nowadays of people looking for something to do."

"Yes ; but of few who can do anything. And Maclew's the last man to put up with incompetence. You must come and see him with me. He's not an easy customer, but he and I are old members of the Grolier Club and he lets me bring a friend to see his library occasionally. I've always promised to take Anne, some day when she's going on to Washington."

Kate's heart gave a sharp downward plunge. That "Take Anne" reverberated in her like a knell. What a fool she had been to bring the subject up! If she had not mentioned Horace Maclew's name Landers might never have thought of his library again; at least not of the promise to take Anne there. Well, it was a lesson to hold her tongue, to let things follow their course without fearing or interfering. Happily Anne, more and more absorbed in her painting, seemed to have no idea of a visit to Washington; she had never mentioned such a plan, beyond once casually saying: "Oh, the Washington magnolias . . . some spring I must go there and paint them."

Some spring . . . well, that was pleasantly indefinite. For Chris was not likely to remain long with Horace Maclew. Where had Chris ever remained long? Kate Clephane did not know, now, whether to tremble at that impermanence or be glad of it. She did not know what to think about anything, now that the thought of Chris had suddenly reintroduced itself into the smooth-running wheels of her existence.

Then, as the days passed, her reassurance returned again, and it was with a stupefied start that one afternoon, crossing the Park on her way to the studio, she once more caught sight of Lilla Gates. This time the person for whom she had presumably been waiting was with her, and the two stood in close communion. The man's back was turned, but his figure, his attitude, were so familiar to Kate that she stopped short, trembling lest she should see his face.

She did not see it. He and Mrs. Gates were in the act of leave-taking. Their hands met, they lingered for a last word, and then separated, each hastening away in a direction other than Kate's. She continued to stand motionless after they had vanished, uncertain yet certain. It was Chris—but of course it was Chris! He came often to New York, then, in spite of what he had said about the difficulty of getting away. If he had said that, it was probably just because he wanted to keep his comings and goings from Mrs. Clephane's knowledge. And that again would tally with what she suspected as to his motives. She turned sick, and stood with compressed lips and lowered head, as if to close her senses against what was coming. At length she roused herself and walked on.

Lilla . . . Lilla . . . Chris and Lilla!

She kept on her way northward, following the less frequented by-ways of the Park. It was early yet, and she wanted to walk off her agitation before joining Anne at the studio.

Lilla . . . Lilla . . . Chris and Lilla!

Something must be done about it, something must be said—it was impossible that this affair, whatever it was, should go on unchecked. But had she, Kate Clephane, any power to prevent it? Probably not—her intervention might

serve only to precipitate events. Well, at least she must know
what was coming—must find out what the others knew . . .
Her excitement increased instead of subsiding: as she walked
on she felt the tears running down her face. Life had
seemed, at last, so simple, so merciful, so soothing; and here
were all the old mysteries and duplicities pressing on her
again. She stopped, out of breath, and finding herself at the
extreme northern end of the Park, with the first street-lights
beginning to gem the bare trees. The need to be with Anne
suddenly seized her. Perhaps, by dropping a careless word or
two, she might learn something from her daughter—learn at
least if the baleful Lilla were using the girl as a confidant, as
that brief scene in the studio had once suggested. On that
point, at any rate, it was the mother's right, her duty even, to
be informed. She had made no appointment to meet Anne
that afternoon; and she hastened her pace, fearing to find
that her daughter had already left the studio . . .

A light through the transom reassured her. She put her key
in the lock, threw off her cloak in the little entrance-hall, and
pushed open the door beyond. The studio was unlit except
by the city's constellated lamps, hung like a golden vintage
from an invisible trellising of towers and poles, and by the
rosy gleam of the hearth. Anne's easel had been pushed
aside, and Anne and another person were sitting near each
other in low chairs, duskily outlined against the fire. As Mrs.
Clephane crossed the threshold a man's voice was saying
gaily: "What I want is a rhyme for *astrolabe*. I must have it!
And apparently there is none; at least none except *babe*. And
so there won't be any poem. That's always my luck. I find
something . . . or somebody . . . who's just what I want, and
then . . ."

Kate Clephane stood still, enveloped by the voice. It was
the first time she had heard those laughing confiding

inflexions addressed to any ear but hers. Southern sunshine scorched her; the air seemed full of flowers. She hung there for a moment, netted in tightening memories; then she loosed her hold on the door-handle and advanced a few steps into the room. Her heels clicked on the bare floor, and the two by the fire rose and turned to her. She fancied her daughter's glance conveyed a faint surprise—was it even a faint annoyance at her intrusion?

"Mother, this is Major Fenno. I think you know him," the girl said.

Chris came forward, simple, natural, unembarrassed. There was no trace of constraint in his glance or tone; he looked at Mrs. Clephane almost fraternally.

"Dear Mrs. Clephane—a rhyme for *astrolabe!*" he entreated, with that half-humorous way he had of flinging the lasso of his own thought over anybody who happened to stray within range; and then, with one of his usual quick transitions: "I got a chance to run over to New York unexpectedly, and I heard you were in town, and went to see you. At your house they told me you might be here, so I came, and Miss Clephane was kind enough to let me wait."

"I was afraid you weren't coming," the girl added, looking gravely at her mother.

In spite of the blood drumming in her head, and the way his airy fib about having heard she was in town had drawn her again into the old net of their complicities, Kate was steadied by his composure. She looked from him to Anne; and Anne's face was also composed.

"I had the luck," Chris added, "to meet Miss Clephane after I was invalided home. She took pity on me when I was in hospital on Long Island, and I've wanted to thank her ever since. But my boss keeps me on a pretty short chain, and I can't often get away."

"It's wonderful," said the girl, with her quiet smile, "how you've got over your lameness."

"Oh, well—" he had one of his easy gestures— "lameness isn't the hardest thing in the world to get over. Especially not with the care I had."

Silence fell. Kate struggled to break it, feeling that she was expected to speak, to say something, anything; but there was an obstruction in her throat, as if her voice were a ghost vainly struggling to raise its own grave-stone.

Their visitor made the automatic motion of consulting his wrist-watch. "Jove! I hadn't an idea it was so late. I've got barely time to dash for my train!" He stood looking in his easy way from mother to daughter; then he turned once more to Kate.

"Aren't you coming over to see the great Maclew library one of these days? I was just telling Miss Clephane—"

"Uncle Fred has always promised to take me," the girl threw in.

"Well, that settles it; doesn't it, Mrs. Clephane?" This time he wavered a second before the "Mrs.", and then carried it off triumphantly. "As soon as you can make a date, will you wire me? Good!" He was holding out his hand. Kate put hers in it; she did not mind. It was as if she had laid a stone in his palm.

"It's a go, then?" he repeated gaily, as he shook hands with Anne; and the door closed on him.

"Major Fenno"—. Kate repeated the name slowly as she turned back toward the fire. She had never heard of his military rank. "Was he wounded?" she asked her daughter suddenly.

"At Belleau Wood—didn't you know? I thought you might have—he was mentioned in despatches. He has the Legion of Honour and the D.S.M." Anne's voice had an unwonted vibration. "But he never talks of all that; all he cares about is his writing," she added.

She was gathering up her brushes, rubbing her pallet with a rag, going through all the habitual last gestures with her usual somewhat pedantic precision. She found something wrong with one of the brushes, and bent over the lamp with it, her black brows jutting. At that moment she reminded her mother of old Mrs. Clephane; somehow, there was an odd solace in the likeness.

"If he comes for anybody it's for Lilla," the mother thought, as her eyes rested on her daughter's stern young profile; and again she felt the necessity of clearing up the mystery. On the whole, it might be easier to question Anne, now that the name had been pronounced between them.

Major Fenno—and he had been wounded . . . And all he cared about was his writing.

X

After all, she was not going to be able to question Anne about Lilla. As she faced the situation the next day—as she faced the new Chris in her path—Kate Clephane saw the impossibility of using him as a key to her daughter's confidence. There was one thing much closer to her now than any conceivable act of Chris's could ever be; and that was her own relation to Anne. She simply could not talk to Anne about Chris—not yet. It was not that she regarded that episode in her life as a thing to be in itself ashamed of. She was not going, even now, to deny or disown it; she wanted only to deny and disown Chris. Quite conceivably, she might have said to her daughter: "Yes, I loved once—and the man I loved was not your father." But to say it about Chris! To see the slow look of wonder in those inscrutable depths of Anne's eyes: a look that said, not "I blame you", or even "I disapprove you", but, so much more scathingly, just: "You, mother—and *Chris?*"

Yes; that was it. It was necessary for her pride and dignity, for her moral safety almost, that what people like Enid Drover would have called her "past" should remain uniden-

tified, unembodied—or at least not embodied in Chris
Fenno. Yet to know—to know!

There were, of course, other sources of enlightenment; if
there were anything in her theory of a love-affair between
Lilla and Chris, the family were probably not unaware of it.
Kate had the sense that they never had their eyes off Lilla
for long. But it was all very well to plan to talk to them—
the question remained, how to begin? Before trying to find
out about Lilla she would first have to find out about them.
What did she know of any one of them? Nothing more, she
now understood, than their glazed and impenetrable sur-
faces.

She was still a guest among them; she was a guest even in
her daughter's house. It was the character she had herself
chosen; in her dread of seeming to assert rights she had
forfeited, to thrust herself into a place she had deserted, she
had perhaps erred in the other sense, held back too much,
been too readily content with the easy part of the week-end
visitor.

Well—it had all grown out of the other choice she had
made when, years ago, she had said: "Thy gods shall *not* be
my gods." And now she but dimly guessed who their gods
were. At the moment when her very life depended on her
knowing their passwords, holding the clue to their labyrinth,
she stood outside the mysterious circle and vainly groped for
a way in.

Nollie Tresselton, of course, could have put the clue in her
hand; but to speak to Nollie was too nearly like speaking to
Anne. Not that Nollie would betray a confidence; but to be
divined and judged by her would be almost as searing an
experience as being divined and judged by Anne. And so
Kate Clephane continued to sit there between them, hugging
her new self in her anxious arms, turning its smooth face

toward them, and furtively regulating its non-committal gestures and the sounds that issued from its lips.

Only the long nights of dreamless sleep were gone; and her heart stood still each time she slipped the key into the studio door.

"Mother, Uncle Fred wants to take us to Baltimore next week to see the Maclew library; you and Lilla and me."

Anne threw it over her shoulder as she stood before her easel, frowning and narrowing her lips at the difficulty of a branch of red pyrus japonica in a brass pot, haloed with the light of the sunlit window.

Kate, behind her, was leaning back indolently in a deep wicker armchair. She started, and echoed in a blank voice: "Next week?"

"Well, you see, I've promised to spend a few days in Washington with Madge Glenver, who has taken a house at Rock Creek for the spring. This is just the moment for the magnolias; and I thought we might stop at Baltimore on the way, and Uncle Fred could bring you and Lilla back from there."

It sounded perfectly simple and sensible; Anne spoke of it in her usual matter-of-course tone. Her mother tried for the same intonation in answering, with a faint touch of surprise: "Lilla too?"

Anne turned around completely and smiled. "Oh, Lilla particularly! You mustn't speak of it yet, please—not even to Aunt Enid—but there's a chance . . . a chance of Lilla's marrying."

Kate's heart gave a great bound of relief or resentment— which? Why, relief, she instantly assured herself. She had been right then—that was the key to the mystery! And why not? After all, what did it matter to her? Had she, Kate, ever imagined that Chris's love-affairs would cease when she passed from his life? Wasn't it most probably in pursuit of a new one that he had left her? To think so had been, at any rate, in spite of the torturing images evoked, more bearable than believing he had gone because he was tired of her. For years, as she now saw, she had been sustained by her belief in that "other woman"; only, that she should take shape in Lilla was unbelievably humiliating.

Anne continued to smile softly down on her mother. In her smile there was something veiled and tender, as faint as sunlight refracted from water—a radiance striking up from those mysterious depths that Kate had never yet reached. "We should all be so glad if it happened," the girl continued; and Kate said to herself: "What she's really thinking of when she smiles in that way is her own marriage . . ." She remembered the cryptic allusion of the football-faced youth at the Opera, and the way those vigilant lids of Anne's had shut down on her vision.

"Of course—poor Lilla!" Mrs. Clephane absently assented. Inwardly she was saying to herself that it would be impossible for her to go to Baltimore on that particular errand. Chris and Lilla—Chris and Lilla! The coupled names began again to jangle maddeningly through her brain. She stood up and moved away to the window. No, she couldn't!

"Next week, dear? It doesn't matter—but I think you'll have to go without me." She spoke from the window, without turning her head toward her daughter, who had gone back to the easel.

"Oh—." There was distinct disappointment in Anne's voice.

"The fact is I've made two or three dinner engagements; I don't think I can very well break them, do you? People have been so awfully kind—all my old friends," Kate stammered, while the "couldn't, couldn't" kept booming on in her ears. "Besides," she added, "why not take Nollie instead? A young party will be more amusing for Mr. Maclew."

Anne laughed. "Oh, I don't believe he'll notice Nollie and me," she said with a gay significance; but added at once: "Of course you must do exactly as you please. That's the foundation of our agreement, isn't it?"

"Our agreement?"

"To be the two most perfect pals that ever were."

Mrs. Clephane sprang up impulsively and moved toward her daughter. "We *are* that, aren't we, Anne?"

Anne's lids dropped; she nodded, screwed her mouth up, and opened her other eyes—her painter's eyes—on the branch of pyrus with its coral-like studding of red cups. "From the very first," she agreed.

The young party went, Fred Landers beaming in attendance. The family thought it a pity that Mrs. Clephane should miss such a chance, for Horace Maclew was chary of exhibiting his books. But there was something absent-minded and perfunctory in the tone of these regrets; Kate could see that the family interest was passionately centred in Lilla. And she felt, more and more, that in the circumstances she herself was better out of the way. For, at the last moment, the party had been invited to stay at Horace Maclew's; and to have assisted, in an almost official capacity, at the betrothal of Chris and Lilla, with all the solemnity and champagne likely to ensue in such a setting, was more than her newly healed nerves could have endured. It was easier to sit at home and wait, and try to prepare herself for this new and unbelievable situation. Chris and Lilla—!

It was on the third day that Aline, bringing in the breakfast-tray with a bunch of violets (Anne's daily attention since she had been gone), produced also a telegram; as on that far-off morning, four months ago, when the girl's first message had come to her mother with the same flowers.

Kate held the envelope for a moment before opening it, as she had done on that other occasion—but not because she wanted to prolong her illusion. This time there was no illusion in the thin envelope between her fingers; she could feel through it the hard knife-edge of reality. If she delayed she did so from cowardice. Chris and Lilla—

She tore open the envelope and read: "Engaged to Horace Maclew madly happy Lilla."

The telegram fluttered to the floor, and Kate Clephane leaned back on her pillows, feeling a little light-headed.

"Is Madame not well?" Aline sharply questioned.

"Oh, yes; perfectly well. Perfectly well!" Kate repeated joyously. But she continued to lean back, staring vacantly ahead of her, till Aline admonished her, as she had done when the other message came, that the chocolate would be getting cold.

A respite—a respite. Oh, yes, it was at least a respite!

XI

There was something so established and reassuring in the mere look of Enid Drover's drawing-room that Kate Clephane, waiting there that afternoon for her sister-in-law to come in, felt a distinct renewal of confidence.

The house was old Mrs. Clephane's wedding gift to her daughter, and everything in it had obviously been selected by some one whose first thought concerning any work of art was to ask if it would chip or fade. Nothing in the solid and costly drawing-room had chipped or faded; it had retained something of Enid's invulnerable youthfulness, and, like herself, had looked as primly old-fashioned in its first bloom as in its well-kept maturity.

It was odd that so stable a setting should have produced that hurricane of a Lilla; and Kate smiled at the thought of the satisfaction with which the very armchairs, in their cushioned permanence, would welcome her back to domesticity.

But Mrs. Drover, when she appeared, took it on a higher plane. Had Lilla ever been unstable, or in any way failed to excel? If so, her mother, and her mother's background, showed no signs of remembering. The armchairs stood there stolidly, as if asking what you meant by such ideas. Enid was a little troubled—she confessed—by the fact that Horace Maclew was a widower, and so much older than her child. "I'm not sure if such a difference of age is not always a risk . . . But then Mr. Maclew is a man of such strong character, and has behaved so generously . . . There will be such opportunities for doing good . . ."

Opportunities for doing good! It was on the tip of Kate's tongue to say: "Ah, that must have been Lilla's reason for accepting him!"; but Mrs. Drover was serenely continuing: "He has given her all the pearls already. She's bringing them back tomorrow to be restrung." And Kate understood that, for the present, the opportunities for doing good lay rather with the bridegroom than the bride.

"Of course," Mrs. Drover went on, "it will be a great sacrifice for her father and me to let her go; though luckily Baltimore is not far off. And it will be a serious kind of life; a life full of responsibilities. Hendrik is afraid that, just at first, Lilla may miss the excitements of New York; but I think I know my child better. When Lilla is *really happy* no one cares less than she does for excitement."

The phrase gave Kate's nerves a sudden twist. It was just what Chris used to say when she urged him to settle down to his painting—at least on the days when he didn't say that excitement was necessary to the artist . . . She looked at her sister-in-law's impenetrable pinkness, and thought: "It might be Mrs. Minity speaking."

Fred Landers had telephoned that he had got back and was coming to dine; she fancied he had it on his mind not to let her feel her solitude while Anne was away; and she said to herself that from him at least she would get a glimpse of the truth.

Fred Landers, as became a friend of the family, was also beaming; but he called Lilla's engagement a "solution" and not a "sacrifice"; and this made it easier for Kate at last to put her question: "How did it happen?"

He leaned back, pulling placidly at his after-dinner cigar, his old-fashioned square-toed pumps comfortably stretched to the fire; and for an instant Kate thought: "It might be pleasant to have him in that armchair every evening." It was the first time such a possibility had occurred to her.

"How did she pull it off, you mean?" He screwed up his friendly blue eyes in a confidential grin. "Well, I'm naturally not initiated; but I suppose in one of the good old ways, Lilla probably knows most of the tricks—and I rather think Nollie Tresselton's been aiding and abetting her. It's been going on for the last six months, I know, and a shooting-box in South Carolina is mixed up with it. Of course they all have a theory that Lilla need only be happy to be good."

"And what do you think about it?"

He shrugged. "Why, I think it's an experiment for which Maclew is to furnish the *corpus vile*. But he's a thick-skinned subject, and it may not hurt him much, and may help Lilla. We can only look on and hope."

Kate sat pondering her next question. At length she said: "Was Mr. Maclew's private secretary there?"

"That fellow Fenno? Yes; he was on duty." She fancied he frowned a little.

"Why do you call him 'that fellow'?"

He turned toward her, and she saw that his friendly brows were beetling. "Is it necessary to speak of him more respectfully? The fact is, I don't fancy him—never did."

"You knew him before, then?" She felt the blood creeping to her forehead, and reached out for a painted hand-screen that she might seem to hold between her eyes and the fire.

Landers reflected. "Oh, yes. I've run across him now and then. I rather fancy he's been mixed up in this too; stirring the brew with the others. That's my impression."

"Yes—I wonder why," said Kate suddenly.

Landers smiled a little, though his brows continued to jut. "To please Anne, perhaps."

"Anne—*Anne?*"

The name, after she had uttered it, continued to ring on between them, and she leaned back, pressing the screen against her closed lids. "Why?" she managed to question.

"Well—a good many people have wanted to please Anne, first and last. I simply conjectured that Fenno might be among them."

"Oh, no; I'm sure you're quite wrong. I wonder—." She hesitated, and then went on with a rush: "The fact is, I wonder you haven't noticed that he and Lilla—"

Landers sat up and flung his cigar-end into the embers. "Fenno and Lilla? By Jove—you might be right. I hadn't thought of it—"

"Well, I have; I've met them together; when they didn't expect to be met—." She hurried it out with a kind of violence. Her heart was beating to suffocation; she had to utter her suspicion, to give it life and substance.

"The idea sheds floods of light—no doubt of that. Poor Maclew! I'm beginning to be sorry for him. But I think the lot of them are capable of taking pretty good care of themselves. On the whole," Landers added with a sudden sigh of relief, "I'm jolly glad it's Lilla—if it's anybody."

"I *know* it's Lilla." Kate spoke with a passionate emphasis. She had to prove to some one that Chris was Lilla's lover in order to believe it herself, and she had to believe it herself in order to dispel the dreadful supposition raised by Landers's words. She found herself, now, able to smile away his

114

suggestion quite easily, to understand that he had meant it only as a random joke. People in America were always making jokes of that kind, juvenile jokes about flirtations and engagements; they were the staple topic of the comic papers. But the shock of finding herself for a second over that abyss sent her stumbling back half-dazed to the safe footing of reality. If she were going to let her imagination run away at any chance word, what peace would there ever be for her?

The next day Nollie Tresselton reappeared, smiling and fresh, like a sick-nurse whose patient has "turned the corner". With Lilla off her hands her keen boyish face had lost its expression of premature vigilance, and she looked positively rejuvenated. She was more outspoken than Landers.

"At last we can talk about it—thank goodness!" And she began. Horace Maclew and Lilla had met the previous autumn, duck-shooting in South Carolina. Lilla was a wonderful shot when she wasn't . . . well, when she was in training . . . and Maclew, like most heavy solemn men of his type, who theoretically admire helpless feminine women, had been bowled over by the sight of this bold huntress, who damned up and down the birds she missed, smoked and drank with the men, and in the evening lay back silent, with lids half-dropped over smouldering sullen eyes, and didn't bore one with sporting chatter or sentimental airs. It had been a revelation, the traditional thunderbolt; only, once back in Baltimore, Maclew had been caught in the usual network of habits and associations; or perhaps other influences had intervened. No doubt, with a man like that, there would be a "settled attachment" in the background. Then Lilla, for a while, was more outrageous than ever, and when he came to New York to see her, dragged him to one of her rowdiest parties, and went away from it in the small hours with another man, leaving Maclew and his super-Rolls to find their way home uncompanioned. After that the suitor had vanished, and it had taken the combined efforts of all the family, and the family's friends, to draw him back. ("And no one helped us more than Major Fenno," Nollie added with a grateful sigh.)

The name, dropping suddenly into their talk, made Lilla and her wooer and all the other figures in the tale shrivel up like toy balloons. Kate Clephane felt her blood rising again; would she never be able to hear Chris mentioned without this rush of the pulses?

"He was so clever and tactful about it," Nollie was going on. "And he really *believes* in Lilla, just as I do. Otherwise, of course, he couldn't have done what he did—when Horace Maclew has been such a friend to him. He believes she'll keep straight, and that they'll be awfully happy. I fancy he knows a good deal about women, don't you?"

"About women like Lilla, perhaps." The words had flashed out before Kate even knew the thought had formed itself. It must have welled up from some depth of bitterness she had long thought dry.

Nollie's eyes looked grieved. "Oh—you don't like him?"

"I haven't seen him for years," Kate answered lifelessly.

"He admires you so much; he says he used to look up to you so when he was a boy. But I daresay he wasn't half as interesting then; he says himself he was a sort of intellectual rolling stone, never sure of what he wanted to be or to do, and always hurting and offending people in his perpetual efforts to find himself. That's how he puts it."

Look up to her when he was a boy! Yes; that's how he *would* put it. And the rest too; how often she had heard that old analogy of the rolling stone and its victims!

"I think the war transformed him; made a man of him. He says so himself. And now he believes he's really found his vocation; he doesn't think of anything but his writing, and some of his poetry seems to me very beautiful. I'm only sorry," Nollie continued thoughtfully, "that he feels obliged to give up his present job. It seems a pity, when he has so little money, and has been looking so long for a post of the sort—"

"Ah . . . he's giving it up?"

"Well, yes; he says he must have more mental elbow-room; for his writing, I mean. He can't be tied down to hours and places."

"Ah, no; he never could—" Again the words had nearly slipped out. The effort to suppress them left Kate dumb for a moment, though she felt that Nollie was waiting for her to speak.

"Then of course he must go," she assented. Inwardly she was thinking: "After all, if I'm right—and this seems to prove I'm right—about him and Lilla, it's only decent of him to give up his job." And her eyes suddenly filled with tears at the thought of his making a sacrifice, behaving at a crucial moment as her old ideal of him would have had him behave. After all, he was perhaps right in saying that the war had made a man of him.

"Yes; but it's a pity. And not only for him, I mean. I think he had a good influence on Lilla," Nollie went on.

Ah, now, really they were too simple—even Nollie was! Kate could hardly keep from shouting it out at her: "But can't you see, you simpleton, that they're lovers, the two of them, and have cooked up this match for their own convenience, and that your stupid Maclew is their dupe, as all the rest of you are?"

But something in her—was it pride or prudence?—recoiled from such an outburst, and from the need of justifying it. In God's name, what did it matter to her—what did it matter?

The risk was removed, the dreadful risk; she was safe again—as safe as she would ever be—unless some suicidal madness drove her to self-betrayal.

With dry lips and an aching smile she said: "You must help me to choose my wedding-present for Lilla."

XII

Anne's sojourn in Washington prolonged itself for a fortnight. Her letters to her mother, though punctual, were inexpressive; but that was not her fault, Kate knew. She had inherited from her father a certain heaviness of pen, an inability to convey on paper shades of meaning or of feeling and having said: "Isn't it splendid about Lilla?" had evidently exhausted the subject, or rather her power of developing it.

At length she returned, bringing with her some studies of magnolias that were freer and more vigorous than any of her previous work. She greeted her mother with her usual tenderness, and to Kate her coming was like a lifting of clouds and opening of windows; the mother had never supposed that anything in her life could ever again strike such deep roots as this passion for her daughter. *Perfect love casteth out fear!* "Does it? *How does any one know?*" she had often incredulously asked herself. But now, for the first time, love and security dwelt together in her in a kind of millennial quiet.

She grudged having to dine out on the evening of Anne's

return; but Mrs. Porter Lanfrey was celebrating Lilla's betrothal by a big dinner, with music afterward, and Anne, arriving by a late train, had barely time to dress before the motor was announced. There was no way of avoiding the festivity; its social significance was immeasurable. Mrs. Lanfrey was one of the hostesses who had dropped Lilla from their lists after the divorce, and Mrs. Lanfrey's yea or nay was almost the last survival of the old social code in New York. Those she invited, at any rate, said that hers was the only house where there was a "tradition" left; and though Lilla, at this, used to growl: "Yes, the tradition of how to bore people," her reinstatement visibly elated her as much as it did her family. To Enid Drover—resplendent in all her jewels—the event had already reversed the parts in her daughter's matrimonial drama, and relegated all the obloquy to the outraged Gates. "Of course this evening shows what Jessie Lanfrey really thinks of Phil Gates," Enid whispered to Mrs. Clephane as the sisters-in-law took off their cloaks in the marble hall; and Kate inwardly emended, with a faint smile: "Or what she really thinks of Horace Maclew."

Mrs. Clephane had entered the vast Lanfrey drawing-room with a shrinking not produced by the presence of most of her own former censors and judges—now transformed into staunch champions or carelessly benevolent acquaintances— but by the dread of seeing, behind Mr. Maclew's momentous bulk, a slighter figure and more vivid face. But the moment of suspense was not long; Chris was not there; nor was his name announced after her arrival. The guests were all assembled; the dining-room doors were thrown open, and Mrs. Lanfrey, taking Mr. Maclew's arm, majestically closed the procession from walnut-and-gold to gold-and-marble—for the Lanfrey house was "tradition" made visible, and even the *menu* was exactly what a previous transmitter of the faith had thought a *menu* ought to be when Mrs. Lanfrey gave her first dinner.

For a moment Kate Clephane felt herself in the faint bewildered world between waking and sleeping. There they all were, the faces that had walled in her youth; she was not sure, at first, if they belonged to the same persons, or had been handed on, as part of the tradition, to a new generation. It even occurred to her that, by the mere act of entering Mrs. Lanfrey's drawing-room, the latter's guests acquired a facial conformity that belonged to the Lanfrey plan as much as the fat prima-donna islanded in a sea of Aubusson who warbled an air from *La Tosca* exactly as a previous fat prima-donna had warbled it on the same spot years before. It seemed as if even Lilla, seated on a gilt sofa beside her betrothed, had smoothed her rebellious countenance to an official smirk. Only Anne and Nollie Tresselton resisted the enveloping conformity; Kate wondered if she herself were not stealthily beginning to resemble Enid Drover. "This is what I ran away from," she thought; and found more reasons than ever for her flight. "And after all, I have Anne back," she murmured blissfully . . . for that still justified the rest. Ah, how fate, in creating Anne, had baffled its own designs against Anne's mother!

On the way home the girl was unusually silent. She leaned back against the cushions and let her lids drop. Was it because she was tired after her long day, or only because she was holding in her vision? Kate could not tell. In the passing flashes of the arc-lights the head at her side, bound about with dark braids, looked as firm and young as a Greek marble; Anne was still at the age when neither weariness nor anxiety mars the surface.

Kate Clephane always respected her daughter's silences,

and never felt herself excluded from them; but she was glad when, as they neared their door, Anne's hand stole out to her. How many old breaches the touch healed! It was almost as if the girl had guessed how often Kate had driven up to that door inertly huddled in her corner, with her husband's profile like a wall between her and the world beyond the windows.

"Dear! You seem to have been gone for months," the mother said as they reached her sitting-room.

"Yes. So much has happened." Anne spoke from far off, as if she were groping through a dream.

"But there'll be time for all that tomorrow. You're dead tired now—you're falling with sleep."

The girl opened her eyes wide, in the way she had when she came out of one of her fits of abstraction. "I'm not tired; I'm not sleepy." She seemed to waver. "Can't I come in and sit with you a little while?"

"Of course, dear." Kate slipped an arm through hers, and they entered the shadowy welcoming room, lit by one veiled lamp and the faint red of the hearth. "After all, this is the best hour of the twenty-four for a talk," the mother said, throwing herself back luxuriously on her lounge. It was delicious, after her fortnight of solitude, to think of talking things over with Anne. "And now tell me about everything," she said.

"Yes; I want to." Anne stood leaning against the chimney-piece, her head on her lifted arm. "There's so much to say, isn't there? Always, I mean—now that you and I are together. You don't know the difference it makes, coming home to you, instead—" She broke off, and crossing the hearth knelt down by her mother. Their hands met, and the girl leant her forehead against Kate's shoulder.

"I've been lonely too!" The confession sprang to Kate's

lips. Oh, if at last she might say it! But she dared not. The bond between her and her daughter was still too fragile; and how would such an avowal sound on her lips? It was better to let Anne guess—

Anne did guess. "You *have* been happy here, haven't you?"

"Happy? Little Anne!"

"And what a beautiful mother you are! Nollie was saying tonight that you're younger looking every day. And nobody wears their clothes as you do. I knew from that old photograph that you were lovely; but I couldn't guess that you hadn't grown any older since it was taken."

Kate lay still, letting the warmth of the words and the embrace flow through her. What praise had ever seemed as sweet? All the past faded in the sunset radiance of the present. "Little Anne," she sighed again. The three syllables summed it all up.

Anne was silent for a moment; then she continued, her cheek still pressed against her mother: "I want you to stay here always, you know; I want the house to belong to you."

"The house—?" Kate sat up with a start. The girl's shoulder slipped from hers and they remained looking at each other, the space between them abruptly widened. "This house—belong to me? Why, what in the world—"

It was the first time such a question had arisen. On her arrival in America, when Landers, at Anne's request, had tentatively broached the matter of financial arrangements, Kate had cut him short with the declaration that she would gladly accept her daughter's hospitality, but preferred not to receive any money beyond the small allowance she had always had from the Clephane estate. After some argument Landers had understood the uselessness of insisting, and had doubtless made Anne understand it; for the girl had never spoken of the subject to her mother.

Kate put out an encircling arm. "What in the world should I do with this house, dear? Besides—need we look so far ahead?"

For a moment Anne remained somewhat passively in her mother's embrace; then she freed herself and went back to lean against the mantel. "That's just it, dear; I think we must," she said. "With such years and years before you—and all that lovely hair!" Her eyes still lingered smilingly on her mother.

Kate sat upright again, and brushed back the lovely hair from her bewildered temples. What did Anne mean? What was it she was trying to say? The mother began to tremble with an undefined apprehension; then the truth flashed over her.

"Dearest—you mean you may be married?"

The girl nodded, with the quick drop of the lids that called up such memories to her mother. "I couldn't write it; I'm so bad at writing. I want you to be happy with me, darling. I'm going to marry Major Fenno."

XIII

Baltimore—the conductor called it out as the train ground its way into the station.

Kate Clephane, on her feet in the long swaying Pullman, looked about her at the faces of all the people in the other seats—the people who *didn't know*. The whole world was divided, now, between people such as those, and the only two who did know: herself and one other. All lesser differences seemed to have been swallowed up in that . . .

She pushed her way between the seats, in the wake of the other travellers who were getting out—she wondered why!—at Baltimore. No one noticed her; she had no luggage; in a moment or two she was out of the station. She stood there, staring in a dazed way at the meaningless traffic of the streets. Where were all these people going, what could they possibly want, or hope for, or strive for, in a world such as she now knew it to be?

There was a spring mildness in the air, and presently, walking on through the hurrying crowd, she found herself in a quiet park-like square, with budding trees, and bulbs pushing up in the mounded flower-beds. She sat down on a bench.

Strength had been given her to get through that first hour with Anne . . . she didn't know how, but somehow, all at once, the shabby years of dissimulation, of manœuvring, of concealing, had leapt to her defence like a mercenary army roused in a righteous cause. She had to deceive Anne, to lull Anne's suspicions, though she were to die in the attempt. And she had not died—

That was the worst of it.

She had never been more quiveringly, comprehensively alive than as she sat there, in that alien place, staring out alone into an alien future. She felt strong and light enough to jump up and walk for miles and miles—if only she had known where to go! They said grief was ageing—well, this agony seemed to have plunged her into a very Fountain of Youth.

No one could possibly know where she was. She had told her daughter that one of the aunts at Meridia was very ill; dying, she believed she had said. To reach Meridia one passed through Baltimore—it had all been simple enough. Luckily she had once or twice talked of the aunts to Anne; had said vaguely: "There was never much intimacy, but some day I ought to go and see them"—so that now it seemed quite natural, and Anne, like all her generation, was too used to sudden comings and goings, and violent changes of plan, to do more than ring up the motor to take her mother to the first train, and recommend carrying a warm wrap.

The hush, the solitude, the sense of being alone and unknown in a strange place to which no one knew she had gone, gradually steadied Kate Clephane's mind, and fragments torn from the last hours began to drift through it, one by one. Curiously enough, it was Anne's awkward little speech about giving her the house that came first—perhaps because it might so easily be the key to the rest.

Kate Clephane had never thought of money since she had
been under her daughter's roof, save on the one occasion
when she had refused to have her allowance increased. Her
disregard of the matter came not so much from conventional
scruples as from a natural gay improvidence. If one were
poor, and lived from hand to mouth, one had to think about
money—worse luck! But once relieved from the need of
doing so, she had dismissed the whole matter from her
thoughts. Safely sheltered, becomingly arrayed, she cared no
more than a child for the abstract power of possession. And
the possession of money, in particular, had always been so
associated in her mind with moral and mental dependence
that after her break with Hylton Davies poverty had seemed
one of the chief attributes of freedom.

It was Anne's suggestion of giving her the house which had
flung a sudden revealing glare on the situation. Anne was
rich, then—very rich! Such a house—one of the few surviv-
ing from the time when Fifth Avenue had been New York's
fashionable quarter—must have grown greatly in value with
the invasion of business. What could it be worth? Mrs.
Clephane couldn't conjecture . . . could only feel that, to
offer it in that way (and with it, of course, the means of living
in it), Anne, who had none of her mother's improvidence,
must be securely and immensely wealthy. And if she were—

The mother stood up and stared about her. What she was
now on the verge of thinking was worse, almost, than all the
dreadful things she had thought before. If it were the money
he wanted, she might conceivably buy him off—that was
what she was thinking! And a nausea crept over her as she
thought it; for he had never seemed to care any more for
money than she did. His gay scorn of it, not only expressed
but acted upon, had been one of his chief charms to her, after
all her years in the Clephane atmosphere of thrifty wealth,

and the showy opulence of the months with Hylton Davies. Chris Fenno, quite simply and naturally, had laughed with her at the cares of the anxious rich, and rejoiced that those, at least, would never weigh on either of them. But that was long ago; long at least in a life as full of chances and changes as his. Compared with the reckless boy she had known he struck her now as having something of the weight and prudence of middle-age. Might not his respect for money have increased with the increasing need of it? At any rate, she had to think of him, to believe it of him, if she could, for the possibility held out her one hope in a welter of darkness.

Her mind flagged. She averted her sickened eyes from the thought, and began to turn once more on the racking wheel of reiteration. *"I must see him . . . I must see him . . . I must see him"* . . . That was as far as she had got. She looked at her watch, and went up to a policeman to ask the way.

He was not to be found at Horace Maclew's, and to her surprise she learned that he did not live there. Careless as he had always been of money in itself, he was by no means averse to what it provided. No one was more appreciative of the amenities of living when they came his way without his having to take thought; and she had pictured him quartered in a pleasant corner of Horace Maclew's house, and participating in all the luxuries of his larder and cellar. But no; a super-butler, summoned at her request, informed her that Major Fenno had telephoned not to expect him that day, and that, as for his home address, the fact was he had never given it.

A new emotion shot through her, half sharper anguish, half relief. If he were not lodged under the Maclew roof, if his private address were not to be obtained there, might it not be because he was involved in some new tie, perhaps actually

living with some unavowable woman? What a solution—
Kate Clephane leapt on it—to be able to return to Anne with
that announcement! It seemed to clear the way in a flash—
but as a hurricane does, by ploughing its path through the
ruins it makes. She supposed she would never, as long as she
lived, be able to think evil of Chris without its hurting her.

She turned away from the wrought-iron and plate-glass
portals that were so exactly what she had known the Maclew
portals would be. Perhaps she would find his address at a
post-office. She asked the way to the nearest one, and vainly
sought for his name in the telephone book. Well, it was not
likely that he would proclaim his whereabouts if what she
suspected were true. But as her eye travelled down the page
she caught his father's name, and an address she remembered. Chris Fenno, though so habitually at odds with his
parents, was fond of them in his easy way—especially fond of
his mother. Kate had often posted letters for him to that
address. She might hear of him there—if necessary she
would ask for Mrs. Fenno.

A trolley carried her to a Quakerish quarter of low plain-
faced brick houses: streets and streets of them there seemed
to be, all alike. Here and there a tree budded before one; but
the house at which she rang had an unbroken view of its
dispirited duplicates. Kate Clephane was not surprised at the
shabbiness of the neighbourhood. She knew that the Fennos,
never well-off according to Clephane standards, had of late
years been greatly straitened, partly, no doubt, through their
son's own exigencies, and his cheerful inability to curtail
them. Her heart contracted as she stood looking down at
Mrs. Fenno's dingy door-mat—the kind on which only tired
feet seem to have wiped themselves—and remembered her
radiant idle months with Mrs. Fenno's son.

She had to ring twice. Then the door was opened by an

elderly negress with gray hair, who stood wiping her hands on a greasy apron, and repeating slowly: "Mr. Chris?"

"Yes. I suppose you can tell me where he lives?"

The woman stared. "Mr. Chris? Where'd he live? Why, right here."

Kate returned the stare. Through the half-open door came the smell of chronic cooking; a mournful waterproof hung against the wall. "Major Fenno—here?"

Major Fenno; yes; the woman repeated it. Mr. Chris they always called him, she added with a toothless smile. Of course he lived there; she kinder thought he was upstairs now. His mother, she added gratuitously, had gone out—stepped round to the market, she reckoned. She'd go and look for Mr. Chris. Would the lady please walk in?

Kate was shown into a small dull sitting-room. All she remembered of it afterward was that there were funny tufted armchairs, blinds half down, a rosewood "what-not," and other relics of vanished ease. Above the fireless chimney stood a too handsome photograph of Chris in uniform.

After all, it was natural enough to find that he was living there. He had always hated any dependence on other people's plans and moods; she remembered how irritably he had spoken of his servitude as Mr. Maclew's secretary, light as the yoke must be. And it was like him, since he was settled in Baltimore, to have returned to his parents. There was something in him—on the side she had always groped for, and occasionally known in happy glimpses—that would make him dislike to live in luxury in the same town in which his father and mother were struggling on the scant income his own follies had reduced them too. He would probably never relate cause and effect, or be much troubled if he did; he would merely say to himself: "It would be beastly wallowing in things here, when it's such hard sledding for the old people"—in the same tone in which he used to say to Kate, on their lazy Riviera Sundays: "If I were at home now I'd be getting ready to take the old lady to church. I always go with her." And no doubt he did. He loved his parents tenderly whenever they were near enough to be loved.

There was a step in the passage. She turned with a start and he came in. At sight of her he closed the door quickly. He was very pale. "Kate!" he said, stopping on the threshold. She had been standing in the window, and she remained there, the width of the room between them. She was silenced by the curious deep shock of remembrance that his actual presence always gave her, and began to tremble lest it should weaken her resolve. "Didn't you expect me?" she finally said.

He looked at her as if he hardly saw her. "Yes; I suppose I did," he answered at length in a slow dragging voice. "I was going to write; to ask when I could see you." As he stood there he seemed like some one snatched out of a trance. To her surprise she felt him singularly in her power. Their parts were reversed for the first time, and she said to herself: "I must act quickly, before he can collect himself." Aloud she asked: "What have you got to say?"

"To say—" he began; and then, suddenly, with a quick change of voice, and moving toward her with outstretched hands: "For God's sake don't take that tone. It's bad enough . . ."

She knew every modulation; he had pleaded with her so often before! His trying it now only hardened her mind and cleared her faculties; and with that flash of vision came the sense that she was actually seeing him for the first time. There he stood, stripped of her dreams, while she registered in a clear objective way all the strength and weakness, the flaws and graces of his person, marked the premature thinning of his smooth brown hair, the incipient crows'-feet about the lids, their too tender droop over eyes not tender enough, and that slight slackness of the mouth that had once seemed a half-persuasive pout, and was now only a sign of secret uncertainties and indulgences. She saw it all, and under the rich glaze of a greater prosperity, a harder maturity, a prompter self-assurance and resourcefulness, she reached to the central failure.

That was what she became aware of—and aware too that the awful fact of actually seeing another human being might happen to one for the first time only after years of intimacy. She averted her eyes as from a sight not meant for her.

"It's bad enough," she heard him repeat.

She turned back to him and her answer caught up his unfinished phrase. "Ah—you do realize how bad it is? That's the reason why you've given up your job? Because you see that you must go? Are you going now—going at once?"

"Going—going?" He echoed the word in his flat sleep-walking voice. "How on earth can I go?"

The question completely hardened whatever his appearance, the startled beaten look of him, had begun to soften in her. She stood gazing at him and laughed.

"How can you go? Are you mad? Why, what else on earth can you do?"

As he stood before her she began to be aware that he had somehow achieved the attitude of dignity for which she was still struggling. He looked like an unhappy man, a cowed man; but not a guilty one.

"If you'd waited I should myself have asked you to let me explain—" he began.

"Explain? What is there to explain?"

"For one thing, why I can't go away—go for good, as you suggest."

"Suggest? I don't suggest! I order it."

"Well—I must disobey your order."

They stood facing each other while she tried to gather up the shattered fragments of her authority. She had said to herself that what lay before her was horrible beyond human imagining; but never once had she imagined that, if she had the strength to speak, he would have the strength to defy her. She opened her lips, but no sound came.

"You seem ready to think the worst of me; I suppose that's natural," he continued. "The best's bad enough. But at any rate, before ordering me to go, perhaps you ought to know that I *did* go—once."

She echoed the word blankly. "Once?"

He smiled a little. "You didn't suppose—or did you?—that I'd drifted into this without a fight; a long fight? At the hospital, where I first met her, I hadn't any idea who she was. I'm not a New Yorker; I knew nothing of your set of people in New York. You never spoke to me of her—I never even knew you had a daughter."

It was true. In that other life she had led she had never spoken to any one of Anne. She had never been able to. From the time when she had returned to Europe, frustrated in her final attempt to get the child back, or even to have one last glimpse of her, to the day when her daughter's cable had summoned her home, that daughter's name had never been uttered by her except in the depths of her heart.

A darkness was about her feet; her head swam. She looked around her vaguely, and put out her hand for something to lean on. Chris Fenno moved a chair forward, and she sat down on it without knowing what she was doing.

He continued to stand in front of her. "You do believe me?" he repeated.

"Oh, yes—I believe you." She was beginning to feel,

now, the relief of finding him less base than he had at first appeared. She lifted her eyes to his. "But afterward—"

"Well; afterward—" He stopped, as if hoping she would help him to fill in the pause. But she made no sign, and he went on. "As I say, we met first in the hospital where she nursed me. It began there. Afterward she asked me to come and see her at her grandmother's. It was only then that I found out—"

"Well, and then—?"

"Then I went away; went as soon as I found out."

"Of course—"

"Yes; of course; only—"

"Only—you came back. You knew; and yet you came back."

She saw his lips hardening again to doggedness. He had dropped into a chair facing hers, and sat there with lowered head, his hands clenched on his knees.

"Naturally you're bound to think the worst of me—"

She interrupted him. "I'm still waiting to know what to think of you. Don't let it be the worst!"

He made a hopeless gesture. "What is the worst?"

"The worst is that, having gone, you should ever have come back. Why did you?"

He stood up, and this time their eyes met. "You have the right to question me about my own feelings; but not about any one else's."

"Feelings? *Your* feelings?" She laughed again. "And my own daughter's—ah, but I didn't mean to name her even!" she exclaimed.

"Well, I'm glad you've named her. You've answered your own question." He paused, and then added in a low voice: "You know what she is when she cares . . ."

"Ah, don't *you* name her—I forbid you! You say you loved

her, not knowing. I believe you . . . I pity you . . . I want to pity you . . . But nothing can change the facts, can change the past. There's nothing for you now but to go."

He stood before her, his eyes on the ground. At last he raised them again, but only for the length of a quick glance. "You think then . . . a past like that . . . irrevocable?"

She sprang to her feet, strong now in her unmitigated scorn. "Irrevocable? Irrevocable? And you ask me this . . . with *her* in your mind? Ah—but you're abominable!"

"Am I? I don't know . . . my head reels with it. She's terribly young; she feels things terribly. She won't give up— she wouldn't before."

"Don't—don't! Leave her out of this. I'm not here to discuss her with you, I'm here to tell you to go, and to go at once."

He made no answer, but turned and walked across the room and back. Then he sank into his chair, and renewed his study of the carpet. Finally he looked up again, with one of the tentative glances she knew so well: those glances that seemed to meet one's answer half-way in their desire to say what one would expect of him. "Is there any use in your taking this tone?"

Again that appeal—it was too preposterous! But suddenly, her eyes on the huddled misery of his attitude, the weakness of his fallen features, she understood that the cry was real; that he was in agony, and had turned to her for help. She crossed the room and laid her hand on his shoulder.

"No; you're right; it's of no use. If you'll listen I'll try to be calm. I want to spare you—why shouldn't I want to?"

She felt her hand doubtfully taken and laid for a moment against his cheek. The cheek was wet. "I'll listen."

"Well, then; I won't reproach you; I won't argue with you. Why should I," she exclaimed with a flash of inspiration, "when all the power is mine? If I came in anger, in abhorrence . . . well, I feel only pity now. Don't reject it—don't reject my pity. This awful thing has fallen on both of us together; as much on me as on you. Let me help you—let us try to help each other."

He pressed the hand closer to his face and then dropped it. "Ah, you're merciful . . . I think I understand the abhorrence better. I've been a cad and a blackguard, and everything else you like. I've been living with the thought of it day and night. Only, now——"

"Well, now," she panted, "let me help you; let me—Chris," she cried, "let me make it possible for you to go. I know there may be all sorts of difficulties—material as well as others—and those at least—"

He looked up at her sharply, as if slow to grasp her words. Then his face hardened and grew red. "You're bribing me? I see. I didn't at first. Well—you've the right to, I suppose; there's hardly any indignity you haven't the right to lay on me. Only—it's not so simple. I've already told you—"

"Don't name her again! Don't make me remember . . . Chris, I want to help you as if this were . . . were any other difficulty . . . Can't we look at it together in that way?"

But she felt the speciousness of her words. How could one face the Gorgon-image of this difficulty as if it were like any other? His silence seemed to echo her thought. Slowly he rose again from his chair, plunged his hands deeply into his pockets, with a gesture she remembered when he was troubled, and went and leaned in the jamb of the window. What was he thinking, she wondered, as he glanced vacantly up and down the long featureless street? Smiling inwardly, perhaps, at the crudeness of her methods, the emptiness of her threats. For, after all—putting the case at its basest—if the money were really what had tempted him, how, with that fortune at his feet, could any offer of hers divert his purpose?

A clock she had not noticed began to tick insistently. It seemed to be measuring out the last seconds before some nightmare crash that she felt herself powerless to arrest. Powerless, at least—

She saw his expression change, and he turned and moved back quickly into the room. "There's my mother coming down the street. She's been to market—my mother does her own marketing." He spoke with a faint smile of irony. "But you needn't be afraid of meeting her. She won't come in here; she never does at this hour. She'll go straight to the kitchen."

Kate had begun to tremble again. "Afraid? Why should I be afraid of your mother? Or she of me? It's you who are afraid now!" she exclaimed.

His face seemed to age as she watched it. "Well, yes, I am," he acknowledged. "I've been a good deal of a nuisance to her first and last; and she's old and ill. Let's leave her out too, if we can."

As he spoke, they heard, through the thin wall, the fumbling of a latch-key in the outer lock. Kate moved to the door; her decision was taken.

"You want to leave her out? Then promise me—give me your word that you'll go. You know you can count on me if you need help. Only you must promise now; if not, I shall call your mother in—I shall tell her everything." Her hand was on the doorknob when he caught it back.

"Don't!"

The street door opened and closed again, a dragging step passed through the narrow hall, and a door was opened into the region from which the negress with the greasy apron had emerged in a waft of cooking.

"Phemia!" they heard Mrs. Fenno call in a tired elderly voice.

"I promise," her son said, loosening his hold on Kate's wrist.

The two continued to stand opposite each other with lowered heads. At length Mrs. Clephane moved away.

"I'm going now. You understand that you must leave at once . . . tomorrow?" She paused. "I'll do all I can for you as long as you keep your word; if you break it I won't spare you. I've got the means to beat you in the end; only don't make me use them—don't make me!"

He stood a few feet away from her, his eyes on the ground. Decidedly, she had beaten him, and he understood it. If there were any degrees left in such misery she supposed that the worst of it was over.

XIV

As Kate Clephane drove up late that night to the house in Fifth Avenue she seemed to be reliving all her former anguished returns there, real or imaginary, from the days when she had said to herself: "Shall I never escape?" to those others when, from far off, she had dreamed of the hated threshold, and yearned for it, and thought: "Shall I never get back?"

She had said she might be late in returning, and had begged that no one should stay up for her. Her wish, as usual, had been respected, and she let herself into the hushed house, put out the lights, and stole up past the door where Anne lay sleeping her last young sleep.

Ah, that thought of Anne's awakening! The thought of seeing Anne's face once again in all its radiant unawareness, and then assisting helpless at the darkening of its light! How would the blow fall? Suddenly and directly, or gradually, circuitously? Would the girl learn her fate on the instant, or be obliged to piece it together, bit by bit, through all the slow agonies of conjecture? What pretext would Chris give for the break? He was skilled enough in evasions and subterfuges—

but what if he had decided to practise them on Anne's mother, and not on Anne? What if the word he had given were already forfeited? What assurance had any promise of his ever conveyed?

Kate Clephane sat in her midnight room alone with these questions. She had forgotten to go to bed, she had forgotten to undress. She sat there, in her travelling dress and hat, as she had stepped from the train: it was as if this house which people called her own were itself no more than the waiting-room of a railway station where she was listening for the coming of another train that was to carry her—whither?

Ah, but she had forgotten—forgotten that she had him in her power! She had said to him: "I've got the means to beat you in the end," and he had bowed his head to the warning and given his word. Why, the mere threat that she would tell his mother had thrown him on her mercy—what would it be if she were to threaten to tell Anne? She knew him . . . under all his emancipated airs, his professed contempt for traditions and conformities, lurked an uneasy fear of being thought less than his own romantic image of himself . . . No; even if his designs on Anne were wholly interested, it would kill him to have her know. There was no danger there.

The bitterness of death was passed; yes—but the bitterness of what came after? What of the time to come, when mother and daughter were left facing each other like two ghosts in a gray world of disenchantment? Well, the girl was young—time would help—they would travel . . . Ah, no; her tortured nerves cried out that there could not be, in any woman's life, another such hour as the one she had just lived through!

Toward dawn she roused herself, undressed, and crawled into bed; and there she lay in the darkness, sharpening her aching wits for the continuation of the struggle.

· · ·

"A telegram—" Aline always said it with the same slightly ironic intonation, as if it were still matter of wonder and amusement to her that any one should be in such haste to communicate with her mistress. Mrs. Clephane, in sables and pearls, with a great house at her orders, was evidently a more considerable person than the stray tenant of the little third-floor room at the Hotel de Minorque, and no one was more competent to measure the distance between them than Aline. But still—a telegram!

Kate opened the envelope with bloodless fingers. "I am going." That was all—there was not even a signature. He had kept his word; and he wanted her to know it.

She felt the loosening of the cords about her heart; a deep breath of relief welled up in her. He had kept his word.

There was a tap on the door, and Anne, radiant, confident, came in.

"You've had a telegram? Not about Aunt Janey—"

Aunt Janey? For a second Kate could not remember, could not associate the question with anything related to the last hours. Then she collected herself, just in time to restrain a self-betraying clutch at the telegram. With a superhuman effort at composure she kept her hands from moving, and left the message lying, face up, on the coverlet between herself and Anne. Yet what if Anne were to read the *Baltimore* above the unsigned words?

"No; it's not about Aunt Janey." She made a farther effort at recollection. "The fact is, the aunts had a panic . . . an absurd panic . . . Aunt Janey's failed a good deal, of course; it's the beginning of the end. But there's no danger of anything sudden—not the least . . . I'm glad I went, though; it comforted them to see me . . . And it was really rather wrong of me not to have been before."

Ah, now, at last she remembered, and how thankfully, that she had, after all, been to Meridia; had, automatically, after leaving Chris, continued her journey, surprised and flattered the aunts by her unannounced appearance, and spent an hour with them before taking the train back to New York. She had had the wit, at the time, to see how useful such an alibi might be, and then, in the disorder of her dreadful vigil, had forgotten about it till Anne's question recalled her to herself. The complete gap in her memory frightened her, and made her feel more than ever unfitted to deal with what might still be coming—what must be coming.

Anne still shed about her the reflected radiance of her bliss. "I'm so glad it's all right—so glad you went. And of course, dear, you didn't tell them anything, did you?"

"Tell them anything—?"

"About me." The lids dropped, the lashes clasped her vision. How could her mother have forgotten? —that flutter of the lids seemed to say.

"Darling! But of course not." Kate Clephane brought the words out with dry lips. Her hand stole out to Anne's, then drew back, affecting to pick up the telegram. She could not put her hand in her daughter's just yet.

The girl sat down beside her on the bed. "I want it to be our secret, remember—just yours and mine—till he comes next week. He can't get away before."

Ah, thank God for that! The mother remembered now that Anne had told her this during their first talk—the talk of which, at the time, no details had remained in her shattered mind. Now, as she listened, those details came back, bit by bit, phantasmagorically mingled.

No one was to be told of the engagement; no, not even Nollie Tresselton; not till Chris came to New York. And that was not to be for another week. He could not get away sooner, and Anne had decreed that he must see her mother before their betrothal was made public. "I suppose I'm absurdly out-of-date—but I want it to be like that," the girl had said; and Kate Clephane understood that it was out of regard for her, with the desire to "situate" her again, and once for all, as the head of the house, that her daughter had insisted on this almost obsolete formality, had stipulated that her suitor should ask Mrs. Clephane's consent in the solemn old-fashioned way.

The girl bent nearer, her radiance veiled in tenderness. "If you knew, mother, how I want you to like him—" ah, the familiar cruel words!—"You did, didn't you, in old times, when you used to know him so well? Though he says he was just a silly conceited boy then, and wonders that anybody could endure his floods of nonsense . . ."

Ah, God, how long would it go on? Kate Clephane again reached out her hand, and this time clasped her daughter's with a silent nod of assent. Speech was impossible. She moistened her parched lips, but no sound came from them; and suddenly she felt everything slipping away from her in a great gulf of oblivion.

"Mother! You're ill—you're over-tired . . ." She was just aware, through the twilight of her faintness, that Anne's arm was under her, that Anne was ringing the bell and moistening her forehead.

BOOK THREE

XV

Fantastic shapes of heavy leaf-shadows on blinding whiteness. Torrents of blue and lilac and crimson foaming over the branches of unknown trees. Azure distances, snow-peaks, silver reefs, and an unbroken glare of dead-white sunshine merging into a moonlight hardly whiter. Was there never any night, real, black, obliterating, in all these dazzling latitudes in which two desperate women had sought refuge?

They had "travelled." It had been very interesting; and Anne was better. Certainly she was much better. They were on their way home now, moving at a leisurely pace—what was there to return for?—from one scene of gorgeous unreality to another. And all the while Anne had never spoken—never really spoken! She had simply, a day or two after Mrs. Clephane's furtive trip to Baltimore, told her mother that her engagement was broken: "by mutual agreement" were the stiff old-fashioned words she used. As no one else, even among their nearest, had been let into the secret of that fleeting bond, there was no one to whom explanations were due; and the girl, her curt confidence to her mother once

147

made, had withdrawn instantly into the rigid reserve she had maintained ever since. Just so, in former days, Kate Clephane had seen old Mrs. Clephane meet calamity. After her favourite daughter's death the old woman had never spoken her name. And thus with Anne; her soul seemed to freeze about its secret. Even the physical resemblance to old Mrs. Clephane reappeared, and with it a certain asperity of speech, a sharp intolerance of trifles, breaking every now and again upon long intervals of smiling apathy.

During their travels the girl was more than ever attentive to her mother; but her solicitude seemed the result of a lesson in manners inculcated long ago (with the rest of her creed) by old Mrs. Clephane. It was impossible for a creature so young and eager to pass unseeingly through the scenes of their journey; but it was clear that each momentary enthusiasm only deepened the inner pang. And from all participation in that hidden conflict between youth and suffering the mother continued to feel herself shut out.

Nevertheless, she began to imagine that time was working its usual miracle. Anne's face was certainly less drawn— Anne's manner perhaps a shade less guarded. Lately she had begun to sketch again . . . she had suggested one day their crossing from Rio to Marseilles, continuing their wanderings in the Mediterranean . . . had spoken of Egypt and Crete for the winter . . .

Mrs. Clephane acquiesced, bought guide-books, read up furtively, and tried to temper zeal with patience. It would not do to seem too eager; she held her breath, waiting on her daughter's moods, and praying for the appearance of the "some one else" whose coming mothers invoke in such contingencies. That very afternoon, sitting on the hotel balcony above a sea of flowers, she had suffered herself to wonder if Anne, who was off on a long riding excursion with a party of young people, might not return with a different look, the clear happy look of the last year's Anne. The young English planter to whose *hacienda* they had gone had certainly interested her more than any one they had hitherto met.

The mother, late that evening, was still alone on the balcony when, from behind her, Anne's shadow fell across the moonlight. The girl dropped into a seat. No, she wasn't tired—wasn't hungry—they had supped, on the way back, at a glorious place high up over Rio. Yes, the day had been wonderful; the beauty incredible; and the moonlit descent through the forest . . . Anne lapsed into silence, her profile turned from her mother. Perhaps—who could tell? Her silence seemed heavy with promise. Suddenly she put out a hand to Kate.

"Mother, I want to make over all my money to you. It would have been yours if things had been different. It *is* yours, really; and I don't want it—I hate it!" Her hand was trembling.

Mrs. Clephane trembled too. "But, Anne—how absurd! What can it matter? What difference can it make?"

"All the difference." The girl lowered her voice. "It's because I was too rich that he wouldn't marry me." It broke from her in a sob. "I can't bear it—I can't bear it!" She stretched her hand to the silver splendours beneath them. "All this beauty and glory in the world—and nothing in me but cold and darkness!"

Kate Clephane sat speechless. She remembered just such flashes of wild revolt in her own youth, when sea and earth and sky seemed joined in a vast conspiracy of beauty, and within her too all was darkness. For months she had been praying for this hour of recovered communion with her daughter; yet now that it had come, now that the barriers were down, she felt powerless to face what was beyond. If it had been any other man! Paralysed by the fact that it was just that one, she continued to sit silent, her hand on Anne's sunken head.

"Why should you think it's the money?" she whispered at last, to gain time.

"I know it—I know it! He told Nollie once that nothing would induce him to marry a girl with a fortune. He thought it an impossible position for a poor man."

"Did he tell *you* so?"

"Not in so many words. But it was easy to guess. When he wrote to . . . to give me back my freedom, he said he'd been mad to think we might marry . . . that it was impossible . . . there would always be an obstacle between us . . ." The girl lifted her head, her agonized eyes on her mother's. "What obstacle could there be but my money?"

Kate Clephane had turned as cold as marble. At the word "obstacle" she stood up, almost pushing the girl from her. In that searching moonlight, what might not Anne read in her eyes?

"Come indoors, dear," she said.

Anne followed her mechanically. In the high-ceilinged shadowy room Mrs. Clephane sat down in a wooden rocking-chair and the girl stood before her, tall and ghostly in her white linen riding-habit, the dark hair damp on her forehead.

"Come and sit by me, Anne."

"No. I want you to answer me first—to promise."

"But, my dear, what you suggest is madness. How can I promise such a thing? And why should it make any difference? Why should any man be humiliated by the fact of marrying a girl with money?"

"Ah, but Chris is different! You don't know him."

The mother locked her hands about the chair-arms. She sat looking down at the bare brick floor of the room, and at

Anne's two feet, slim and imperious, planted just before her in an attitude of challenge, of resistance. She did not dare to raise her eyes higher. *"I don't know him!"* she repeated to herself.

"Mother, answer me—you've got to answer me!" The girl's low-pitched voice had grown shrill; her swaying tall white presence seemed to disengage some fiery fluid. Kate Clephane suddenly recalled the baby Anne's lightning-flashes of rage, and understood what reserves of violence still underlay her daughter's calm exterior.

"How can I answer? I know what you're suffering—but I can't pretend to think that what you propose would make any difference."

"You don't think it was the money?"

Kate Clephane drew a deep breath, and clasped the chair-arms tighter. "No."

"What *was* it, then?" Anne had once more sunk on her knees beside her mother. "I can't bear not to know. I can't bear it an hour longer," she gasped out.

"It's hard, dear . . . I know how hard . . ." Kate put her arms about the shuddering body.

"What shall I do, mother? I've written, and he doesn't answer. I've written three times. And yet I know—"

"You know?"

"He *did* love me, mother."

"Yes, dear.

"And there wasn't any one else; I know that too."

"Yes."

"No one else that he cared about . . . or who had any claim . . . I asked him that before I promised to marry him."

"Then, dear, there's nothing more to say—or to do. You can only conclude that he gave you back your freedom because he wanted his."

"But it was all so quick! How can anybody love one day, and not the next?"

Kate winced. "It does happen so—sometimes."

"I don't believe it—not of him and me! And there *was* the money; I know that. Mother, let me try; let me tell him that you've agreed to take it all back; that I shall have only the allowance you choose to make me."

Mrs. Clephane again sat silent, with lowered head. She had not foreseen this torture.

"Don't you think, dear, as you've written three times and had no answer, that you'd better wait? Better try to forget?"

The girl shook herself free and stood up with a tragic laugh. "You don't know me either, mother!"

That word was crueller than the other; the mother shrank from it as if she had received a blow.

"I do know that, in such cases, there's never any remedy but one. If your courage fails you, there's your pride."

"My pride? What's pride, if one cares? I'd do anything to get him back. I only want you to do what I ask!"

Kate Clephane rose to her feet also. Her own pride seemed suddenly to start up from its long lethargy, and she looked almost defiantly at her defiant daughter.

"I can't do what you ask."

"You won't?"

"I can't."

"You want me to go on suffering, then? You want to kill me?" The girl was close to her, in a white glare of passion. "Ah, it's true—why should you care what happens to me? After all, we're only strangers to each other."

Kate Clephane's first thought was: "I mustn't let her see how it hurts—" not because of the fear of increasing her daughter's suffering, but to prevent her finding out how she could inflict more pain. Anne, at that moment, looked as if the discovery would have been exquisite to her.

The mother dared not speak; she feared her whole agony would break from her with her first word. The two stood facing each other for a moment; then Mrs. Clephane put her hand out blindly. But the girl turned from it with a fierce "Don't!" that seemed to thrust her mother still farther from her, and swept out of the room without a look.

XVI

Anne had decreed that they should return home; and they returned.

The day after the scene at Rio the girl had faltered out an apology, and the mother had received it with a silent kiss. After that neither had alluded to the subject of their midnight talk. Anne was as solicitous as ever for her mother's comfort and enjoyment, but the daughter had vanished in the travelling companion. Sometimes, during those last weary weeks of travel, Kate Clephane wondered if any closer relation would ever be possible between them. But it was not often that she dared to look ahead. She felt like a traveller crawling along a narrow ledge above a precipice; a glance forward or down might plunge her into the depths.

As they drew near New York she recalled her other return there, less than a year before, and the reckless confidence with which she had entered on her new life. She recalled her first meeting with her daughter, her sense of an instant understanding on the part of each, and the way her own past had fallen from her at the girl's embrace.

Now Anne seemed remoter than ever, and it was the

mother's past which had divided them. She shuddered at the fatuity with which she had listened to Enid Drover and Fred Landers when they assured her that she had won her daughter's heart. "She's taken a tremendous fancy to you—" Was it possible that that absurd phrase had ever satisfied her? But daughters, she said to herself, don't take a fancy to their mothers! Mothers and daughters are part of each other's consciousness, in different degrees and in a different way, but still with the mutual sense of something which has always been there. A real mother is just a habit of thought to her children.

Well—this mother must put up with what she had, and make the most of it. Yes; for Anne's sake she must try to make the most of it, to grope her own way and the girl's through this ghastly labyrinth without imperilling whatever affection Anne still felt for her. So a conscientious chaperon might have reasoned—and what more had Kate Clephane the right to call herself?

They reached New York early in October. None of the family were in town; even Fred Landers, uninformed of the exact date of their return, was off shooting with Horace Maclew in South Carolina. Anne had wanted their arrival to pass unperceived; she told her mother that they would remain in town for a day or two, and then decide where to spend the rest of the autumn. On the steamer they languidly discussed alternatives; but, from the girl's inability to decide, the mother guessed that she was waiting for something— probably a letter. "She's written to him after all; she expects to find the answer when we arrive."

They reached the house and went upstairs to their respective apartments. Everything in Anne's establishment was as discreetly ordered as in a club; each lady found her correspondence in her sitting-room, and Kate Clephane, while she glanced indifferently over her own letters, sat with an an-guished heart wondering what message awaited Anne.

They met at dinner, and she fancied the girl looked paler and more distant than usual. After dinner the two went to Kate's sitting-room. Aline had already laid out some of the presents they had brought home: a Mexican turquoise orna-ment for Lilla, an exotic head-band of kingfishers' feathers for Nollie, an old Spanish chronicle for Fred Landers. Mother and daughter turned them over with affected inter-est; then talk languished, and Anne rose and said goodnight.

On the threshold she paused. "Mother, I was odious to you that night at Rio."

Kate started up with an impulsive gesture. "Oh, my darling, what does that matter? It was all forgotten long ago."

"I haven't forgotten it. I'm more and more ashamed of what I said. But I was dreadfully unhappy . . ."

"I know, dear, I know."

The girl still stood by the door, clutching the knob in an unconscious hand. "I wanted to tell you that now I'm cured—quite cured." Her smile was heartbreaking. "I didn't follow your advice; I wrote to him. I told him—I pre-tended—that you were going to accept my plan of giving you back the money, and that I should have only a moderate allowance, so that he needn't feel any inequality . . . any sense of obligation . . ."

Kate listened with lowered head. "Perhaps you were right to write to him."

"Yes, I was right," Anne answered with a faint touch of self-derision. "For now I know. It was not the money; he has told me so. I've had a letter."

"Ah—"

"I'm dismissed," said the girl with an abrupt laugh.

"What do you mean, dear, when you say I was right?"

"I mean that there was another woman." Anne came close to her, with the same white vehement face as she had shown during their nocturnal talk at Rio.

Kate's heart stood still. "Another woman?"

"Yes. And you made me feel that you'd always suspected it."

"No, dear . . . really . . ."

"You *didn't?*" She saw the terrible flame of hope rekindling in Anne's eyes.

"Not—not about any one in particular. But of course, with a man . . . a man like that . . ." (Should she go on, or should she stop?)

Anne was upon her with a cry. *"Mother, what kind of a man?"*

Fool that she was, not to have foreseen the consequences of such a slip! She sat before her daughter like a criminal under cross-examination, feeling that whatever word she chose would fatally lead her deeper into the slough of avowal.

Anne repeated her question with insistence. "You knew him before I did," she added.

"Yes; but it's so long ago."

"But what makes you suspect him now?"

"Suspect? I suspect nothing!"

The girl stood looking at her fixedly under dark menacing brows. "I do, then! I wouldn't allow myself to before; but all the while I knew there was another woman." Between the sentences she drew short panting breaths, as though with every word speech grew more difficult. "Mother," she broke out, "the day I went to Baltimore to see him the maid who opened the door didn't want to let me in because there'd been a woman there two days before who'd made a scene. A scene—that's what she said! Isn't it horrible?" She burst into tears.

157

Kate Clephane sat stupefied. She could not yet grasp the significance of the words her daughter was pouring out, and repeated dully: "You went to Baltimore?" How secret Anne must be, she thought, not only to have concealed her visit at the time, but even to have refrained from any allusion to it during their stormy talk at Rio! How secret, since, even in moments of seeming self-abandonment, she could refrain from revealing whatever she chose to keep to herself! More acutely than ever, the mother had the sense of being at arm's length from her child.

"Yes, I went to Baltimore," said Anne, speaking now in a controlled incisive voice. "I didn't tell you at the time because you were not well. It was just after you came back from Meridia, and had that nervous break-down—you remember? I didn't want to bother you about my own affairs. But as soon as I got his letter saying the engagement was off I jumped into the first train, and went straight to Baltimore to see him."

"And you did?" It slipped from Kate irresistibly.

"No. He was away; he'd left. But I didn't believe it at the time; I thought the maid-servant had had orders not to let me in . . ." She paused. "Mother, it was too horrible; she took me for the woman who had made the scene. She said I looked just like her."

Kate gasped: "The negress said so?"

Her question seemed to drop into the silence like a shout; it was as if she had let fall a platter of brass on a marble floor.

"The negress?" Anne echoed.

Kate Clephane sank down into the depths of her chair as if she had been withered by a touch. She pressed her elbows against her side to try to hide the trembling of her body.

"How did you know it was a negress, mother?"

Kate sat helpless, battling with confused possibilities of fear; and in that moment Anne leapt on the truth.

"It was *you*, mother—you were the other woman? You went to see him the day you said you'd been to Meridia?" The girl stood before her now like a blanched Fury.

"I did go to Meridia!" Kate Clephane declared.

"You went to Baltimore too, then. You went to his house; you saw him. You were the woman who made the scene." Anne's voice had mounted to a cry; but suddenly she seemed to regain a sense of her surroundings. At the very moment when Kate Clephane felt the flash of the blade over her head it was arrested within a hair's-breadth of her neck. Anne's voice sank to a whisper.

"Mother—you did that? It was really you—it was your doing? You've always hated him, then? Hated him enough for that?"

Ah, that blessed word—*hated!* When the other had trembled in the very air! The mother, bowed there, her shrunken body drawn in on itself, felt a faint expanding of the heart.

"No, dear; no; not hate," she stammered.

"But it *was* you?" She suddenly understood that, all the while, Anne had not really believed it. But the moment for pretense was past.

"I did go to see him; yes."

"To persuade him to break our engagement?"

"Anne—"

"Answer me, please."

"To ask him—to try to make him see . . ."

The girl interrupted her with a laugh. "You made him break our engagement—you did it. And all this time—all these dreadful months—you let me think it was because he was tired of me!" She sprang to her mother and caught her by the wrists. Her hot fingers seemed to burn into Kate's shivering flesh.

"Look at me, please, mother; no, straight in the eyes. I want to try to find out which of us you hated most; which of us you most wanted to see suffer."

The mother disengaged herself and stood up. "As for suffering—if you look at me, you'll see I've had my share."

The girl seemed not to hear. "But why—why— why?" she wailed.

A reaction of self-defence came over Kate Clephane. Anne's white-heat of ire seemed to turn her cold, and her self-possession returned.

"What is it you want me to tell you? I did go to see Major Fenno—yes. I wanted to speak to him privately; to ask him to reconsider his decision. I didn't believe he could make you happy. He came round to my way of thinking. That's all. Any mother would have done as much. I had the right—"

"The right?" Anne shrilled. "What right? You gave up all your rights over me when you left my father for another man!"

Mrs. Clephane rose with uncertain steps, and moved toward the door of her bedroom. On the threshold she paused and turned toward her daughter. Strength had come back to her with the thought that after all the only thing that mattered was to prevent this marriage. And that she might still do.

"The right of a friend, then, Anne. Won't you even allow me that? You've treated me as a friend since you asked me to come back. You've trusted me, or seemed to. Trust me now. I did what I did because I knew you ought not to marry Major Fenno. I've known him for a great many years. I knew he couldn't make you happy—make any woman happy. Some men are not meant to marry; he's one of them. I know enough of his history to know that. And you see he recognized that I was right—"

Anne was still staring at her with the same fixed implacable brows. Then her face broke up into the furrows of young anguish, and she became again a helpless grief-tossed girl, battling blindly with her first sorrow. She flung up her arms, buried her head in them, and sank down by the sofa. Kate watched her for a moment, hesitating; then she stole up and laid an arm about the bowed neck. But Anne shook her off and sprang up.

"No—no—no!" she cried. They stood facing each other, as on that other cruel night.

"You don't know me; you don't understand me. What right have you to interfere with my happiness? Won't you please say nothing more now? It was my own fault to imagine that we could ever live together like mother and daughter. A relation like that can't be improvised in a day." She flung a tragic look at her mother. "If you've suffered, I suppose it was my fault for asking you to make the experiment. Excuse me if I've said anything to hurt you. But you must leave me to manage my life in my own way." She turned toward the door.

"Goodnight—my child," Kate whispered.

XVII

Two days later Fred Landers returned.

Mrs. Clephane had sent a note begging him to call her up as soon as he arrived. When his call came she asked if she might dine with him that night, and he replied that she ought to have come without asking. Anne, he supposed, would honour him too?

No, she answered; Anne, the day before, had gone down to the Drovers' on Long Island. She would probably be away for a few days. And would Fred please ask no one else to dine? He assured her that such an idea would never have occurred to him.

He received her in the comfortable shabby drawing-room which he had never changed since his mother and an old-maid sister had vanished from it years before. He indulged his own tastes in the library upstairs, leaving this chintzy room, with its many armchairs, the Steinway piano and the family Chippendale, much as Kate had known it when old Mrs. Landers had given her a bridal dinner. The memory of that dinner, and of Mrs. Landers, large, silvery, demonstrative, flashed through Mrs. Clephane's mind. She saw herself in an elaborately looped gown, proudly followed by her husband, and enclosed in her hostess's rustling embrace, while her present host, crimson with emotion and admiration, hung shyly behind his mother; and the memory gave her a pang of self-pity.

In the middle of the room she paused and looked about her. "It feels like home," she said, without knowing what she was saying.

A flush almost as agitated as the one she remembered mounted to Landers's forehead. She saw his confusion and pleasure, and was remotely touched by them.

"You see, I'm homeless," she explained with a faint smile.

"Homeless?"

"Oh, I can't remember when I was ever anything else. I've been a wanderer for so many years."

"But not any more," he smiled.

The double mahogany doors were thrown open. Landers, with his stiff little bow, offered her an arm, and they passed into a dusky flock-papered dining-room which seemed to borrow most of its lighting from the sturdy silver and monumental cut-glass of the dinner-table. A bunch of violets, compact and massive, lay by her plate. Everything about Fred Landers was old-fashioned, solid and authentic. She sank into her chair with a sense of its being a place of momentary refuge. She did not mean to speak till after dinner—then she would tell him everything she thought. "How delicious they are!" she murmured, smelling the violets.

In the library, after dinner, Landers settled her in his deepest armchair, moved the lamp away, pressed a glass of old Chartreuse on her, and said: "And now, what's wrong?"

The suddenness and the perspicacity of the question took

her by surprise. She had imagined he would leave the preliminaries to her, or at any rate beat about the subject in a clumsy effort to get at it. But she perceived that, awkward and almost timorous as he remained in smaller ways, the mere habit of life had given him a certain self-assurance at important moments. It was she who now felt a tremor of reluctance. How could she tell him—what could she tell him?"

"Well, you know, I really *am* homeless," she began. "Or at least, in remaining where I am I'm forfeiting my last shred of self-respect. Anne has told me that her experiment has been a mistake."

"What experiment?"

"Having me back."

"Is that what she calls it—an experiment?"

Mrs. Clephane nodded.

Fred Landers stood leaning against the mantelpiece, an unlit cigar in his hand. His face expressed perplexity and perturbation. "I don't understand. What has happened? She seemed to adore you."

"Yes; as a visitor; a chaperon; a travelling companion."

"Well—that's not so bad to begin with."

"No; but it has nothing on earth to do with the real relation between a mother and daughter."

"Oh, *that*—"

It was her turn to flush. "You agree with Anne, then, that I've forfeited all right to claim it?"

He seemed embarrassed. "What do you mean by claiming it?"

She hesitated a moment; then she began. It was not the story she had meant to tell; she had hardly opened her lips before she understood that it would be as impossible to tell that to Fred Landers as to Anne. For an instant, as he welcomed her to the familiar house, so full of friendly memories, she had had the illusion of nearness to him, the sense of a brotherly reassuring presence. But as she began to speak of Chris every one else in her new life except her daughter became remote and indistinct to her. She supposed it could not be otherwise. She had chosen to cast her lot elsewhere, and now, coming back after so many years, she found the sense of intimacy and confidence irreparably destroyed. What did she really know of the present Fred Landers, or he of her? All she found herself able to say was that when she had heard that Anne meant to marry Chris Fenno she had thought it her duty to try to prevent the marriage; and that the girl had guessed her interference and could not forgive her. She elaborated on this, lingering over the relatively insignificant details of her successive talks with her daughter in the attempt to delay the moment when Landers should begin to question her.

She saw that he was deeply disturbed, but perhaps not altogether sorry. He had never liked Chris, she knew, and the news of the engagement was clearly a shock to him. He said he had seen and heard nothing of Fenno since Anne and her mother had left. Landers, who could not recall that either Horace Maclew or Lilla had ever mentioned him, had concluded that the young man was no longer a member of their household, and probably not even in Baltimore. If he were, Lilla would have been sure to keep her hold on him; he was too useful a diner and dancer to be lost sight of—and much more in Lilla's line, one would have fancied, than in Anne's.

Kate Clephane winced at the unconscious criticism. "He gave me his word that he would go," she said with a faint sigh of relief.

Fred Landers continued to lean meditatively against the chimney-piece.

"You said nothing at all to Anne herself at the time?" he asked, after another interval.

"No. Perhaps I was wrong; but I was afraid to. I felt I didn't know her well enough—yet."

Instantly she saw how he would interpret her avowal, and her colour rose again. She must have felt, then, that she knew Major Fenno better; the inference was inevitable.

"You found it easier to speak to Fenno?"

She hesitated. "I cared so much less for what he felt."

"Of course," he sighed. "And you knew damaging things about him? Evidently, since he broke the engagement when you told him to."

Again she faltered. "I knew something of his past life—enough to be sure he wasn't the kind of husband for Anne. I made him understand it. That's all."

"Ah. Well, I'm not surprised. I suspected he was trying for her, and I own I hated the idea. But now I suppose there's no help for it—"

"No help?" She looked up in dismay.

"Well—is there? To be so savage with you she must be pretty well determined to have him back. How the devil are you going to stop it?"

"I can't. But *you*—oh, Fred, you must!"—Her eyes clung imploringly to his troubled face.

"But I don't know anything definite! If there *is* anything—anything one can really take hold of—you'll have to tell me. I'll do all I can; but if I interfere without good reason, I know it will only make Anne more determined. Have you forgotten what the Clephanes are like?"

She had lowered her head again, and sat desolately staring at the floor. With the little wood-fire playing on the hearth, and this honest kindly man looking down at her, how safe and homelike the room seemed! Yet her real self was not in it at all, but blown about on a lonely wind of anguish, outside in the night. And so it would always be, she supposed.

"Won't you tell me exactly what there is against him?" she heard Landers repeat.

The answer choked in her throat. Finally she brought out: "Oh, I don't know . . . women . . . the usual thing . . . He's light . . ."

"But is it all just hearsay? Or have you proof—proof of any one particular rotten thing?"

"Isn't his giving up and going away sufficient proof?"

"Not if he comes back now when she sends for him."

The words shot through her like a stab. "Oh, but she mustn't—she can't!"

"You're fairly sure he will come if she does?"

Kate Clephane put up her hands and pressed them against her ears. She could not bear to hear another question. What had been the use of coming to Fred Landers? He had no help to give her, and his insight had only served to crystallize her hazy terrors. She rose slowly from her armchair and held out her hand with a struggling smile.

"You're right. I suppose there's nothing more to do."

"But you're not going?"

"Yes; I'm tired. And I want to be by myself—to think. I must decide about my own future."

"Your own future? Oh, nonsense! Let all this blow over. Wait till Anne comes back. The chief thing, of course, is that you should stay with her, whatever happens."

She put her hand in his. "Goodbye, Fred. And thank you."

"I'll do all I can, you know," he said, as he followed her down the stairs. "But you mustn't desert Anne."

The taxi he had called carried her back to her desolate house.

XVIII

Her place was beside Anne—that was all she had got out of Fred Landers. And in that respect she was by no means convinced that her instinct was not surer than his, that she was not right in agreeing with her daughter that their experiment had been a failure.

Yet, even if it had, she could not leave Anne now; not till she had made sure there was no further danger from Chris. Ah—if she were once certain of that, it would perhaps be easiest and simplest to go! But not till then.

She did not know when Anne was coming back; no word had come from her. Mrs. Clephane had an idea that the house-keeper knew; but she could not ask the house-keeper. So for another twenty-four hours she remained on, with a curious sense of ghostly unconcern, while she watched Aline unpack her trunks and "settle" her into her rooms for the winter.

It was on the third day that Nollie Tresselton telephoned. She was in town, and asked if she might see Mrs. Clephane at once. The very sound of her voice brought reassurance; and Kate Clephane sat counting the minutes till she appeared.

She had come up from the Drovers', as Kate had guessed; and she brought an embarrassed message of apology from Anne. "She couldn't write—she's too upset. But she's so sorry for what she said . . . for the way she said it. You must try to forgive her . . ."

"Oh, forgive her—that's nothing!" the mother cried, her eyes searching the other's face. But Nollie's vivid features were obscured by the embarrassment of the message she had brought. She looked as if she were tangled in Anne's confusion.

"That's nothing," Kate Clephane repeated. "I hurt her horribly too—I had to. I couldn't expect her to understand."

Mrs. Tresselton looked relieved. "Ah, you do see that? I knew you would! I told her so" She hesitated, and then went on, with a slight tremor in her voice: "Your taking it in that way will make it all so much easier—"

But she stopped again, and Kate, with a sinking heart, stood up. "Nollie; she wants me to go?"

"No, no! How could you imagine it? She wants you to look upon this house as yours; she has always wanted it."

"But she's not coming back to it?"

The younger woman laid a pleading hand on Mrs. Clephane's arm. "Aunt Kate—you must be patient. She feels she can't; not now, at any rate."

"Not now? Then it's *she* who hasn't forgiven?"

"She would, you know—oh, so gladly!—she'd never think again of what's happened. Only she fears—"

"Fears?"

"Well—that your feeling about Chris is still the same . . ."

Mrs. Clephane caught at the hand that lay on her arm. "Nollie! She knows where he is? She's seen him?"

"No; but she means to. He's been very ill—he's had a bad time since the engagement was broken. And that makes her feel still more strongly—" The younger woman broke off and looked at Mrs. Clephane compassionately, as if trying to make her understand the hopelessness of the struggle. "Aunt Kate, really . . . what's the use?"

"The use? Where is he, Nollie? Here—now—in New York?"

Mrs. Tresselton was silent; the pity in her gaze had turned to a guarded coolness. Of course Nollie couldn't understand—never would! Of course they were all on Anne's side. Kate Clephane stood looking helplessly about her. The memory of old scenes under that same roof—threats, discussions, dissimulations and inward revolts—arose within her, and she felt on her shoulders the whole oppression of the past.

"Don't think," Nollie continued, her expression softening, "that Anne hasn't tried to understand . . . to make allowances. The boy you knew must have been so different from the Major Fenno we all like and respect—yes, respect. He's 'made good', you see. It's not only his war record, but everything since. He's worked so hard—done so well at his various jobs—and Anne's sure that if he had the chance he would make himself a name in the literary world. All that naturally makes it more difficult for her to understand your objection—or your way of asserting it."

Mrs. Clephane lifted imploring eyes to her face. "I don't expect Anne to understand; not yet. But you must try to, Nollie; you must help me."

"I want to, Aunt Kate." The young woman stood before her, affectionately perplexed. "If there's anything . . . anything really wrong . . . you ought to tell me."

"I *do* tell you," Kate panted.

"Well—what is it?"

Silence fell—always the same silence. Kate glanced desperately about the imprisoning room. Every panel and moulding of its walls, every uncompromising angle or portly curve of its decorous furniture, seemed equally leagued against her, forbidding her, defying her, to speak.

"Ask Fred Landers," she said, at bay.

"But I have; I saw him on my way here. And he says he doesn't know—that you wouldn't explain."

"Why should I have to explain? I've said Major Fenno ought not to marry Anne. I've known him longer than any of you. Isn't it likely that I know him better?"

The words came from her precipitate and shrill; she felt she was losing all control of her face and voice, and lifted her handkerchief to her lips to hide their twitching.

"Aunt Kate—!" Nollie Tresselton gasped it out on a new note of terror; then she too fell silent, slowly turning her eyes away.

In that instant Kate Clephane saw that she had guessed, or if not, was at least on the point of guessing; and fresh alarm possessed the mother. She tried to steady herself, to raise new defences against this new danger. "Some men are not meant to marry: they're sure to make their wives unhappy. Isn't that reason enough? It's a question of character. In those ways, I don't believe character ever changes. That's all."

"That's all." The word was said. She had been challenged again, and had again shrunk away from the challenge.

Nollie Tresselton drew a deep breath of relief. "After knowing him so well as a boy, you naturally don't want to say anything more; but you think they're unsuited to each other."

"Yes—that's it. You do see?"

The younger woman considered; then she took Mrs. Clephane by the hand. "I do see. And I'll try to help—to persuade Anne to put off deciding. Perhaps after she's seen him it will be easier . . ."

Nollie was again silent, and Mrs. Clephane understood that, whatever happened, the secret of Chris's exact whereabouts was to be kept from her. She thought: "Anne's afraid to have me meet him again," and there was a sort of fierce satisfaction in the thought.

Nollie was gathering up her wrap and hand-bag. She had to get back to Long Island, she said; Kate understood that she meant to return to the Drovers'. As she reached the door a last impulse of avowal seized the older woman. What if, by giving Nollie a hint of the truth, she could make sure of her support and thus secure Anne's safety? But what argument against the marriage would be more efficacious on Nollie's lips than on her own? One only—the one that no one must ever use. The terror lest Nollie, possessed of that truth, and sickened by it, should after all reveal it in a final effort to prevent the marriage, prevailed over Mrs. Clephane's other fears. Once Nollie knew, Anne would surely get to know; the horror of that possibility sealed the mother's lips.

Nollie, from the threshold, still looked at her wistfully, expectantly, as if half-awaiting the confession; but Mrs. Clephane held out her hand without a word.

"I must find out where he is." It was Kate's first thought after the door had closed on her visitor. If he were in New York—and he evidently was—she, Kate Clephane, must run him down, must get speech with him, before he had been able to see her daughter.

But how was she to set about it? Fred Landers did not even know if he were still with Horace Maclew or not—for the mere fact of Maclew's not alluding to him while they were together meant nothing, less than nothing. And even if he had left the Maclews, the chances were that Lilla knew where he was, and had already transmitted Anne's summons.

Mrs. Clephane consulted the telephone-book, but of course in vain. Then, after some hesitation, she rang up Horace Maclew's house in Baltimore. No one was there, but she finally elicited from the servant who answered the telephone that Mrs. Maclew was away on a motor trip. Perhaps Mr. Maclew could be reached at his country-place . . . Kate tried the country-place, but Mr. Maclew had gone to Chicago.

The sense of loneliness and helplessness closed in on her more impenetrably than ever. Night came, and Aline reminded her that she had asked to have her dinner brought up on a tray. Solitary meals in John Clephane's dining-room were impossible to her.

"I don't want any dinner."

Aline's look seemed to say that she knew why, and her mistress hastily emended: "Or just some bouillon and toast. Whatever's ready—"

She sat down to it without changing her dress. Every gesture, every act, denoting intimacy with that house, or the air of permanence in her relation to it, would also have been impossible. Again she had the feeling of sitting in a railway station, waiting for a train to come in. But now she knew for what she was waiting.

At the close of her brief meal Aline entered briskly with fruit and coffee. Her harsh face illuminated with curiosity, she handed her mistress a card. "The gentleman is downstairs. He hopes Madame will excuse the hour." Her tone seemed to imply: "Madame, in this case, will excuse *everything!*" and Kate cast a startled glance at the name.

He had come to her, then—had come of his own accord! She felt dizzy with relief and fear. Fear uppermost—yes; was she not always afraid of him?

XIX

Chris Fenno stood in the drawing-room. The servant who received him had turned on a blast of lamps and wall-lights, and in the hard overhead glare he looked drawn and worn, like a man recovering from severe illness. His clothes, too, Kate fancied, were shabbier; everything in his appearance showed a decline, a defeat.

She had not much believed in his illness when Nollie spoke of it; the old habit of incredulity was too strong in her. But now his appearance moved her. She felt herself responsible, almost guilty. But for her folly, she thought, he might have been standing before her with a high head, on easy terms with the world.

"You've been ill!" she exclaimed.

His gesture brushed that aside. "I'm well now, thanks." He looked her in the face and added: "May we have a few minutes' talk?"

She faltered: "If you think it necessary." Inwardly she had already begun to tremble. When his blue eyes turned to that harsh slate-gray, and the two perpendicular lines deepened between his brows, she had always trembled.

"You've made it necessary," he retorted, his voice as harsh as his eyes.

"I?"

"You've broken our compact. It's not my doing. I stuck to my side of it." He flung out the short sentences like blows.

Her heart was beating so wildly that she could not follow what he said. "What do you mean?" she stammered.

"That you agreed to help me if I gave up Anne. God knows what your idea of helping me was. To me it meant only one thing: your keeping quiet, keeping out of the whole business, and trusting me to carry out my side of the bargain—as I did. I broke our engagement, chucked my job, went away. And you? Instead of keeping out of it, of saying nothing, you've talked against me, insinuated God knows what, and then refused to explain your insinuations. You've put me in such a position that I've got to take back my word to you, or appear to your daughter and your family as a man who has run away because he knew he couldn't face the charge hanging over him."

It was only in the white heat of anger that he spoke with such violence, and at such length; he seemed spent, and desperately at bay, and the thought gave Kate Clephane courage.

"Well—*can* you face it?" she asked.

His expression changed, as she had so often seen it change. From menace it passed to petulance and then became almost pleading in its perplexity. She said to herself: "It's the first time I've ever been brave with him, and he doesn't know how to take it." But even then she felt the precariousness of the advantage. His ready wit had so often served him instead of resolution. It served him now.

"You do mean to make the charge, then?" he retorted.

She stood silent, feeling herself defeated, and at the same

time humiliated that their angry thoughts should have dragged them down to such a level.

"Don't sneer—" she faltered.

"Sneer? At what? I'm in dead earnest—can't you see it? You've ruined me—or very nearly. I'm not speaking now of my feelings; that would make you sneer, probably. At any rate, this is no time for discussing them. I'm merely putting my case as a poor devil who has to earn his living, a man who has his good name to defend. On both counts you've done me all the harm you could."

"I had to stop this marriage."

"Very well. I agreed to that. I did what I'd promised. Couldn't you let it alone?"

"No. Because Anne wouldn't. She wanted to ask you to come back. She saw I couldn't bear it— she suspected me of knowing something. She insisted."

"And you sacrificed my good name rather—"

"Oh, I'd sacrifice anything. You'd better understand that."

"I do understand it. That's why I'm here. To tell you I consider that what you've done has freed me from my promise."

She stretched out her hands as if to catch him back. "Chris—no, stay! You can't! You can't! You know you can't!"

He stood leaning against the chimney-piece, his arms crossed, his head a little bent and thrust forward, in the attitude of sullen obstinacy that she knew so well. And all at once in her own cry she heard the echo of other cries, other entreaties. She saw herself in another scene, stretching her arms to him in the same desperate entreaty, with the same sense of her inability to move him, even to reach him. Her tears overflowed and ran down.

"You don't mean you'll tell her?" she whispered.

He kept his dogged attitude. "I've got to clear myself—somehow."

"Oh, don't tell her, don't tell her! Chris, don't tell her!"

As the cry died on her lips she understood that, in uttering it, she had at last cast herself completely on his mercy. For it was not impossible that, if other means failed, he would risk justifying himself to Anne by revealing the truth. There were times when he was reckless enough to risk anything. And if Kate were right in her conjecture—if he had the audacity he affected—then his hold over her was complete, and he knew it. If any one else told Anne, the girl's horror would turn her from him at once. But what if he himself told her? All this flashed on Kate Clephane in the same glare of enlightenment.

There was a long silence. She had sunk into a chair and hidden her face in her hands. Presently, through the enveloping cloud of her misery, she felt his nearness, and a touch on her shoulder.

"Kate—won't you try to understand; to listen quietly?"

She lifted her eyes and met his fugitively. They had lost their harshness, and were almost frightened. "I was angry when I came here—a man would be," he continued. "But what's to be gained by our talking to each other in this way? You were awfully kind to me in old times; I haven't forgotten. But is that a reason for being so hard on me now? I didn't bring this situation on myself—you're my witness that I didn't. But here it is; it's a fact; we've got to face it."

She lowered her eyes and voice to whisper painfully: "To face Anne's love for you?"

"Yes."

"Her determination—?"

"Her absolute determination."

His words made her tremble again; there had always been

moments when his reasonableness alarmed her more than his anger, because she knew that, to be so gentle, he must be certain of eventually gaining his point. But she gathered resolution to say: "And if I take back my threats, as you call them? If I take back all I've said—'clear' you entirely? That's what you want, I understand? If I promise that," she panted, "will you promise too—promise me to find a way out?"

His hand fell from her shoulder, and he drew back a step. "A way out—now? But there isn't any."

Mrs. Clephane stood up. She remembered wondering long ago—one day when he had been very tender—how cruel Chris could be. The conjecture, then, had seemed whimsical, almost morbid; now she understood that she had guessed in him from the outset this genius for reaching, at the first thrust, to the central point of his antagonist's misery.

"You've seen my daughter, then?"

"I've seen her—yes. This morning. It was she who sent me here."

"If she's made up her mind, why did she send you?"

"To tell you how she's suffering. She thinks, you know—" He wavered again for a second or two, and then brought out: "She's very unhappy about the stand you take. She thinks you ought to say something to . . . to clear up . . ."

"What difference will it make, if she means to marry you?"

"Why—the immense difference of her feeling for you. She's dreadfully hurt . . . she's very miserable. . . ."

"But absolutely determined?"

Again he made an embarrassed gesture of acquiescence.

Kate Clephane stood looking about the rich glaring room. She felt like a dizzy moth battering itself to death against that implacable blaze. She closed her lids for an instant.

"I shall tell her, then; I shall tell her the truth," she said suddenly.

He stood in the doorway, his hard gaze upon her. "Well, tell her—do tell her; if you want never to see her again," he said.

XX

He must have been very sure of her not acting on his final challenge, or he would not have dared to make it. That was the continuous refrain of Kate Clephane's thoughts as the train carried her down to Long Island the next morning.

"He's convinced I shall never tell her; but what if I do?" The thought sustained her through the long sleepless night, and gave her the strength and clearness of mind to decide that she must at once see Anne, however little her daughter might desire the meeting. After all, she still had that weapon in her depleted armoury: she could reveal the truth.

At the station she found one of the Drover motors, and remembered with a start that it was a Saturday, and that she would probably come upon a large house-party at her sister-in-law's. But to her relief she learned that the motor had only brought a departing visitor to the up-train. She asked to be driven back in it, and in a few moments was rolling between the wrought-iron gates and down the long drive to the house. The front door stood open, and she went into the hall. The long oak tables were so laden with golf-sticks, tennis racquets

and homespun garments that she saw she had been right in
guessing she would encounter a houseful. But it was too late
to turn back; and besides, what did the other people matter?
They might, if they were numerous enough, make it easier
for her to isolate herself with Anne.

The hall seemed empty; but as she advanced she saw a
woman's figure lazily outstretched in a deep armchair before
the fire. Lilla Maclew rose from the chair to greet her.

"Hallo—Aunt Kate?" Mrs. Clephane caught the embarrassment in her niece's rich careless voice, and guessed that
the family had already been made aware of the situation
existing between Anne and Anne's mother, and probably,
therefore, of the girl's engagement. But Lilla Maclew was
even more easy, self-confident and indifferent than Lilla
Gates had been. The bolder dash of peroxyde on her hair,
and the glint of jewels on her dusky skin, made her look like
a tall bronze statue with traces of gilding on it.

"Hallo," she repeated, rather blankly; "have you come to
lunch?"

"I've come to see Anne," Anne's mother answered.

Lilla's constraint visibly increased, and with it her sullen
reluctance to make any unnecessary effort. One hadn't married money, her tone proclaimed, to be loaded up like this
with family bothers.

"Anne's out. She's gone off with Nollie to a tennis match
or something. I'm just down; we played bridge till nearly
daylight, and I haven't seen anybody this morning. I suppose
mother must be somewhere about."

She glanced irritably around her, as if her look ought to
have been potent enough to summon her mother to the spot;
and apparently it was, for a door opened, and Mrs. Drover
appeared.

"Kate! I didn't know you were here! How did you come?"

Her hostess's mild countenance betrayed the same embarrassment as Lilla's, and under it Mrs. Clephane detected the
same aggrieved surprise. Having at last settled her own
daughter's difficulties, Mrs. Drover's eyes seemed to ask,
why should she so soon be called upon to deal with another
family disturbance? Even juries, after a protracted trial, are
excused from service for seven years; yet here she was being
drawn into the thick of a new quarrel when the old one was
barely composed.

"Anne's out," she added, offering a cool pink cheek to her
sister-in-law.

"May I wait, then? I came to see her," Kate said timidly.

"Of course, my dear! You must stay to lunch." Mrs.
Drover's naturally ceremonious manner became stiff with
apprehension. "You look tired, you know; this continuous
travelling must be very exhausting. And the food! . . . Yes;
Anne ought to be back for lunch. She and Nollie went off to
the Glenvers' to see the tennis finals; didn't they, Lilla? Of
course I can't *promise* they'll be back . . . but you must
stay . . ." She rang and gave orders that another seat should
be put at table. "We're rather a large party; you won't mind?
The men are off at a polo practice at Hempstead. Dawson,
how many shall we be for lunch?" she asked the butler.
Under her breath she added: "Yes; champagne." If we ever
need it, she concluded in a parenthetic glance, it will be
today!

The hall was already filling up with a jocund bustle of
Drovers and Tresseltons. Young, middle-aged and elderly,
they poured out of successive motors, all ruddy, prosperous,
clamouring for food. Hardly distinguishable from the family
were the week-end friends returning with them from one
sportive spectacle or another. As Kate Clephane stood among
them, going through the mechanical gestures of greeting and

small-talk, she felt so tenuous and spectral that she almost wondered how she could be visible to their hearty senses. They were all glad to see her, all a little surprised at her being there, and all soon forgetful of their own surprise in discussing the more important questions of polo, tennis and lunch. Once more she had the impression of being hurried with them down a huge sliding stairway that perpetually revolved upon itself, and once more she recalled her difficulty in telling one of them from another, and in deciding whether it was the Tresseltons or the Drovers who had the smallest noses.

"But Anne—where's Anne?" Hendrik Drover enquired, steering the tide of arrivals toward the shining stretch of a long luncheon-table. He put Mrs. Clephane at his left, and added, as he settled her in her seat: "Anne and Nollie went off early to the Glenver finals. But Joe was there too—weren't you, Joe?"

He did not wait for Joe Tresselton's answer, but addressed himself hurriedly to the lady on his right. Kate had the feeling that they all thought she had committed an error of taste in appearing among them at that particular moment, but that it was no business of theirs, after all, and they must act in concert in affecting that nothing could be more natural. The Drovers and Tresseltons were great at acting in concert, and at pretending that whatever happened was natural, usual, and not of a character to interfere with one's lunch. When a member of the tribe was ill, the best doctors and most expensive nurses were summoned, but the illness was spoken of as a trifling indisposition; when misfortune befell any one of them, it was not spoken of at all. Taking Lilla for granted had brought this art to the highest point of perfection, and her capture of Horace Maclew had fully confirmed its usefulness.

All this flashed through Kate Clephane while she refused the champagne ordered on her behalf, and pretended to eat Maryland chicken and corn *soufflé;* but under the surface-rattle of her thoughts a watchful spirit brooded haggardly on the strangeness and unreality of the scene. She had come, in agony of soul, to seek her daughter, to have speech with her at all costs; and the daughter was away watching a tennis match, and no one seemed surprised or concerned. Life, even Anne's life, was going on in its usual easy way. The girl had found her betrothed again, and been reunited to him; what would it matter to her, or to her approving family, if the intruder who for a few months had gone through the pretence of being one of them, and whose delusion they had good-naturedly abetted, should vanish again from the group? As she looked at them all, so obtuse and so powerful, so sure of themselves and each other, her own claim to belong to them became incredible even to herself. She had made her choice long ago, and she had not chosen them; and now their friendly indifference made the fact clear.

Well—perhaps it also made her own course clearer. She was as much divided from them already as death could divide her. Why not die, then—die altogether? She would tell Anne the truth, and then go away and never see her again; and that would be death . . .

"Ah, here they are!" Hendrik Drover called out genially. Lunch was over; the guests, scattered about in the hall and billiard-room, were lighting their cigarettes over coffee and liqueurs. Mrs. Clephane, who had drifted out with the rest, and mechanically taken her cup of coffee as the tray passed her, lifted her head and saw Anne and Nollie Tresselton. Anne entered first. She paused to take off her motor coat, glanced indifferently about her, and said to Mrs. Drover: "You didn't wait for us, Aunt Enid? We were so late that we stopped to lunch at Madge's—." Then she saw her mother and her pale cheek whitened.

Mrs. Clephane's eyes filled, and she stood motionless. Everything about her was so blurred and wavering that she dared not stir, or even attempt to set down her cup.

"Mother!" the girl exclaimed. With a quick movement she made her way through the cluster of welcoming people, and went up with outstretched arms to Mrs. Clephane.

For a moment the two held each other; then Mrs. Drover, beaming up to them, said benevolently: "Your mother must be awfully tired, Anne. Do carry her off to your own quarters for a quiet talk—" and dazed, trembling, half-fearing she was in a dream from which the waking would be worse than death, Mrs. Clephane found herself mounting the stairs with her daughter.

On the first landing she regained her senses, said to herself: "She thinks I've come to take back what I said," and tried to stiffen her soul against this new form of anguish. Anne moved silently at her side. After the first cry and the first kiss she had drawn back into herself, perhaps obscurely conscious of some inward resistance in her mother. But when the bedroom door had closed on them she drew Mrs. Clephane down into an armchair, dropped on her knees beside it, and whispered: "Mother—how could you and I ever give each other up?"

The words sounded like an echo of the dear unuttered things the mother had heard said to herself long ago, in her endless dialogues with an invisible Anne. No tears rose to her eyes, but their flood seemed to fill her thirsty breast. She drew Anne's head against it. "Anne . . . little Anne . . ." Her fingers crept through the warm crinklings of hair, wound about the turn of the temples, and slipped down the cheeks. She shut her eyes, softly saying over her daughter's name.

185

Anne was the first to speak. "I've been so unhappy. I wanted you so to come."

"Darling, you were sure I would?"

"How could I tell? You seemed so angry."

"With you? Never, child!"

There was a slight pause; then, raising herself, the girl slipped her arms about her mother's neck.

"Nor with him, any longer?"

The chill of reality smote through Mrs. Clephane's happy trance. She felt herself turning again into the desolate stranger who had stood below watching for Anne's return.

"Mother—you see, I want you both," she heard the girl entreating; and *"Now!"* the inward voice admonished her.

Now indeed was the time to speak; to make an end. It was clear that no compromise would be of any use. Anne had obviously imagined that her mother had come to forgive and be forgiven, and that Chris was to be included in the general amnesty. On no other terms would any amnesty be accepted. Through the girl's endearments Kate felt, as never before, the steely muscles of her resolution.

Anne pressed her closer. "Can't we agree, mother, that I must take my chance—and that, if the risks are as great as you think, you'll be there to help me? After all, we've all got to buy our own experience, haven't we? And perhaps the point of view about . . . about early mistakes . . . is more indulgent now than in your time. But I don't want to discuss that," the girl hurried on. "Can't we agree not to discuss anything—not even Chris—and just be the perfect friends we were before? You'd say yes if you knew the difference it has made, this last year, to have you back!" She lifted her face close to Mrs. Clephane's to add, with a half-whimsical smile: "Mothers oughtn't ever to leave their daughters."

Kate Clephane sat motionless in that persuasive hold. It

did not seem to her, at the moment, as if she and her child were two, but as if her whole self had passed into the young body pressed pleadingly against her.

"How can I leave her—how can I ever leave her?" was her only thought.

"You see," the cajoling voice went on, "when I asked you to come back and live with me, though I did want you to, most awfully, I wasn't as sure . . . well, as sure as Uncle Fred was . . . that the experiment would be a success—a perfect success. My life had been rather lonely, but it had been very independent too, in spite of Granny, and I didn't know how well I should behave to my new mother, or whether she'd like me, or whether we'd be happy together. And then you came, and the very first day I forgot all my doubts—didn't *you?*"

Kate Clephane assented: "The very first day."

"And every day afterward, as I saw how right Uncle Fred had been, and how perfectly he'd remembered what you were, and what you would have been to me if we hadn't been separated when I was a baby, I was more and more grateful to you for coming, and more and more anxious to make you forget that we hadn't always been together."

"You did make me forget it—"

"And then, suddenly, the great gulf opened again, and there I was on one side of it, and you on the other, just as it was in all those dreary years when I was without you; and it seemed as if it was you who had chosen again that we should be divided, and in my unhappiness I said dreadful things . . . I know I did . . ."

Kate felt as if it were her own sobs that were shaking her daughter's body. She held her fast, saying over and over, as a mother would to a child that has fallen and hurt itself: "There, there . . . don't cry." She no longer knew what she herself was feeling. All her consciousness had passed into Anne. This young anguish, which is the hardest of all to bear, must be allayed: she was ready to utter any words that should lift that broken head from her breast.

"My Anne—how could I ever leave you?" she whispered. And as she spoke she felt herself instantly caught in the tight net of her renunciation. If she did not tell Anne now she would never tell her—and it was exactly on this that Chris had counted. He had known that she would never speak.

XXI

It had been decided that Mrs. Clephane must, of course, stay over the Sunday; on Monday morning she would return to town with Anne. Meanwhile Aline was summoned with week-end raiment; and Kate Clephane, after watching the house-party drive off to a distant polo match, remained alone in the great house with her sister-in-law.

Mrs. Drover's countenance, though worn from the strain of incessant hospitality, had lost its look of perturbation. It was clear that the affectionate meeting between mother and daughter had been a relief to the whole family, and Mrs. Drover's ingenuous eye declared that since now, thank heaven, that matter was settled, there need be no farther pretence of mystery. She invited her sister-in-law to join her in her own sitting-room over a quiet cup of tea, and as she poured it out observed with a smile that she supposed the wedding would take place before Christmas.

"The wedding? Anne's wedding?"

"Why, my dear, isn't everything settled? We all supposed that was what you'd come down for. She told us of her

189

engagement as soon as she arrived." Wrinkles of apprehension reluctantly reformed themselves on Mrs. Drover's brow. "At least you might have let me have my tea without this new worry!" her look seemed to protest. "Hendrik has the highest opinion of Major Fenno, you know," she continued, in a tone that amicably sought to dismiss the subject.

Kate Clephane put down her untasted cup. What could she answer? What was the use of answering at all?

Misled by her silence, Mrs. Drover pursued with a clearing brow: "Of course nowadays, with the cut of everything changing every six months, there's no use in ordering a huge trousseau. Besides, Anne tells me they mean to go to Europe almost immediately; and whatever people say, it *is* more satisfactory to get the latest models on the spot . . ."

"Oh, Enid—Anne mustn't marry him!" Kate Clephane cried, starting to her feet.

Mrs. Drover set down her own cup. Lines of disapproval hardened about her small concise mouth; but she had evidently resolved to restrain herself to the last limit of sisterly forbearance.

"Now, my dear, do sit down again and drink your tea quietly. What good will all this worrying do? You look feverish—and as thin as a rail. Are you sure you haven't picked up one of those dreadful tropical microbes? . . . Of course, I understand your being unhappy at parting so soon again with Anne . . . She feels it too; I know she does. It's a pity you couldn't have been together a little longer, just you two; but then— And, after all, since Anne wants you to keep the Fifth Avenue house for yourself, why shouldn't the young people buy that property just round the corner? Then the lower floors of the two houses could be thrown into one for entertaining. I'm not clever about plans, but Lilla'll tell you exactly how it could be done. She's got hold of such a clever young architect to modernize their Baltimore house. Of course, though Horace didn't realize it, it was *all* library; no room for dancing. And I daresay Anne—not that Anne ever cared much for dancing . . . But I hear Major Fenno likes going out, and a young wife can't make a greater mistake than to have a dull house if her husband is fond of gaiety. Lilla, now, has quite converted Horace—"

Kate Clephane had reseated herself and was automatically turning the spoon about in her cup. "It won't happen; it can't be; he'll never dare." The thought, flashing in on her aching brain, suddenly quieted her, helped her to compose her features, and even to interject the occasional vague murmur which was all her sister-in-law needed to feed her flow of talk. The mention of the Maclews and their clever architect had served to deflect the current of Mrs. Drover's thoughts, and presently she was describing how wonderfully Lilla managed Horace, and how she and the architect had got him to think he could not live without the very alterations he had begun by resolutely opposing, on the ground that they were both extravagant and unnecessary.

"Just an innocent little conspiracy, you know . . . They completely got the better of him, and now he's delighted, and tells everybody it was his own idea," Mrs. Drover chuckled; and then, her voice softening, and a plump hand reassuringly out-stretched to Mrs. Clephane: "You'll see, my dear, after you get over the first loneliness, what a lovely thing it is to have one's child happily married."

"It won't happen; it can't be; he'll never dare!" the other mother continued to murmur to herself.

Horace Maclew, among numerous other guests, arrived for dinner. He sat nearly opposite Mrs. Clephane, and in the strange whirl and dazzle that surrounded her she instinctively

anchored her gaze on his broad frame and ponderous countenance. What had his marriage done to him, she wondered,
and what weight had it given him in the counsels of his new
family? She had known of him but vaguely before, as the
conscientious millionaire who collects works of art and re-
lieves suffering; she imagined him as having been brought up
by equally conscientious parents, themselves wealthy and
scrupulous, and sincerely anxious to transmit their scruples,
with their millions, to their only son. But other influences
and tendencies had also been in play; one could fancy him
rather heavily adjusting them to his inherited principles, with
the "After all" designed to cover venial lapses. His marriage
with Lilla must have been the outcome, the climax, of these
private concessions, and have prepared him to view most of
the problems of life from an easier angle. Undoubtedly,
among the men present, though no quicker-witted than the
others, he would have been the one most likely to understand Kate Clephane's case, could she have put it to him. But
to do so—one had only to intercept their glances across the
table to be sure of it—would have been to take Lilla also into
her confidence; and it suddenly became clear to Mrs.
Clephane that no recoil of horror, and no Pharisaical disapproval, would be as intolerable to her as Lilla's careless stare
and Lilla's lazy: "Why, what on earth's all the fuss about?
Don't that sort of thing happen all the time?"

It did, no doubt; Mrs. Clephane had already tried to adjust
her own mind to that. She had known such cases; everybody
had; she had seen them smoothed over and lived down; but
that she and Anne should ever figure as one of them was
beyond human imagining. She would have felt herself
befouled to the depths by Lilla's tolerance.

Her unquiet eyes wandered from Horace Maclew to her
daughter. Anne shone with recovered joy. Her anxiety had

left only the happy traces of a summer shower on a drooping garden. Every now and then she smiled across the table at her mother, and Kate felt herself irresistibly smiling back. There was something so rich, dense and impregnable in the fact of possessing Anne's heart that the mother could not remember to be alarmed when their eyes met.

Suddenly she noticed that Anne was absorbed in conversation with one of her neighbours. This was the Reverend Dr. Arklow, Rector of St. Stephen's, the New York church of the Clephane and Drover clan. Old Mrs. Clephane had been a pillar of St. Stephen's, and had bequeathed a handsome sum to the parish. Dr. Arklow, formerly the curate, had come back a few years previously as Rector of the church, and was now regarded as one of the foremost lights of the diocese, with a strong possibility of being named its Coadjutor, or possibly Bishop of the American Episcopal Churches in Europe.

The Drovers and all their tribe took their religion with moderation: they subscribed handsomely to parochial charities, the older members of the family still went to church on Sunday mornings, and once in the winter each of the family invited the Rector to a big dinner. But their relations with him, though amicable, were purely formal, and Kate concluded that his presence at one of the Drover week-ends was to be attributed to the prestige he had acquired as a certain Coadjutor or possible Bishop. The Drover social scheme was like a game of chess in which Bishops counted considerably more than Rectors.

The Rector of St. Stephen's struck Mrs. Clephane, who had met him only once before, as a man accustomed to good company, and eager to prove it. He had a face as extensive as Mr. Maclew's but running to length instead of width. His thin gray hair was carefully brushed back from a narrow benevolent forehead, and though he loved a good cigar, and wore a pepper-and-salt suit on his travels, he knew his value as a decorative element, and was fastidiously clerical on social occasions. His manly chest seemed outspread to receive the pectoral cross, and all his gestures were round and full, like the sleeves for which they were preparing.

As he leaned back, listening to Anne with lowered lids, and finger-tips thoughtfully laid against each other, his occasional faint smile and murmur of assent suggested to Mrs. Clephane that the girl was discussing with him the arrangements for the wedding; and the mother, laying down her fork, closed her eyes for an instant while the big resonant room reeled about her. Then she said to herself that, after all, this was only what was to be expected, and that if she hadn't the courage to face such a possibility, and many others like it, she would assuredly never have the courage to carry out the plan which, all through the afternoon and evening, had been slowly forming in her mind. That plan was simply, for the present, to hold fast to Anne, and let things follow their course. She would return to New York the next day with Anne, she would passively assist at her daughter's preparations—for an active share in them seemed beyond her powers —and she would be there when Chris came, and when they announced the engagement. Whatever happened, she would be there. She would let Chris see at once that he would have to reckon with that. And how would he be able to reckon with it? How could he stand it, day after day? They would perhaps never exchange another word in private—she prayed they might not—but he would understand by her mere presence what she meant, what she was determined on. He would understand that in the end he would have to give up Anne because she herself would never do so. The struggle between them would become a definite, practical, circumscribed thing; and, knowing Chris as she did, she felt almost sure she could hold out longer than he.

This new resolve gave her a sort of light-headed self-confidence: when she left the dinner-table she felt so easy and careless that she was surprised to see that the glass of champagne beside her plate was untouched. She felt as if all its sparkles were whirling through her.

On the return of the gentlemen to the drawing-room Dr. Arklow moved to her side, and she welcomed him with a smile. He opened with some mild generalities, and she said to herself that he was too anxiously observant of the social rules to speak of her daughter's marriage before she herself alluded to it. For a few minutes she strove to find a word which should provide him with an opening; but to say to any one: "My daughter is going to be married" was beyond her, and they lingered on among slumbrous platitudes.

Suddenly Anne drifted up, sat down an on arm of her mother's chair, and took her mother's hand. Kate's eyes filled, and through their mist she fancied she saw Dr. Arklow looking at her attentively. For the first time it occurred to her that, behind the scrupulous social puppet, there might be a simple-hearted man, familiar with the humble realities of pain and perplexity, and experienced in dealing with them. The thought gave her a sense of relief, and she said to herself: "I will try to speak to him alone. I will go to see him when we get to New York." But meanwhile she merely continued to smile up at her daughter, and Dr. Arklow to say: "Our young lady has been telling me about the big tennis finals. There's no doubt all these sports are going to be a great factor in building up a healthier, happier world."

None of the three made any allusion to Anne's engagement.

XXII

"**M**iss Anne Clephane weds War Hero. Announces engagement to Major Christopher Fenno, D.S.M., Chevalier of Legion of Honour."

The headline glared at Kate Clephane from the first page of the paper she had absently picked up from the table of her sitting-room. She and Anne, that morning, had journeyed back from Long Island in Hendrik Drover's motor, separated by his genial bulk, and shielded by it from the peril of private talk. On the day before—that aching endless Sunday—Anne, when with her mother, had steadily avoided the point at issue. She seemed too happy in their reunion to risk disturbing its first hours; perhaps, Kate thought, she was counting on the spell of that reunion to break down her mother's opposition. But as they neared New York every mile brought them closer to the reality they were trying not to see; and here it was at last, deriding the mother from those hideous headlines. She heard Anne's step behind her, and their glance crossed above the paragraph. A flush rose to the girl's cheek, while her eyes hesitatingly questioned her mother.

The decisive moment in their struggle was at hand. Kate felt that everything depended on her holding fast to the line she had resolved to follow, and her voice sounded thin and small in the effort to steady it.

"Is Major Fenno in New York?"

"No. He went back to Baltimore on Saturday." Anne wavered. "He's waiting to hear from me . . . before he comes."

A hope leapt up in the mother's breast, then sank its ineffectual wings. She glanced back slowly at the newspaper.

"This announcement was made with your permission?"

The unwonted colour still burned in the girl's cheek. She made a motion of assent, and added, after another pause: "Uncle Hendrik and Aunt Enid thought it only fair."

"Fair to Major Fenno?"

"Yes."

The silence prolonged itself. At length the mother brought out: "But if you've announced your engagement he has a right to be with you."

Anne looked at her almost timidly. "I wanted first . . . we both wanted . . . to feel that when he came you would . . . would be ready to receive him."

Kate Clephane turned away from her daughter's eyes. The look in them was too intolerably sweet to her. Anne was imploring her approval—Anne could not bear to be happy without it. Yes; but she wanted her other happiness also; she wanted that more than anything else; she would not hesitate to sacrifice her mother to it if there were no other way.

All this rushed over Kate in a final flash of illumination. "I want you both!" Anne had said; but she wanted Chris Fenno infinitely the more.

"Dear—" At her mother's first syllable Anne was at her side again, beseechingly. Kate Clephane lifted her hands to the girl's shoulders. "You've made your choice, dearest. When Major Fenno comes of course I will receive him." Her lips felt dry and stiff as she uttered her prevarication. But all her old arts of casuistry had come back; what was the use of having practised them so long if they were not to serve her now? She let herself yield to Anne's embrace.

That afternoon, as Mrs. Clephane sat alone upstairs, Fred Landers telephoned to ask if she would receive him. Anne was out, and her mother sent word that when Mr. Landers came he was to be shown up to her sitting-room. He entered it, presently, with outstretched hands and a smile of satisfaction.

"Well, it's all settled, then? Thank God! You've done just the right thing; I knew you would."

Her hand fell lifelessly into his; she could not answer.

He drew up an armchair to the little autumnal fire, and continued to contemplate her approvingly.

"I know how hard it must have been. But there was only one thing to be considered: Anne needs you!"

"She needs Major Fenno more."

"Oh, well—that's the law of life, isn't it?" His tone seemed to say: "At any rate, it's the one you obeyed in your own youth." And again she found no answer.

She was conscious that the gaze he still fixed on her had passed from benevolence to wistfulness. "Do you still mind it so awfully?"

His question made her tears rise; but she was determined not to return upon the past. She had proved the uselessness of the attempt.

"Anne has announced her engagement. What more is there to say? You tell me she needs me; well, here I am with her."

"And you don't know how she appreciates it. She rang me up as soon as you got back this morning. She's overcome by your generosity in going down to the Drovers' after what had taken place between you—after her putting herself so completely in the wrong." He paused again, as if weighing his next words. "You know I'm not any keener than you are about this marriage; but, my dear, I believe it had to be."

"Had to be?"

His capacious forehead crimsoned with the effort to explain. "Well, Anne's a young woman of considerable violence of feeling . . . of . . . of . . . In short, there's no knowing what she might have ended by doing if we'd all backed you up in opposing her. And I confess I didn't feel sure enough of the young man to count on his not taking advantage of her . . . her impetuosity, as it were, if he thought there was no other chance . . . You understand?"

She understood. What he was trying to say was that, on the whole, given the girl's self-will, and taking into account her . . . well, her peculiar heredity . . . taking into account, in fact, Kate Clephane herself . . . the family had probably adopted the safest course in accepting the situation.

"Not that I mean to imply—of course not! Only the young people nowadays settle most questions for themselves, don't they? And in this case . . . Well, all's well that ends well. We all know that some of the most successful marriages have had . . . er . . . rather risky preliminaries."

Kate Clephane sat listening in a state of acquiescent lassitude. She felt as if she had been given a drug which had left her intelligence clear but paralyzed her will. What was the use of arguing, discussing, opposing? Later, of course, if everything else failed, Fred Landers was after all the person she would have to turn to, to whom her avowal would have to be made; but for the moment he was of no more use to her than any of the others. The game she had resolved to play must be played between herself and Chris Fenno; everything else was the vainest expenditure of breath.

"You do agree, don't you?" she heard Landers rather nervously insisting; and: "Oh, I daresay you're right," she assented.

"And the great thing, you know, is that Anne shouldn't lose you, or you lose Anne, because of this. All the rest will arrange itself somehow. Life generally does arrange things. And if it shouldn't—"

He stood up rather awkwardly, and she was aware of his advancing toward her. His face had grown long and solemn, and his broad bulk seemed to have narrowed to the proportions of the lank youth suffused with blushes who had taken shelter behind his mother when old Mrs. Landers had offered a bridal banquet to the John Clephanes.

"If it doesn't work out for you as we hope . . . there's my house . . . that's been waiting for you for ever so long . . . though I shouldn't ever have ventured to suggest it . . ."

"Oh—" she faltered out, the clutch of pain relaxing a little about her heart.

"Well, well," her visitor stammered, rubbing his hands together deprecatingly, "I only suggest it as a sort of last expedient . . . a forlorn hope . . ." His nervous laugh tried to give the words a humorous turn, but his eyes were still grave. Kate rose and put her hand in his.

"You're awfully good to me," was all she found to say. Inwardly she was thinking, with a fresh thrill of anguish: "And now I shall never be able to tell him—never!"

He had caught the note of dismissal in her voice, and was trying to gather up the scattered fragments of his self-possession. "Of course, at our age . . . *my* age, I mean . . . all that kind of thing is rather. . . But there: I didn't want you to feel there was no one you could turn to. That's all. You won't bear me a grudge, though? Now then; that's all right. And you'll see: this other business will shake down in time. Bound to, you know. I daresay the young man has merits that you and I don't see. And you'll let me go on dropping in as usual? After all, I'm Anne's guardian!" he ended with his clumsy laugh.

"I shall want you more than ever, Fred," Mrs. Clephane said simply.

The next evening, as she looked down the long dinner-table from her seat at its head, she was fantastically reminded of the first family dinner over which she had presided after her marriage.

The background was the same; the faces were the same, or so like that they seemed merely rejuvenated issues of the same coinage. Hendrik Drover sat in his brother-in-law's place; but even that change was not marked enough to disturb the illusion. Hendrik Drover's heavy good-natured face belonged to the same type as John Clephane's; one saw that the two had gone to the same schools and the same University, frequented the same clubs, fished the same salmon rivers; Hendrik Drover might have been the ghost of John Clephane revisiting the scene of his earthly trials in a mood softened by celestial influences. And as for herself— Kate Clephane—if she had conformed to the plan of life prepared for her, instead of turning from it and denying it, might she not reasonably have hoped to reappear on the scene in the form of Enid Drover?

These grotesque fancies had begun to weave their spirals through her brain only after a first impact had emptied it of everything else, swept it suddenly clear of all meaning and all reason. That moment had come when Chris Fenno had entered in the wake of the other guests; when she had heard his name announced like that of any other member of the family; had seen him advance across the interminable length of the room, all the lights in it converging upon him as she felt that all the eyes in it converged on her; when she had seen Anne at his side, felt her presence between them, heard the girl's voice, imperious, beseeching: "Mother—here's Chris," and felt her hand drop into that other hand with the awful plunge that the heart makes when a sudden shock flings it from its seat.

She had lived through all that; she and he had faced each other; had exchanged greetings, she supposed; had even, perhaps, said something to each other about Anne, and about their future relation. She did not know what; she judged only, from the undisturbed faces about them, that there had been nothing alarming, nothing to scandalize or grieve; that it had all, to the tribal eye, passed off decently and what they called "suitably". Her past training had served her—his boundless assurance had served him. It was what the French called "a moment to pass"; they had passed it. And in that mad world beyond the abyss, where she now found herself, here they all were with the old faces, saying the same old things with the same old complacency, eating their way through the same Clephane courses, expressing the same approval of the Clephane cellar ("It was Hendrik, you know, who advised John to lay down that ninety-five Clicquot," she caught Enid Drover breathing across the bubbles to her son-in-law). It was all, in short, as natural and unnatural, as horrible, intolerable and unescapable, as if she had become young again, with all her desolate and unavoidable life stretching away ahead of her to—this.

And, in the mad phantasmagoria, there was Chris himself,

symbolizing what she had flown to in her wild escape; representing, in some horrible duality, at once her sin and its harvest, her flight and her return. At the thought, her brain began to spin again, and she saw her own youth embodied before her in Anne, with Anne's uncompromising scorns and scruples, Anne's confident forward-looking gaze.

"Ah, well," she heard Hendrik Drover say as they rose from the table, "these occasions will come round from time to time in the best-regulated families, and I suppose we all feel—" while, at the other side of the table, Enid Drover, pink and melting from a last libation, sighed to Horace Maclew: "I only wish dear mother and John could have been here with us!" and Lilla, overhearing her, bracketed the observation in an ironic laugh.

It had all gone off wonderfully; thanks to Anne's tact the meeting between her mother and her betrothed had been thickly swaddled in layer on layer of non-conducting, non-explosive "family". A sense of mutual congratulation was in the air as the groups formed themselves again in the drawing-room. The girl herself moved from one to another, pale, vigilant, radiant; Chris Fenno, in a distant corner, was settled with coffee-cup and cigarette at Lilla Maclew's side; Mrs. Clephane found herself barricaded behind Hendrik Drover and one of the older Tresseltons. They were the very two men, she remembered, between whom she had spent her evening after that first family dinner in which this one was so hallucinatingly merged.

Not until the party was breaking up, and farewells filled the hall, did she suddenly find herself—she knew not how—isolated in the inner drawing-room with Chris Fenno. He stood there before her, and she seemed to hear his voice for the first time.

"I want to thank you . . ." He appeared to feel it was a bad beginning, and tried again. "Shan't I have the chance, someday soon, of finding you—for a word or two, quietly?" he asked.

She faced him, erect and unflinching; she dragged her eyes up to his.

"A chance? But as soon as you like—as many chances as you like! You'll always find me—I shall always be here. I'm never going to leave Anne," she announced.

It had been almost worth the agony she had bought it with to see the look in his eyes when he heard that.

XXIII

Extreme exhaustion — the sense of having reached the last limit of endurable emotion—plunged Kate Clephane, that night, into a dreamless sleep. It was months and months since she had reached those nethermost levels below sound or image or any mental movement; and she rose from them revived, renewed—and then suddenly understood that they had been only a grief-drugged mockery.

The return to reality was as painful as that of a traveller who has fallen asleep in the snow. One by one she had to readjust all her frozen faculties to the unchanged and intolerable situation; and she felt weaker, less able to contend with it. The thought that that very day she might have to face Chris Fenno paralyzed her. He had asked to see her alone—and she lay there, in the desolate dawn, rehearsing to herself all the cruel things he would find to say; for his ways of being cruel were innumerable. The day before she had felt almost light-heartedly confident of being able to outface, to outlast him; of her power of making the situation even more intolerable to him than he could make it to her. Now, in the merciless morning light, she had a new view of their respective situations. Who had suffered most the previous evening, he or she? Whose wakening that morning was most oppressed by fears? He had proposed to have a talk with her; he had had the courage to do that; and she felt that by having that courage he had already gained another point in their silent struggle.

Slowly the days dragged by; their hours were filled, for mother and daughter, by the crowding obligations and preoccupations natural to such times. Mrs. Clephane was helping her daughter with the wedding preparations; a spectacle to charm and edify the rest of the family.

Chris Fenno, two or three days after the announcement of the engagement, had returned to Baltimore, where he had accepted a temporary job on a newspaper, and where he had that, and other matters, to wind up before his marriage. During his stay in New York, Mrs. Clephane had had but two or three brief glimpses of him, and always in the presence of others. It was natural that he should wish to devote the greater part of his time to his betrothed. He and Anne went off in the early afternoon, and when they returned were, on each evening, engaged to dine with some member of the family. It was easy for Mrs. Clephane to excuse herself from these entertainments. The fact of her having presided at the dinner at which the engagement was announced had sealed it with her approval; and at the little dinners organized by Nollie Tresselton and the other cousins her presence was hardly expected, and readily dispensed with.

All this fitted in with the new times. The old days of introspections and explanations were over; the era of taking things for granted was the only one that Anne's generation knew, and in that respect Anne was of her day.

After the betrothal dinner she had said a tender goodnight to her mother, and the next evening, as she rushed up to dress after her long outing with Chris, had stopped at Kate's door to wave a loving hand and call out: "He says you've been so perfect to him—" That was all. Kate Clephane's own memories told her that to some natures happiness comes like a huge landslide burying all the past and spreading a fresh surface to life's sowings: and it was from herself, she reflected, that Anne had inherited her capacity for such all-obliterating bliss.

The days passed, and Chris Fenno at length came back. He was staying with the Joe Tresseltons, and there was a constant coming and going of the young people between the two houses. Opportunities were not lacking to see Mrs. Clephane in private, and for the first days after his return she waited in numb terror for the inevitable, the incalculable moment. But it did not come; and gradually she understood that it never would. His little speech had been a mere formula; he had nothing to say to her; no desire was farther from him than the wish to speak with her alone. What she had dreaded past expression, but supposed to be inevitable, he had probably never even seriously considered. Explanations? What was the use of explanations? He had gained his point; the thing now was to live at peace, with everybody.

She saw that all her calculations had been mistaken. She had fancied that her tactics would render his situation intolerable; that if only she could bear to spend a few weeks in his presence she would demonstrate to him the impossibility of his spending the rest of his life in hers. But his reasoning reached a good deal farther, and embraced certain essential elements in human nature that hers had left out. He had said to himself—she was sure of it now—: "The next few weeks

will be pretty bad, but after that I'll have the upper hand."
He had only to hold out till the wedding; after that she would
be a mere mother-in-law, and mothers-in-law are not a
serious problem in modern life. How could she ever have
imagined that he would not see through her game and
out-manœuvre her, when he had done it so often before, and
when his whole future depended on his doing it just once
more! She felt herself beaten at every point.

Unless—unless she told the truth to Anne. Every day was
making that impossible thing more impossible; yet every day
was bringing them nearer to the day when not to do so—if all
other measures failed—would be most impossible of all. She
seemed to have reached that moment when, one morning,
Anne came into her room and caught her by the hand.

"Dearest—you've got to come with me this very minute."

Kate, yielding to the girl's hand, was drawn along the
corridor to her bedroom. There, on the bed, in a dazzle of
whiteness, lay the wedding-dress.

"Will you help me to try it on?" Anne asked.

Kate Clephane rang the Rectory bell and found herself in the
Rectory sitting-room. As she sat there, among photogravures
of Botticelli Virgins and etchings of English cathedrals, she
could not immediately remember why she had come, and
looked with a kind of detached curiosity at the volumes of
memoirs and sermons on the table at her elbow, at the
perpendicular Gothic chairs against the wall, and the Morris
armchairs which had superseded them. She had not been in a
rectory sitting-room since the committee meeting at the
Merrimans', on the day when she had received Anne's cable.

Her lapse of memory lasted only for a few seconds, but
during that time she relived with intensity the sensations of
that other day, she felt her happy heart dancing against the

message folded under her dress, she saw the southern sun gilding the dull faces about the table, and smelt the violets and mimosa in Mrs. Merriman's vases. She woke again to the present just as an austere parlour-maid was requesting her to step this way.

Dr. Arklow's study was full of books, of signed photographs of Church dignitaries, of more English cathedrals, of worn leather armchairs and scattered pipes and tobacco-pouches. The Rector himself, on the hearth, loomed before her at once bland and formidable. He had guessed, of course, that she had come to talk about the date and hour of the wedding, and all the formulas incidental to such visits fell from his large benevolent lips. The visit really passed off more easily than she had expected, and she was on her feet again and feeling him behind her like a gentle trade-wind accustomed to waft a succession of visitors to the door, when she stopped abruptly and faced him.

"Dr. Arklow—"

He waited benevolently.

"There's something else—a case I've always wanted to put to you . . ."

"Dear Mrs. Clephane—do put it now." He was waving her back into her armchair; but she stood before him, unconscious of the gesture.

"It's about a friend of mine—"

"Yes: a friend? Do sit down."

She sat down, still unaware of her movements or his.

"A most unhappy woman . . . I told her I would ask . . . ask what could be done . . . She had an idea that you could tell her . . ."

He bowed expectantly.

Her parched lips brought out: "Of course it's confidential," and his gesture replied that communications, in that room, were always held to be so. "Whatever I can do—" he added.

"Yes. My friend thought—her position is really desperate." She stopped, her voice failing her; then the words came forth in panting jerks. "She was most unhappily married . . . things went against her—everything did. She tried . . . tried her best . . . Then she met him . . . it was too difficult . . . He was her lover; only for a short time. After that her life was perfectly . . . was all it should be. She never saw him—oh, for years. Now her daughter wants to marry him . . ."

"Marry him? *The same man?*" The Rector's voice swelled above her like a wave; his presence towered, blurred and gigantic. She felt the tears in her throat; but again she was seized by the besetting desire that her secret should not be guessed, and a desperate effort at self-control drove the tears back and cleared her voice.

Dr. Arklow still loomed and brooded. "And the man—"

A slow flush of agony rose to her forehead; but she remembered that she was seated with her back to the light, and took courage. "He—he is determined." She paused, and then went on: "It's too horrible. But at first he didn't know . . . when he first met the girl. Neither of them knew. And when he found out—"

"Yes?"

"Then—it was too late, he said. The girl doesn't know even now; she doesn't dream; and she's grown to care—care desperately."

"That's his defence?"

Her voice failed her again, and she signed her assent.

There was another long pause. She sat motionless, looking down at her own interlocked hands. She felt that Dr. Arklow was uneasily pacing the hearth-rug; at last she was aware that he was once more standing before her.

"The lady you speak of—your friend—is she here?"

She started. *"Here?"*

"In New York, I mean?"

"No; no; she's not here," Kate cried precipitately. "That's the reason why I offered to come—"

"I see." She thought she caught a faint note of relief in his voice. "She wished you to consult me?"

"Yes."

"And she's done everything—everything, of course, to stop this abomination?"

"Oh, everything . . . everything."

"Except to tell her daughter?"

She made another sign of assent.

Dr. Arklow cleared his throat, and declared with emphasis: "It is her duty to tell her daughter."

"Yes," Kate Clephane faltered. She got to her feet and looked about her blindly for the door.

"She must tell her daughter," the Rector repeated with rising vehemence. "Such a shocking situation must be avoided; avoided at all costs."

"Yes," she repeated. She was on the threshold now; automatically she held out her hand.

"Unless," the Rector continued uncertainly, his eyes upon her, "she is absolutely convinced that less harm will come to all concerned if she has the courage to keep silence— always." There was a pause. "As far as I can see into the blackness of it," he went on, gaining firmness, "the whole problem turns on that. I may be mistaken; perhaps I am. But when a man has looked for thirty or forty years into pretty nearly every phase of human suffering and error, as men of my cloth have to do, he comes to see that there must be adjustments . . . adjustments in the balance of evil. Compromises, politicians would call them. Well, I'm not afraid of the word." He stood leaning against the jamb of the door; her hand was on the doorknob, and she listened with lowered head.

"The thing in the world I'm most afraid of is sterile pain," he said after a moment. "I should never want any one to be the cause of that."

She lifted her eyes with an effort, and saw in his face the same look of understanding she had caught there for a moment while she talked with him at the Drovers' after dinner.

"Sterile pain—" she murmured. She had crossed the threshold now; she felt that he was holding out his hand. His face once more wore the expression of worldly benevolence that was as much the badge of his profession as his dress. After all, she perceived, he was glad that she had said nothing more definite, glad that their talk was safely over. Yet she had caught that other look.

"If your friend were here; if there were anything I could do for her, or say to her—anything to help—"

"Oh, she's not here; she won't be here," Kate repeated.

"In that case—" Again she caught the relief in his voice.

"But I will tell her—tell her what you've said." She was aware that they were shaking hands, and that he was averting his apprehensive eyes from hers. "For God's sake," the eyes seemed to entreat her, "let's get through with this before you betray yourself—if there's anything further to betray."

At the front door he bowed her out, repeating cordially: "And about a date for Anne's wedding as soon as you and she are absolutely decided, remember I'm completely at your service."

The door closed, and she found herself in the street.

XXIV

She turned away from the Rectory and walked aimlessly up Madison Avenue. It was a warm summer-coloured October day. At Fifty-ninth Street she turned into the Park and wandered on over the yellowing leaf-drifts of the ramble. In just such a state of blind bewilderment she had followed those paths on the day when she had first caught sight of Chris Fenno and Lilla Gates in the twilight ahead of her. That was less than a year ago, and she looked back with amazement at the effect which that chance encounter had had on her. She seemed hardly to be suffering more now than she had suffered then. It had seemed unbearable, impossible, at the moment, that Chris Fenno should enter, even so episodically, so remotely, into her new life; and here he was, ensconced in its very centre, in complete possession of it.

She tried to think the situation out; but, as always, her trembling thoughts recoiled, just as she had seen Dr. Arklow's recoil.

Every one to whom she had tried to communicate her secret without betraying it had had the same instantaneous revulsion. "Not that—don't tell me that!" their averted eyes, their shrinking voices seemed to say. It was too horrible for any ears.

How then was she to obey Dr. Arklow's bidding and impart the secret to Anne? He had said it as positively as if he were handing down a commandment from Sinai: "The daughter must be told."

How easy to lay down abstract rules for other people's guidance: "The daughter" was just an imaginary person—a convenient conversational pawn. But Kate Clephane's daughter—her own Anne! She closed her eyes and tried to face the look in Anne's as the truth dawned on her.

"You—*you*, mother? The mother I've come to adore—the mother I can't live without, even with all my other happiness? *You?*"

Yes—perhaps that would be the worst of it, the way Anne would look at her and say *"You?"* For, once the girl knew the truth, her healthy youth might so revolt from Chris's baseness, Chris's duplicity, that the shock of the discovery would be its own cure. But when the blow had fallen, when Anne's life had crashed about her, and the ruins been cleared away—what then of her mother? Why, her mother would be buried under those ruins; her life would be over; but a hideous indestructible image of her would remain, overshadowing, darkening the daughter's future.

"This man you are going to marry has—"

No; Kate Clephane could go no farther than that. Such confessions were not to be made; were not for a daughter's ears. She began the phrase to herself again and again, but could not end it . . .

And, after all, she suddenly thought, Dr. Arklow himself, having given the injunction, had at once qualified, had virtually withdrawn it. In declaring that such an abomination must at all costs be prevented he had spoken with the firmness of a priest; but almost at once the man had intervened, and had suggested to the hypothetical mother the alternative of not speaking at all, if only she could be sure of never betraying herself in the future, of sacrificing everything to the supreme object of avoiding what he called sterile pain. Those tentative, half-apologetic words now effaced the others in Kate's mind. Though spoken with the accent of authority—and almost under his breath—she knew they represented what he really felt. But where should she find the courage to conform to them?

She had left the Park, aimlessly, unseeingly, and was walking eastward through a half-built street in the upper Nineties. The thought of returning home—re-entering that house where the white dress still lay on the bed—was unbearable. She walked on and on . . . Suddenly she came upon an ugly sandstone church-front with a cross above the doorway. The leathern swing-doors were flapping back and forth, women passing in and out. Kate Clephane pushed open one of the doors and looked in. The day was fading, and in the dusky interior lights fluttered like butterflies about the paper flowers of the altar. There was no service, but praying figures were scattered here and there. Against the brown-washed walls of the aisles she observed a row of confessionals of varnished wood, like cigar-boxes set on end; before one or two, women were expectantly kneeling. Mrs. Clephane wondered what they had to tell.

Leaning against one of the piers of the nave she evoked all those imaginary confessions, and thought how trivial, how childish they would seem, compared to what she carried in her breast . . . What a help it must be to turn to somebody who could tell one firmly, positively what to do—to be able to lay down one's moral torture like a heavy load at the end of the day! Dr. Arklow had none of the authority which the habit of the confessional must give. He could only vaguely sympathize and deplore, and try to shuffle the horror out of sight as soon as he caught an unwilling glimpse of it. But these men whose office it was to bind and to unbind—who spoke as the mere impersonal mouth-pieces of a mighty Arbitrator, letting neither moral repugnance nor false delicacy interfere with the sacred task of alleviation and purification—how different must they be! Her eyes filled at the thought of laying her burden in such hands.

And why not? Why not entrust her anonymous secret to one of those anonymous ears? In talking to Dr. Arklow she had felt that both he and she were paralyzed by the personal relation, and all the embarrassments and complications arising from it. When she spoke of her friend in distress, and he replied with the same evasive formula, both were conscious of the evasion, and hampered by it. And so it had been from the first—there was not an ear into which she dared pour her agony. What if, now, at once, she were to join those unknown penitents? It was possible, she knew—she had but a step to take . . .

She did not take it. Her unrest drove her forth again into the darkening street, drove her homeward with uncertain steps, in the mood of forlorn expectancy of those who, having failed to exert their will, wait helplessly on the unforeseen. After all, how could one tell? Chris must, in his own degree, be suffering as she was suffering. Why not stick to her old plan of waiting, holding on, enduring everything, in the hope of wearing him out? She reached the door of her house, set her teeth, and went in. Overhead, she remembered with a shudder, the white dress waited, with all that it implied . . .

The drawing-room was empty, and she went up to her own room. There, as usual, the fire shone invitingly, fresh flowers opened in the lamplight. All was warmth, peace, intimacy. As she sat down by the fireside she seemed to see Fred Landers's heavy figure in the opposite armchair, his sturdy square-toed boots turned to the hearth. She remembered how, one day, as he sat there, she had said to herself that it might be pleasant to see him there always. Now, in the extremity of her loneliness, the thought returned. Since then he had confessed his own hope to her—shyly, obliquely, apologetically; but under his stammering words she had recognized the echo of a long desire. She knew he had always loved her; had not Anne betrayed that it was her guardian who had persuaded her to recall her unknown mother? Kate Clephane owed him everything, then—all her happiness and all her sorrow! He knew everything of her life—or nearly everything. To whom else could she turn with the peculiar sense of security which that certitude gave? She felt sorry that she had received his tentative advance so coldly, so inarticulately. After all, he might yet be her refuge—her escape. She closed her eyes, and tried to imagine what life would be—years and years of it—at Fred Landers's side. To feel the nearness of that rugged patient kindness; would it not lighten her misery, make the thoughts and images that were torturing her less palpable, less acute, less real?

She sat there for a long time, brooding. Now and then a step passing her door, or a burst of voices on the landing, told her that Anne was probably receiving some of her friends in her own rooms at the other end of the passage. The wedding presents were already arriving; Anne, with a childish pleasure that was unlike her usual aloofness from material things, had set them out on a long table in her sitting-room. The mother pictured the eager group inspecting and admiring, the talk of future plans, the discussion of all the details of the wedding. The date for it would soon be fixed; ostensibly, her own visit to Dr. Arklow had been made for the purpose. But at the last moment her courage had failed her, and she had said vaguely, in leaving, that she would let him know.

As she sat there, she saw her daughter's pale illuminated face as though it were before her. Anne's happiness shone through her, making her opaque and guarded features luminous and transparent; and the mother could measure, from her own experience, the amount of heat and force that fed that incandescence. She herself had always had a terrible way of being happy—and that way was Anne's.

She simply could not bear to picture to herself the change, in Anne's face, from ecstasy to anguish. She had seen that change once, and the sight had burned itself into her eyeballs. To destroy Anne's happiness seemed an act of murderous cruelty. What did it matter—as the chances of life went—of what elements such happiness was made? Had she, Kate Clephane, ever shrunk from her own bliss because of the hidden risks it contained? She had played high, staked everything—and lost. Could she blame her daughter for choosing to take the same risks? No; there was, in all great happiness, or the illusion momentarily passing for it, a quality so beatific, so supernatural, that no pain with which it might have to be paid could, at the time, seem too dear; could hardly, perhaps, ever seem so, to headlong hearts like hers and Anne's.

Her own heart had begun to tremble and dilate with her new resolve; the resolve to accept the idea of Anne's marriage, to cease her inward struggle against it, and try to be in reality what she was already pretending to be: the acquiescent, approving mother . . . After all, why not? Legally, technically, there was nothing wrong, nothing socially punishable, in the case. And what was there on the higher, the more private grounds where she pretended to take her stand

and deliver her judgment? Chris Fenno was a young man—she was old enough to be, if not his mother, at least his mother-in-law. What had she ever hoped or expected to be to him but a passing incident, a pleasant memory? From the first, she had pitched their relation in that key; had insisted on the difference in their ages, on her own sense of the necessary transiency of the tie, on the fact that she would not have it otherwise. Anything rather than to be the old woman clutching at an impossible prolongation of bliss—anything rather than be remembered as a burden instead of being regretted as a delight! How often had she told him that she wanted to remain with him like the memory of a flowering branch brushed by at night? "You won't quite know if it was lilac or laburnum, or both—you'll only know it was something vanishing and sweet." Vanishing and sweet—that was what she had meant to be! And she had kept to her resolution till the blow fell—

Well, and was he so much to blame for its falling? She herself had been the witness of his resistance, of his loyal efforts to escape. The vehemence of Anne's passion had thwarted him, had baffled them both; if he loved her as passionately as she loved him, was he not justified in accepting the happiness forced upon him? And how refuse it without destroying the girl's life?

"If any one is to be destroyed, oh God, don't let it be Anne!" the mother cried. She seemed at last to have reached a clearer height, a more breathable air. Renunciation—renunciation. If she could attain to that, what real obstacle was there to her daughter's happiness?

"I would sell my soul for her—why not my memories?" she reflected.

The sound of steps and voices outside had ceased. From the landing had come a "Goodbye, dearest!" in Nollie

219

Tresselton's voice; no doubt she had been the last visitor to leave, and Anne was now alone; perhaps alone with her betrothed. Well; to that thought also Kate Clephane must accustom herself; by and bye they would be always alone, those two, in the sense of being nearer to each other than either of them was to any one else. The mother could bear that too. Not to lose Anne—at all costs to keep her hold on the girl's confidence and tenderness: that was all that really mattered. She would go to Anne now. She herself would ask the girl to fix the date for the wedding.

She got up and walked along the deep-piled carpet of the corridor. The door of Anne's sitting-room was ajar, but no sound came from within. Every one was gone, then; even Chris Fenno. With a breath of relief the mother pushed the door open. The room was empty. One of the tall vases was full of branching chrysanthemums and autumn berries. In a corner stood a tea-table with scattered cups and plates. The Airedale drowsed by the hearth. As she stood there, Kate Clephane saw the little Anne who used to sit by that same fire trying to coax the red birds through the fender. The vision melted the last spot of resistance in her heart. The door of Anne's bedroom was also ajar, but no sound came from there either. Perhaps the girl had gone out with her last visitors, escaping for a starlit rush up the Riverside Drive before dinner. These sudden sallies at queer hours were a way the young people had.

The mother listened a moment longer, then laid her hand on the bedroom door. Before her, directly in the line of her vision, was Anne's narrow bed. On it the wedding-dress still lay, in a dazzle of whiteness; and between Mrs. Clephane and the bed, looking also at the dress, stood Anne and Chris Fenno. They had not heard her cross the sitting-room or push open the bedroom door; they did not hear her now. All their faculties were absorbed in each other. The young man's arms were around the girl, her cheek was against his. One of his hands reached about her shoulder and, making a cup for her chin, pressed her face closer. They were looking at the dress; but the curves of their lips, hardly detached, were like those of a fruit that has burst apart of its own ripeness.

Kate Clephane stood behind them like a ghost. It made her feel like a ghost to be so invisible and inaudible. Then a furious flame of life rushed through her; in every cell of her body she felt that same embrace, felt the very texture of her lover's cheek against her own, burned with the heat of his palm as it clasped Anne's chin to press her closer.

"Oh, not that—not that—not that!" Mrs. Clephane imagined she had shrieked it out at them, and pressed her hands to her mouth to stifle the cry; then she became aware that it was only a dumb whisper within her. For a time which seemed without end she continued to stand there, invisible, inaudible, and they remained in each other's embrace, motionless, speechless. Then she turned and went. They did not hear her.

A dark fermentation boiled up into her brain; every thought and feeling was clogged with thick entangling memories . . . Jealous? Was she jealous of her daughter? Was she physically jealous? Was that the real secret of her repugnance, her instinctive revulsion? Was that why she had felt from the first as if some incestuous horror hung between them?

She did not know—it was impossible to analyze her anguish. She knew only that she must fly from it, fly as far as she could from the setting of these last indelible impressions. How had she ever imagined that she could keep her place at Anne's side—that she could either outstay Chris, or continue to live under the same roof with them? Both projects seemed to her, now, equally nebulous and impossible. She must put the world between them—the whole width of the world was not enough. The very grave, she thought, would be hardly black enough to blot out that scene.

She found herself, she hardly knew how, at the foot of the stairs, in the front hall. Her precipitate descent recalled the early winter morning when, as hastily, almost as unconsciously, she had descended those same stairs, flying from her husband's house. Nothing was changed in the hall: her eyes, once again morbidly receptive of details, noted on the door the same patent locks with which her fingers had then struggled. Now, as then, a man's hat and stick lay on the hall table; on that other day they had been John Clephane's, now they were Chris Fenno's. That was the only difference.

She stood there, looking about her, wondering why she did not push back the bolts and rush out into the night, hatless and cloakless as she was. What else was there to do but to go straight to the river, or to some tram line with its mortal headlights bearing straight down on one? One didn't have to have a hat and cloak to go out in search of annihilation . . .

As she stood there the door-bell rang, and she heard the step of a servant coming to open the door. She shrank back into the drawing-room, and in another moment Enid Drover had rustled in, her pink cheeks varnished with the cold, her furs full of the autumn freshness. Her little eyes were sharp with excitement.

"My dear Kate! I've rushed in with such good news: I shall be late for dinner, Hendrik will be furious. But never mind; I had to tell you. The house next door really *is* for sale! Isn't it too perfect? The agent thinks it could be got for a fairly reasonable price. But Hendrik says it may be snapped up at any minute, and Anne ought to decide at once. Then you could stay on comfortably here, and you and she and Chris would always be together, just as she wants you to be . . .

No; don't send for her; I can't wait. And besides, I want you to have the pleasure of telling her." On the doorstep Mrs. Drover turned to call back: "Remember, Hendrik says she must decide." Her limousine engulfed her.

XXV

$\mathbf{M}$rs. Clephane excused her-
self from coming down to dinner; Aline was to say that she
was very tired, and begged that no one should disturb her.
The next morning, she knew, Chris was returning to Baltimore. Perhaps in his absence she would be able to breathe
more freely, see more clearly.

Anne, as usual, respected her mother's wishes; she neither
came up nor sent to enquire. But the next morning, in the
old way, fresh and shining, she appeared with Mrs.
Clephane's breakfast tray. She wanted to be reassured as to
her mother's health, and Kate, under her solicitous eye,
poured out a cup of tea and forced down a bit of toast.

"You look tired, mother. It's only that?"

"Only that, dear."

"You didn't tell me that Aunt Enid had been in last night
about the house next door—" Anne spoke the least little
reproachfully.

"I'm sorry. I had such a headache that when she left I
went straight to my room. Did she telephone you?"

"Uncle Hendrik did. Isn't it the greatest luck? It will be

such fun arranging it all." The girl paused and looked at her mother. "And this will make you decide, darling, won't it?"

"Decide?"

"To stay on here. To keep this house for yourself. It will be almost like our all being together."

"Yes—almost."

"You will stay, won't you?"

"Stay here? I can't—I can't!" The words escaped before Mrs. Clephane could repress them. Her heart began to rush about in her like a caged animal.

Anne's brows darkened and drew together. "But I don't understand. You told Chris you would—"

"Did I? Perhaps I did. But I must sometimes be allowed to change my mind," Mrs. Clephane murmured, forcing a thin smile.

"To change your mind about being with us! You don't want to, then, after all?"

Mrs. Clephane pushed the tray away and propped herself on her elbow. "No, I don't want to."

"How you say it, mother! As if I were a stranger. I don't understand . . ." The girl's lip was beginning to tremble. "I thought . . . Chris and I both thought . . ."

"I'm sorry. But I must really decide as I think best. When you are married you won't need me."

"And shan't you need me, mother? Not a little?" Anne hesitated, and then ventured, timidly: "You're so alone—so awfully alone."

"I've always been that. It can't be otherwise. You've chosen . . . you've chosen to be married . . ."

Anne stood up and looked down on her with searching imperious eyes. "Is it my being married—or my being married to Chris?"

"Ah—don't let us talk of that again!"

The girl continued to scrutinize her strangely. "Once for all—you won't tell me?"

Mrs. Clephane did not speak.

"Then I shall ask him—I shall ask him in your presence," Anne exclaimed in a shaking voice.

At the sound of that break in her voice the dread of seeing her suffer once more superseded every other feeling in the mother's breast. She leaned against the pillows, speechless for a moment; then she held out her hand, seeking Anne's.

"There's nothing to ask, dear; nothing to tell."

"You don't hate him, mother? You really don't?"

Slowly Kate Clephane articulated: "I don't—hate him."

"But why won't you see him with me, then? Why won't you talk it all out with us once for all? Mother, what *is* it? I must know."

Mrs. Clephane, under her daughter's relentless eyes, felt the blood rising from her throat to her pale lips and drawn cheeks, and to the forehead in which her pulses must be visibly beating. She lay there, bathed in a self-accusing crimson, and it seemed to her that those clear young eyes were like steel blades plunging into the deepest folds of her conscience.

"You don't hate him? But then you're in love with him—you're in love with him, and I've known it all along!" The girl shrilled it out suddenly, and hid her face in her hands.

Kate Clephane lay without speaking. In the first shock of the outcry all her defences had crashed together about her head, and it had been almost a relief to feel them going, to feel that pretences and disguises were at an end. Then Anne's hands dropped to her side, and the mother, meeting her gaze, lost the sense of her own plight in the sight of that other woe. All at once she felt herself strong and resolute; all the old forces of dissimulation were pouring back through her veins. The accusing red faded from her face, and she lay there and quietly met the question in Anne's eyes.

"*Anne!*" she simply said, with a little shrug.

"Oh, mother—mother! I think I must be going mad!" Anne was on her knees at the bedside, her face buried in the coverlet. It was easier to speak to her while her eyes were hidden, and Kate laid a hand on her hair.

"Not mad, dear; but decidedly over-strung." She heard the note of magnanimity in her own voice.

"But can you forgive me—ever?"

"Nonsense, dear; can I do anything else?"

"But then—if you *do* forgive me, really—why must you go away? Why won't you promise to stay with us?"

Kate Clephane lay against her pillows and meditated. Her hand was still in Anne's hair; she held the girl's head gently against the coverlet, still not wishing her own face to be too closely scrutinized. At length she spoke.

"I didn't mean to tell you just yet; and you must tell no one." She paused, and rallied her failing courage. "I can't promise to stay with you, dear, because I may be going to get married too." The first words were the most difficult to say; after that she heard her voice going on steadily. "Fred Landers has asked me to marry him; and I think I shall accept . . . No; don't hug me too hard, child; my head still aches— There; now you understand, don't you? And you won't scold me any more? But remember, it's a secret from every one. It's not to be spoken of till after you're married . . . Now go."

After Anne had left her, subdued but jubilant, she lay there and remembered, with a twinge of humiliation, that the night before she had hurried downstairs in a mad rush to death. Anything—anything to escape from the coil of horror closing in on her! . . . And it had sufficed to her to meet Enid

Drover in the hall, with that silly chatter about the house next door, to check the impulse, drive her back into the life she was flying from . . . She reflected with self-derision that all her suicidal impulses seemed to end in the same way; by landing her in the arms of some man she didn't care for. Then she remembered Anne's illuminated face, and lay listening to the renewed life of the house, the bustle of happy preparations going on all about her.

"Poor Fred! Well—if it's what he wants—" she thought. What she herself wanted, all she now wanted, was never again to see that dreadful question in Anne's eyes. And she had found no other way of evading it.

XXVI

Now that a day for the wedding was fixed, the preparations went on more rapidly. Soon there was only a fortnight left; then only ten days; then a week.

Chris Fenno's parents were to have come to New York to make the acquaintance of their son's betrothed; but though a date had several times been appointed for their visit, Mrs. Fenno, whose health was not good, had never been well enough to come, and finally it was arranged that Anne should go to Baltimore to see them. She was to stay with the Maclews, who immediately seized the opportunity to organize a series of festivities in celebration of the event.

Lilla invited Mrs. Clephane to come with her daughter; but Kate declined, on the plea that she herself was not well. People were beginning to notice how tired and thin she looked. Her glass showed streaks of gray in her redundant hair, and about her lips and eyes the little lines she had so long kept at bay. Everybody in the family agreed that it would be a good thing for her to have a few days' rest before the wedding.

With regard to her own future she had sworn Anne to unconditional secrecy. She explained that she did not intend to give Fred Landers a definite answer till after the wedding, and Anne, who had all the Clephane reticence, understood her wish to keep the matter quiet, and even in her guardian's presence was careful not to betray that she knew of his hopes. She only made him feel that he was more than ever welcome, and touched him by showing an added cordiality at a moment when most girls are deaf and blind to all human concerns but their own.

"It's so like Anne to find time to remember an old derelict just when she might be excused for forgetting that any of us exist." He said it with a gentle complacency as he sat in Mrs. Clephane's sitting-room one evening during Anne's absence. "She's like you—very like you," he added, looking at Kate Clephane with shy beseeching eyes.

She smiled back at him, wondering if she would ever have the courage to tell him that she meant to marry him. He was thinking of that too, she knew. Why not tell him now, at once? She had only to lean forward and lay her hand on his. No words would be necessary. And surely she would feel less alone . . . But she remained silent; it was easier to think of speaking than to speak.

It was he who questioned: "And afterward—have you decided what you're going to do?"

She continued to smile. "There'll be time to decide afterward."

"Anne tells me you've definitely refused to remain in this house."

"This house hasn't many pleasant associations for me."

He coloured as if she had caught him in a failure of tact. "I understand that. But with the young people here . . . or next door . . . she hoped you'd feel less lonely."

Again she perceived that he was trying to remind her of a possible alternative, and again she let the allusion drop, answering merely: "I'm used to being lonely. It's not as bad as people think."

"You've known worse, you mean?" He seldom risked anything as direct as that. "And it would be worse for you, being with Anne after she's married? You still hate the idea as much as ever?"

She rose impatiently and went to lean against the mantelpiece. "Fred, what's the use? I shall never hate it less. But that's all over—I've accepted it."

"Yes, and made Anne so happy."

"Oh, love is what is making Anne happy!" She hardly knew how she brought the word from her lips.

"Well—loving Fenno hasn't made her cease to love you."

"Anne is perfect. But suppose we talk of something else. At my age I find this bridal atmosphere a little suffocating. I shall go abroad again, probably—I don't know."

She turned and looked at herself in the glass above the mantel, seeing the gray streaks and the accusing crows'-feet. And as she stood there, she remembered how once, when she was standing in the same way before a mirror, Chris had come up behind her, and they had laughed at seeing their reflections kiss. How young she had been then—how young! Now, as she looked at herself, she saw behind her the reflection of Fred Landers's comfortable bulk, sunk in an armchair in after-dinner repose, his shirt-front bulging a little, the lamp-light varnishing the top of his head through the thinning hair. A middle-aged couple—perfectly suited to each other in age and appearance. She turned back and sat down beside him.

"Shall we try a Patience?" she said.

He accepted with a wistful alacrity which seemed to say it

was the most he hoped for, and they drew up a table and sat down opposite each other, calmly disposing the little cards in elaborate patterns.

They had been playing for about half an hour when she rumpled up the cards abruptly, and sweeping them together into a passionate heap cried out: "I want it to be a gay wedding—the gayest wedding that ever was! I'm determined it shall be a gay wedding."

She dropped her face into her hands, and sat there propping her elbows on the card-table, and laughing out between her intercrossed fingers: "A really gay wedding, you know . . ."

XXVII

O_{nly} three days more now; for just three days more she and Anne would live under one roof. And then?

The interrogation was not Anne's. The news of Mrs. Clephane's intended marriage had completely restored the girl's serenity. Chris Fenno, detained in Baltimore by his mother's sudden and somewhat alarming illness, had not yet reappeared; it seemed likely now that he would arrive in New York only the day before the wedding. Anne was to have her mother to herself to the last; and with every art of tenderness and dependence she tried to show her appreciation of these final days, sweet with the sweetness of dear things ending, yet without pain because they were not to precede a real separation. Her only anxiety—the alarm about Mrs. Fenno—had been allayed by a reassuring telegram, and she moved within that rainbow bubble that once or twice in life contrives to pass itself off as the real horizon.

The sight of her, Kate Clephane reasoned, ought to have been justification enough. Anything was worth doing or sacrificing to keep the bubble unbroken. And the last three days would pass—the Day itself would pass. The world, after it was over, would go on in the same old way. What was all the flurry about?

Mrs. Drover did not find it easy to maintain so detached an attitude. She, for one, could not conceive how her sister-in-law could remain so calm at such a moment.

"Of course Nollie's wonderfully capable; she and Lilla have taken almost all the worry on their shoulders, haven't they? I never could have struggled alone with that immense list of invitations. But still I don't think you ought to assume that *everything's* settled. After all, there are only three days left! And no one seems to have even begun to think who's going to take you up the aisle . . ."

"Up the aisle?" Mrs. Clephane echoed blankly.

"Well, yes, my dear. There *is* an aisle at St. Stephen's," Enid Drover chirped with one of her rare attempts at irony. "And of course Hendrik must take up the bride, and you must be there, ready to receive her and give her away . . ."

"Give her away?"

"Hadn't you thought of that either?" Mrs. Drover's little laugh had a tinge of condescension. Though all the family had conspired to make Mrs. Clephane forget that she had lived for nearly twenty years outside the social pale, the fact remained; she *had*. And it was on just such occasions as this that she betrayed it, somewhat embarrassingly to her sister-in-law. Not even to know that, when a bride's father was dead, it was her mother who gave her away!

"You didn't expect Hendrik to do it?" Mrs. Drover rippled on, half compassionate, half contemptuous. It was hard to understand how some people contrived to remain in ignorance of the most elementary rules of behaviour!

"Hendrik—well, why shouldn't he?" Kate Clephane said.

Anne was passing through the room, a pile of belated presents in her arms.

"Do you hear, my dear? Your uncle Hendrik will be very much flattered." Mrs. Drover's little eyes grew sharp with the vision of Hendrik's broad back and glossy collar playing the leading part in the ceremony. "The bride was given away by her uncle, Mr. Hendrik Drover, of—" It really would read very well.

"Flattered about what?" Anne paused to question.

"Your mother seems to think it's your uncle who ought to give you away."

"Not you, mother?" Kate Clephane caught the instant drop in the girl's voice. Underneath her radiant security, what suspicion, what dread, still lingered?

"I'm so stupid, dear; I hadn't realized it was the custom."

"Don't you want it to be?"

"I want what you want." Their thin-edged smiles seemed to cross like blades.

"I want it to be you, mother."

"Then of course, dear—"

Mrs. Drover heaved a faintly disappointed sigh. Hendrik would certainly have looked the part better. "Well, *that's* settled," she said, in the tone of one who strikes one more item off an invisible list. "And now the question is, who's to take your mother up the aisle?"

Anne and her mother were still exchanging smiles. "Why, Uncle Fred of course, isn't he?" Anne cried.

"That's the point. If your mother's cousin comes from Meridia—"

Mrs. Clephane brushed aside the possible cousin from Meridia. "Fred shall take me up," she declared; and Anne's smile lost its nervous edge.

"Now, is there anything else left to settle?" the girl gaily challenged her aunt; and Mrs. Drover groaned back: "Anything else? But it seems as if we'd only just begun. If it weren't for Nollie and Lilla I shouldn't feel sure of *anybody's* being at the church when the time comes . . ."

The time had almost come: the sun had risen on the day before the wedding. It rose, mounted up in a serene heaven, bent its golden arch over an untroubled indifferent world, and stooped westward in splendid unawareness. The day, so full of outward bustle, of bell-ringing, telephone calls, rushings back and forth of friends, satellites and servants, had drooped to its close in the unnatural emptiness of such conclusions. Everything was done; every question was settled; every last order given; and Anne, with a kiss for her mother, had gone off with Nollie and Joe Tresselton for one of the crepuscular motor-dashes that clear the cobwebs from modern brains.

Anne had resolutely refused to have either bridesmaids or the conventional family dinner of the bridal eve. She wanted to strip the occasion of all its meaningless formalities, and Chris Fenno was of the same mind. He was to spend the evening alone with his parents at their hotel, and Anne had invited no one but Fred Landers to dine. She had warned her mother that she might be a little late in getting home, and had asked her, in view of Mr. Landers's excessive punctuality, to be downstairs in time to receive and pacify him.

Mrs. Clephane had seen through the simple manœuvre, and had not resented it. After all, it would be the best opportunity to tell Fred Landers what she had decided to tell him. As she sat by the drawing-room fire listening for the door-bell she felt a curious sense of aloofness, almost of pacification. It might be only the quiet of exhaustion; she half-suspected it was, but she was too exhausted to feel sure. Yet one thing was clear to her; she had suffered less savagely since she had known that Dr. Arklow had guessed what she was suffering. The problem had been almost too difficult for him; but it was enough that he had perceived its difficulty, had seen that it was too deeply rooted in living fibres to be torn out without mortal hurt.

"Sterile pain . . . I should never want any one to be the cause of sterile pain . . ." That phrase of his helped her even now; her mind clung fast to it as she sat waiting for Landers's ring.

It came punctually, even sooner than the hour, as Anne had foreseen; and in another moment he was advancing across the room in his slow bulky way, with excuses for his early arrival.

"But I did it on purpose. I was sure Anne would be late—"

"Anne! She isn't even in—"

"I knew it! They're all a pack of vagabonds. And I hoped you'd be punctual," he continued, letting himself down into an armchair as if he were lowering a bale of goods over the side of a ship. "After all, you and I belong to the punctual generation."

She winced a little at being so definitely relegated to the rank where she belonged. Yes: he and she were nearly of an age. She remembered, in her newly-married precocity, thinking of him as a shy shambling boy, years younger than herself. Now he had the deliberate movements of the elderly, and though he shot, fished, played golf, and kept up the activities common to his age, his mind, in maturing, had grown heavier, and seemed to have communicated its prudent motions to his body. She shut her eyes for a second from the vision. Her own body still seemed so supple, free and imponderable. If it had not been for her looking-glass she would never have known she was more than twenty.

She glanced up at the clock; a quarter to eight. Very likely Anne would not be back for another half hour. How would the evening ever drag itself to an end?

They exchanged a few words about the wedding, but the topic was intolerable to Mrs. Clephane. She had managed to face the situation as a whole: to consider its details was still beyond her. Yet if she left that subject, just beyond it lay the question her companion was waiting to ask; and that alternative was intolerable too. She got up from her seat, moved aimlessly across the room, straightened a flower in a vase, put out a superfluous wall-light.

"That's enough illumination—at our age," she said, coming back to her seat.

"Oh—you!" He threw all his unspoken worship into the word. "With that hair of yours . . ."

"My hair—my hair!" Her hands went up to the rich mass as if she would have liked to tear it from her head. At that moment she hated it, as she did everything else that mocked her with the barren illusion of youth.

Fred Landers had coloured to the edge of his own thin hair; no doubt he was afraid of her resenting even this expression of admiration. His embarrassment irritated yet touched her, and raising her eyes she looked into his.

"I never knew till the other day that it's to you I owe the fact of being here," she said.

He was evidently unprepared for this, and did not know whether to be distressed or gratified. His faint blush turned to crimson.

"To me?"

"Oh, well—I'm not sorry it should be," she rejoined, her voice softening.

"But it's all nonsense. Anne was determined to get you back."

"Yes; because you told her she must. She owned up frankly. She said she wasn't sure, at first, how the plan would work; but you were. You backed me for all you were worth."

"Oh, if you mean that; of course I backed you. You see, she didn't know you; and I did."

She continued to look at him thoughtfully, almost tenderly. "Very few people have taken the trouble to care what became of me. And you hadn't seen me for nearly twenty years."

"No; but I remembered; and I knew you'd had a rotten bad start."

"Lots of women have that, and nobody bothers. But you did; you remembered and you brought me here."

She turned again, restlessly, and went and stood by the chimney-piece, resting her chin on her hand.

Landers smiled up at her, half deprecatingly. "If I did, don't be too hard on me."

"Why should I be? I've had over a year. As happiness goes, that's a lifetime."

"Don't speak as if yours were over."

"Oh, it's been good enough to be worth while!"

He sat silent for a while, meditatively considering his honest boot-tips. At length he spoke again, in a tone of sudden authority, such as came into his voice when business matters were being discussed. "You mustn't come back alone to this empty house."

She looked slowly about her. "No; I never want to see this house again."

"Where shall you go, then?"

"After tomorrow? There's a steamer sailing for the Mediterranean the next day. I think I shall just go down and get on board."

"Alone?"

She shed a sudden smile on him. "Will you come with me?"

At the question he sprang up out of his armchair with the headlong haste of a young man. The movement upset a little table at his elbow; but he let the table lie.

"By God, yes!" he shouted, reaching out to her with both hands.

She shrank back a little, not from reluctance but from a sense of paralyzing inadequacy. "It's I who am old now," she thought with a shiver.

"What—you really would come with me? The day after tomorrow?" she said.

"I'd come with you today, if there was enough of it left to get us anywhere." He stood looking at her, waiting for her to speak; then, as she remained silent, he slowly drew back a step or two. "Kate—this isn't one of your jokes?"

As she returned his look she was aware that her sight of him was becoming faintly blurred. "Perhaps it was, when I began. It isn't now." She put her hands in his.

XXVIII

In the stillness of the sleeping house she sat up with a start, plucked out of a tormented sleep. "But it can't be—it can't be—it can't be!"

She jumped out of bed, turned on the light, and stared about her. What secret warning had waked her with that cry on her lips? She could not recall having dreamed: she had only tossed and fought with some impalpable oppression. And now, as she stood there, in that hideously familiar room, the silence went on echoing with her cry. All the excuses, accommodations, mitigations, mufflings, disguisings, had dropped away from the bare fact that her lover was going to marry her daughter, and that nothing she could do would prevent it.

A few hours ago she had still counted on the blessed interval of time, the lulling possibilities of delay. She had kissed Anne goodnight very quietly, she remembered. Then it was eleven o'clock of the night before; now it was the morning of the day. A pitch-black winter morning: there would be no daylight for another three hours. No daylight—but the Day was here!

She glanced at the clock. Half-past four. The longing seized her to go and look at Anne for the last time; but the next moment she felt that hardly a sight in the world would be less bearable.

She turned back into her room, wrapped herself in her dressing-gown, and went and sat in the window.

What did Fifth Avenue look like nowadays at half-past four o'clock of a winter morning? Much as it had when she had kept the same vigil nearly twenty years earlier, on the morning of her flight with Hylton Davies. That night too she had not slept, and for the same reason: the thought of Anne. On that other day she had deserted her daughter for the first time—and now it seemed as though she were deserting her again. One betrayal of trust had led inexorably to the other.

Fifth Avenue was much more brilliantly lit than on that other far-off morning. Long streamers of radiance floated on the glittering asphalt like tropical sea-weeds on a leaden sea. But overhead the canopy of darkness was as dense, except for the tall lights hanging it here and there with a planetary glory.

The street itself was empty. In old times one would have heard the desolate nocturnal sound of a lame hoof-beat as a market-gardener's cart went by: they always brought out in the small hours the horses that were too bad to be seen by day. But all that was changed. The last lame horse had probably long since gone to the knacker's yard, and no link of sound was left between the Niagara-roar of the day and the hush before dawn.

On that other morning a hansom-cab had been waiting around the corner for young Mrs. Clephane. It had all been very well arranged—Hylton Davies had a gift for arranging. His yacht was a marvel of luxury: food, service, appointments. He was the kind of man who would lean across the table to say confidentially: "I particularly recommend that sauce." He had the soul of a club steward. It was curious to be thinking of him now . . .

She remembered that, as she jumped into the hansom on that fateful morning, she had thought to herself: "Now I shall never again hear my mother-in-law say: 'I do think, my dear, you make a mistake not to humour John's prejudices a little more.' " She had fixed her mind with intensity on the things she most detested in the life she was leaving; it struck her now that she had thought hardly at all of the life she was going to. Above all, that day, she had crammed into her head every possible thought that might crowd out the image of little Anne: John Clephane's bad temper, his pettiness about money, his obstinacy, his obtuseness, the detested sound of his latch-key when he came home, flown with self-importance, from his club. "Thank God," she remembered thinking, "there can't possibly be a latch-key on a yacht!"

Now she suddenly reminded herself that before long she would have to get used to the click of another key. Dear Fred Landers! That click would symbolize all the securities and placidities: all the thick layers of affection enfolding her from loneliness, from regret, from remorse. It comforted her already to know that, after tomorrow, there would always be some one between herself and her thoughts. In that mild warmth she would bask like one of those late bunches of grapes that have just time, before they drop, to turn from sourness to insipidity.

Now again she was at the old game of packing into her mind every thought that might crowd out the thought of Anne; but her mind was like a vast echoing vault, and the thoughts she had to put into it would not have filled the palm of her hand.

Where would she and Landers live? A few months of travel, no doubt; and then—New York. Could she picture him anywhere else? Would it be materially possible for him to give up his profession—renounce "the office"? Her mind refused to see him in any other setting. And yet—and yet . . . But no; it was useless to linger on that. Nothing, nothing that she could invent would crowd out the thought of Anne.

She sat in the window, and watched the sky turn from black to gray, and then to the blank absence of colour before daylight . . .

In the motor, on the way to St. Stephen's, the silence had become oppressive, and Kate suddenly laid her hand on her daughter's.

"My darling, I wish you all the happiness there ever was in the world—happiness beyond all imagining."

"Oh, mother, take care! Not too much! You frighten me . . ." Through the white mist of tulle Kate caught the girl's constrained smile. She had been too vehement, then? She had over-emphasized? Doubtless she would never get exactly the right note. She heard herself murmuring vaguely: "But there can't be too much, can there?" and Anne's answer: "Oh, I don't know . . ." and mercifully that brought them to the verge of the crimson carpet and the awning.

In the vestibule of the church they were received into a flutter of family. No bridesmaids; but Fred Landers and Hendrik Drover, stationed there as participants in the bridal procession, amid a cluster of Drovers and Tresseltons who had lingered for a glimpse of the bride before making their way to the front pews. A pervading lustre of pearls and tall hats; a cloud of expensive furs, a gradual vague impression of something having possibly gone wrong, and no one wishing to be the first to suggest it. Finally Joe Tresselton approached to say in Mrs. Clephane's ear: "He's not here yet—"

Anne had caught the whisper. Her mother saw her lips

whiten as they framed a laugh. "Chris late? How like him! Or is it that we're too indecently punctual—?"

Oh, the tidal rush in the mother's breast! The *Not here! Not here! Not here!* shouted down at her from every shaft and curve of the vaulting, rained down on her from the accomplice heavens! And she had called the sky indifferent! But of course he was not here—he would not be here. She had always known that she would wear him out in the end. Her case was so much stronger than his. In a flash all her torturing doubts fell away from her.

All about her, wrist-watches were being furtively consulted. Anne stood between the groups, a pillar of snow.

"Anne always *is* indecently punctual," Nollie Tresselton laughed; Uncle Hendrik mumbled something ponderous about traffic obstruction. Once or twice the sexton's black gown fluttered enquiringly out of an aisle door and back; the bridal group began to be aware of the pressure, behind them, of late arrivals checked in the doorway till the procession should have passed into the church.

Kate Clephane caught Fred Landers's eyes anxiously fixed on her; she suspected her own of shooting out rays of triumph, and bent down hurriedly to straighten a fold of Anne's train. *Not here! Not here! Not here!* the sky shouted down at her. And none of them—except perhaps Anne—knew why . . . Anne—yes; Anne's suffering would be terrible. But she was young—she was young; and some day she would know what she had been saved from . . .

The central doors were suddenly flung open; the Mendelssohn march rolled out. Mrs. Clephane started up from her stooping posture to signal to Fred Landers that the doors must be shut . . . The music stopped . . . since the bridegroom was not coming.

But the folds of Anne's train were already slipping through

her mother's fingers, Anne was in motion on Uncle Hendrik's stalwart arm. The rest of the family had drifted up to their front pews: Fred Landers, a little flushed, stood before Mrs. Clephane, his arm bent to receive her hand. The bride, softly smiling, drew aside to let her mother pass into the church before her. At the far end of the nave, on the chancel-steps, two figures had appeared against a background of lawn sleeves and lilies.

Blindly Kate Clephane moved forward, keeping step with Landers's slow stride. At the chancel-steps he left her, taking his seat with Mrs. Drover. The mother stood alone and waited for her daughter.

XXIX

The Drovers had wanted Mrs. Clephane to return to Long Island with them that afternoon; Nollie Tresselton had added her prayer; Anne herself had urged her mother to accept.

"How can I drive away thinking of you here all alone?" the girl had said; and Kate had managed to smile back: "You won't be thinking of me at all!" and had added that she wanted to rest, and have time to gather up her things before sailing.

It had been settled, in the last days before the wedding, that she was to go abroad for the winter: to Italy, perhaps, or the south of France. The young couple, after a brief dash to Florida, were off for India, by Marseilles and Suez; it seemed only reasonable that Mrs. Clephane should not care to remain in New York. And Anne knew—though no one else did—that when her mother went abroad she would not go alone. Nothing was to be said . . . not a word to any one; though by this time—an hour after bride and groom had driven away to the Palm Beach express—Chris Fenno was no doubt in the secret.

Anne had left without anxiety; she understood her mother's wish to keep her plans to herself, and respected it. And in a few days now the family would be reassembling at St. Stephen's for another, even quieter wedding.

Aline came downstairs to the long drawing-room, where Mrs. Clephane was sitting alone in a litter of fallen rose-petals, grains of rice and ends of wedding-cake ribbon. Beyond, in the dining-room, the servants were moving away the small tables, and carrying off the silver in green-lined baskets.

The housekeeper had come in to give the butler the address of the hospital to which Mrs. Fenno wished the flowers to be sent, and a footman was already removing the baskets and bouquets from the drawing-room.

"Madame will be much more comfortable upstairs than in all this untidiness; and Mr. Landers has telephoned to ask if he may see Madame in about half an hour."

Aline, of course, knew everything; news reached her by every pore, as it circulates through an Eastern bazaar. Erect in the handsome dress that Mrs. Clephane had given her for the wedding, she smiled drily but approvingly upon her mistress. It was understood that Mr. Landers was *un bon parti;* and the servants' hall knew him to be generous. So did Aline, whose gown was fastened by the diamond arrow he had offered her that morning.

"There's a nice fire in Madame's sitting-room," she added persuasively.

Kate Clephane sat motionless, without looking up. She heard what the maid was saying, and could have repeated her exact words; but they conveyed no meaning.

"Madame must come up," Aline again insisted.

The humiliation of being treated like a sick person at length roused Mrs. Clephane, and she got to her feet and followed the maid. On the way upstairs she said to her: "Presently I will tell you what I shall need on the steamer." Then she turned into the sitting-room, and Aline softly closed the door on her.

The fire was burning briskly; Anne's last bunch of violets stood on the low table near the lounge. Outside the windows the winter light was waning. Kate Clephane, sitting down on the lounge, remembered that the room had worn that same look of soothing intimacy on the day when Anne had first led her into it, little more than a year ago; and she remembered that, then, also, Fred Landers had joined her there, hurriedly summoned to reassure her loneliness. It was curious, in what neatly recurring patterns events often worked themselves out.

The door opened and he came in. He still wore his wedding clothes, and the dark morning coat and the pearl in his tie suited him, gave him a certain air of self-confidence and importance. He looked like a man who would smooth one's way, manage all the tiresome details of life admirably, without fuss or bluster. The small point of consciousness left alive in Kate Clephane registered the fact, and was dimly comforted by it. Steamer chairs, for instance, and the right table in a ventilated corner of the dining-saloon—one wouldn't have to bother about anything . . .

"I wish we could have got off tomorrow," he said, sitting down beside her, and looking at her with a smile. "I would have, you know, if you'd thought it feasible. Why shouldn't we have been married in Liverpool?"

"Or on board! Don't they provide a registry office on these modern boats?" she jested with pale lips.

"But next week—next week I shall carry you off," he continued with authority.

"Yes; next week." She tried to add a word of sympathy, of

affection; the word he was waiting for. But she could only turn her wan smile on him.

"My dear, you're dead-beat; don't you want me to go?"

She shook her head.

"No? You'd rather I stayed—you really would?" His face lit up. "You needn't pretend with me, Kate, you know."

"Needn't I? Are you sure? All my life I seem never to have done anything but pretend," she suddenly exclaimed.

"Well, you needn't now; I'm sure." He sealed it with his quiet smile, leaning toward her a little, but without moving his chair nearer. There was something infinitely reassuring in the way he took things for granted, without undue emphasis or enthusiasm.

"Lie down now; let me pull that shawl up. A cigarette—may I? I suppose there'll be tea presently? We needn't talk about plans till tomorrow."

She tried to smile back. "But what else is there to talk about?" Her eyes rested on his face, and she read in it his effort to remain the unobtrusive and undemanding friend. The sight gave her a little twinge of compunction. "I mean, there's nothing to say about me. Let's talk about you," she suggested.

The blood mounted to his temples, congesting his cheekbones and the elderly fold above his stiff collar. He made a movement as if to rise, and then settled back resolutely into his chair. "About me? There's nothing to say about me either—except in relation to you. And there there's too much! Don't get me going. Better take me for granted."

"I do; that's my comfort." She was beginning to smile on him less painfully. "All your goodness to me—"

But now he stood up, his pink deepening to purple.

"Oh, not that, please! It rather hurts; even at my age. And

I assure you I can be trusted to remind myself of it at proper intervals."

She raised herself on her elbow, looking up at him in surprise.

"I've hurt you? I didn't mean to."

"Well—goodness, you know! A man doesn't care to be eternally reminded of his goodness; not even if it's supposed to be all he has to offer—in exchange for everything."

"Oh—*everything!*" She gave a little shrug. "If ever a woman came to a man empty-handed . . ."

With a slight break in his voice he said: "You come with yourself."

The answer, and his tone, woke in her a painful sense of his intense participation in their talk and her own remoteness from it. The phrase "come with yourself" shed a lightning-flash of irony on their reciprocal attitude. What self had she left to come with? She knew he was waiting for an answer; she felt the cruelty of letting his exclamation drop as if unheard; but what more had she to say to him—unless she should say everything?

The thought shot through her for the first time. Had she really meant to marry him without his knowing? Perhaps she had; she was not sure; she felt she would never again be very sure of her own intentions. But now, through all the confusion and exhaustion of her mind, one fact had become abruptly clear: that she would have to tell him. Whether she married him or not seemed a small matter in comparison. First she must look into those honest eyes with eyes as honest.

"Myself?" she said, echoing his last word. "What do you know of that self, I wonder?"

He continued to stand before her in the same absorbed

and brooding attitude. "All I need to know is how unhappy you've been."

She leaned on her arm, still looking up at him. "Yes; I've been unhappy; horribly unhappy. Beyond anything you can imagine. Beyond anything you've ever guessed."

This did not seem to surprise him. He continued to return her gaze with the same tranquil eyes. "But I rather think I *have* guessed," he said.

Something in his voice seemed to tell her that after all she had not been alone in her struggle; it was as if he had turned a key in the most secret ward of her heart. Oh, if he had really guessed—if she were to be suddenly lifted beyond that miserable moment of avowal into a quiet heaven of understanding and compassion!

"You have guessed—you've understood?"

Yes; his face was still unperturbed, his eyes were indulgent. The tears rushed to her own; she wanted to sit down and cry her heart out. Instead, she got to her feet and went to him with outstretched hands. She must thank him; she would find the words now; she would be able to tell him what that perfect trust was to her, or at least what it would be when the present was far enough away for anything on earth to help her.

"Oh, Fred—you knew all the while? You saw I tried to the utmost, you saw I couldn't do anything to stop it?"

He had her hands in his, and was holding them against his breast. "Stop it—the marriage? Is that what's troubling you?" He was speaking now as if to a frightened disconsolate child. "Of course you couldn't stop it. I know how you must have loathed it; all you must have suffered. But Anne's happiness had to come first."

He did understand, then; did pity her! She let herself lie in his hold. The relief of avowal was too exquisite, now that all peril ˸ ᶜ explanation was over and she could just yield herself up to ...ᵢ pity. But though he held her she no longer saw him; all her attention was centred on her own torturing problem. She thought of him only as of some one kinder and more understanding than any one else, and her heart overflowed.

"But wasn't it just cowardice on my part? Wasn't it wicked of me not to dare to tell her?"

"Of course it wasn't wicked. What good would it have done? It's hard that she made the choice she did; but a girl with a will like Anne's has to take her chance. I always felt you'd end by seeing it. And you will, when you're less tired and overwrought. Only trust me to look after you," he said.

Her tears rose and began to run down. She would have liked to go on listening without having to attend to what he said. But again she felt that he was waiting for her to speak, and she tried to smile back at him. "I do trust you . . . you do help me. You can't tell the agony of the secret . . ." She hardly knew what she was saying.

"It needn't be a secret now. Doesn't that help?"

"Your knowing, and not loathing me? Oh, *that*—" She gave a faint laugh. "You're the only one of them all who's not afraid of me."

"Afraid of you?"

"Of what I might let out—if they hadn't always stopped me. That's my torture now; that I let them stop me. It always will be. I shall go over it and over it; I shall never be sure I oughtn't to have told them."

"Told *what?*"

"Why—what you know."

She looked up at him, surprised, and saw that a faint veil had fallen over the light in his eyes. His face had grown pale and she felt that he was holding her hands without knowing that he held them.

"I know you've been most unhappy . . . most cruelly treated . . ." He straightened his shoulders and looked at her. "That there've been things in the past that you regret . . . must regret . . ." He paused, as if waiting for her to speak; then, with a visible effort, went on: "In all those lonely years—when you were so friendless—I've naturally supposed you were not always . . . alone . . ."

She freed herself gently and moved away from him.

"Is that all?"

She was conscious in him of a slowly dawning surprise. "All—what else is there?"

"What else? The shame . . . the misery . . . the truth . . ."

For a moment he seemed hardly to take in the words she was flinging at him. He looked like a man who has not yet felt the pain of the wound he has received.

"I certainly don't know—of any shame," he answered slowly.

"Then you don't know anything. You don't know any more than the others." She had almost laughed out as she said it.

He seemed to be struggling with an inconceivable idea: an idea for which there were no terms in his vocabulary. His lips moved once or twice before he became articulate. "You mean: some sort of complicity—some sort of secret—between you and—and Anne's husband?"

She made a faint gesture of assent.

"Something—" he still wavered over it—"something you ought to have told Anne before . . . before she . . ." Abruptly he broke off, took a few steps away from her, and came back. "Not you—not you and that man?" She was silent.

The silence continued. He stood without moving, turned away from her. She had dropped down on the foot of the lounge, and sat gazing at the pattern of the carpet. He put his hands over his eyes. Presently, hearing him move, she looked up. He had uncovered his eyes and was staring about the room as if he had never seen it before, and could not remember what had brought him there. His face had shrunk and yellowed; he seemed years older.

As she looked at him, she marvelled at her folly in imagining even for a moment that he had read any farther into her secret than the others. She remembered his first visit after her return; remembered how she had plied him with uncomfortable questions, and detected in his kindly eyes the terror of the man who, all his life, has tried to buy off fate by optimistic evasions. Fate had caught up with him now—Kate Clephane would have given the world if it had not been through her agency. Sterile pain—it appeared that she was to inflict it after all, and on the one being who really loved her, who would really have helped her had he known how!

He moved nearer, and stood in front of her, forcing a thin smile. "You'll think me as obtuse as the rest of them," he said.

She could not find anything to answer. Her tears had stopped, and she sat dry-eyed, counting the circles in the carpet. When she had reached the fifteenth she heard him speaking again in the same stiff concise tone. "I—I was unprepared, I confess."

"Yes. I ought to have known—" She stood up, and continued in a low colourless voice, as if the words were being dictated to her: "I meant to tell you; I really did; at least I suppose I did. But I've lived so long with the idea of the thing that I wasn't surprised when you said you knew— knew everything. I thought you meant that you'd guessed. There were times when I thought everybody must have guessed—"

"Oh, God forbid!" he ejaculated.

She smiled faintly. "I don't know that it much matters. Except that I want to keep it from Anne—that I must keep it from her now. I daresay it was wicked of me not to stop the marriage at any cost; but when I tried to, and saw her agony, I couldn't. The only way would have been to tell her outright; and I couldn't do that—I couldn't! Coming back to her was like dying and going to heaven. It *was* heaven to me here till he came. Then I tried . . . I tried . . . But how can I ever make you understand? For nearly twenty years no one had thought much of me—I hadn't thought much of myself. I'd never really forgiven myself for leaving Anne. And then, when she sent for me, and I came, and we were so happy together, and she seemed so fond of me, I thought . . . I thought perhaps after all it hadn't made any difference. But as soon as the struggle began I saw I hadn't any power—any hold over her. She told me so herself: she said I was a stranger to her. She said I'd given up any claim on her, any right to influence her, when I went away and left her years ago. And so she wouldn't listen to me. That was my punishment: that I couldn't stop her."

"Oh, Anne—Anne can look out for herself. What do I care for Anne?" he exclaimed harshly. "But you—you—you—and that man!" He dropped down into his armchair and hid his eyes again.

She waited a minute or two; then she ventured: "Don't mind so much."

He made no answer. At length he lifted his head, but without looking directly at her.

"It was—long ago?"

"Yes. Six years—eight years. I don't know . . ." She heard herself pushing the date back farther and farther, but she could not help it.

"At a time when you were desperately lonely and unhappy?"

"Oh—not much more than usual." She added, after a moment: "I don't claim any extenuating circumstances."

"The cad—the blackguard! I—"

She interrupted him. "Not that either—quite. When he first met Anne he didn't know; didn't know she was even related to me. When he found out he went away; he went away twice. She made him come back. She reproached me for separating them. Nothing could have stopped her except my telling her. And I couldn't tell her when I saw how she cared."

"No—" There was a slight break in the harshness of his voice.

Again she was silent, not through the wish to avoid speaking, but from sheer inability to find anything more to say.

Suddenly he lifted his miserable eyes, and looked at her for a second. "You've been through hell," he said.

"Yes. I'm there still." She stopped, and then, drawn by the pity in his tone, once more felt herself slipping down the inevitable slope of confession. "It's not only *that* hell—there's another. I want to tell you everything now. It was not only for fear of Anne's suffering that I couldn't speak; it was because I couldn't bear the thought of what she would think of me if I did. It was so sweet being her mother—I couldn't bear to give it up. And the triumph of your all thinking she'd done right to bring me back—I couldn't give that up either, because I knew how much it counted in her feeling for me. Somehow, it turned me once more into the person I was meant to be—or thought I was meant to be. That's all. I'm glad I've told you . . . Only you mustn't let it hurt you; not for long . . ."

After she had ended he continued to sit without moving;

she had the impression that he had not heard what she had said. His attention, his receptive capacity, were still engrossed by the stark fact of her confession: her image and Chris Fenno's were slowly burning themselves into his shrinking vision. To assist at the process was like peeping into a torture-chamber, and for the moment she lost the sense of her own misery in the helpless contemplation of his. Sterile pain, if ever there was—

At last she crossed over to where he sat, and laid a touch on his shoulder.

"Fred—you mustn't let this hurt you. It has done me good to tell you . . . it has helped. Your being so sorry has helped. And now it's all over . . . it's ended . . ."

He did not change his attitude or even look up again. She still doubted if he heard her. After a minute or two she withdrew her hand and moved away. The strain had been too great; she had imposed on him more than he could bear. She saw that clearly now: she said to herself that their talk was over, that they were already leagues apart. Her sentimental experience had shown her how often two people still in the act of exchanging tender or violent words are in reality at the opposite ends of the earth, and she reflected, ironically, how much success in human affairs depends on the power to detect such displacements. She herself had no such successes to her credit; hers was at best the doubtful gift of discerning, perhaps more quickly than most people, why she failed. But to all such shades of suffering her friend was impervious: he was taking his ordeal in bulk.

She sat down and waited. Curiously enough, she was less unhappy than for a long time past. His pain and his pity were perhaps what she had most needed from him: the centre of her wretchedness seemed the point at which they were meant to meet. If only she could have put it in words simple enough to reach him—but to thank him for what he was suffering would have seemed like mockery; and she could only wait and say to herself that perhaps before long he would go.

After a while he lifted his head and slowly got to his feet. For a moment he seemed to waver; then he crossed the space between them, and stood before her. She rose too, and held out her hand; but he did not appear to notice the gesture, though his eyes were now intensely fixed on her.

"The time will come," he said, "when all this will seem very far off from both of us. That's all I want to think of now."

She looked up, not understanding. Then she began to tremble in all her body; her very lips trembled, and the lids of her dazzled eyes. He was still looking at her, and she saw the dawn of the old kindness in his. He seemed to have come out on the other side of a great darkness. But all she found to say was the denial of what she was feeling. "Oh, no—no— no—"; and she put him from her.

"No?"

"It's enough; enough; what you've just said is enough." She stammered it out incoherently. "Don't you see that I can't bear any more?"

He stood rooted there in his mild obstinate kindness. "There's got to be a great deal more, though."

"Not now—not now!" She caught his hand, and just laid it to her cheek. Then she drew back, with a sense of resolution, of finality, that must have shown itself in her face and air. "Now you're to go; you're to leave me. I'm dreadfully tired." She said it almost like a child who asks to be taken up and carried. It seemed to her that for the first time in her life she had been picked up out of the dust and weariness, and set down in a quiet place where no harm could come.

He was still looking at her, uncertainly, pleadingly. "To-morrow, then? Tomorrow morning?"

She hesitated. "Tomorrow afternoon."

"And now you'll rest?"

"Now I'll rest."

With that—their hands just clasping—she guided him gently to the door, and stood waiting till she heard his step go down the stair. Then she turned back into the room and opened the door of her bedroom.

The maid was there, preparing a becoming teagown. She had no doubt conjectured that Mr. Landers would be coming back for dinner.

"Aline! Tomorrow's steamer—it's not too late to call up the office?"

The maid stood staring, incredulous, the shimmering dress on her arm.

"The steamer—not tomorrow's steamer?"

"The steamer on which I had taken passages," Mrs. Clephane explained, hurriedly reaching for the telephone book.

Aline's look seemed to say that this was beyond all reasonable explanation.

"But those passages—Madame ordered me to give them up. Madame said we were not to sail till next week."

"Never mind. At this season there's no crowd. You must call up at once and get them back."

"Madame is not really thinking of sailing tomorrow? The boat leaves at six in the morning."

Mrs. Clephane almost laughed in her face. "I'm not thinking of doing it; I'm going to do it. Ah, here's the number—" She unhooked the receiver.

XXX

Kate Clephane was wakened by the slant of Riviera sun across her bed.

The hotel was different; it was several rungs higher on the ladder than the Minorque et l'Univers, as its name—the Petit Palais—plainly indicated. The bedroom, too, was bigger, more modern, more freshly painted; and the corner window of the tiny adjoining salon actually clipped a wedge of sea in its narrow frame.

So much was changed for the better in Mrs. Clephane's condition; in other respects, she had the feeling of having simply turned back a chapter, and begun again at the top of the same dull page.

Her maid, Aline, was obviously of the same opinion; in spite of the more commodious room, and the sitting-room with its costly inset of sea, Mrs. Clephane had not recovered her lost prestige in Aline's estimation. "What was the good of all the fuss if it was to end in *this?*" Aline's look seemed to say, every morning when she brought in the breakfast-tray. Even the fact that letters now lay on it more frequently, and that telegrams were no longer considered epoch-making, did not compensate for the general collapse of Aline's plans and ambitions. When one had had a good roof over one's head, and a good motor at one's door, what was the sense of bolting away from them at a moment's notice and coming back to second-rate hotels and rattling taxis, with all the loss of consequence implied? Aline remained icily silent when her mistress, after a few weeks at the Petit Palais, mentioned that she had written to enquire about prices at Dinard for the summer.

Kate Clephane, on the whole, took the change more philosophically. To begin with, it had been her own choice to fly as she had; and that in itself was a help—at times; and then—well, yes,—already, after the first weeks, she had begun to be aware that she was slipping back without too much discomfort into the old groove.

The first month after her arrival wouldn't yet bear thinking about; but it was well behind her now, and habit was working its usual miracle. She had been touched by the welcome her old friends and acquaintances had given her, and exquisitely relieved—after the first plunge—to find herself again among people who asked no questions about her absence, betrayed no curiosity about it, and probably felt none. They were all very much occupied with each other's doings when they were together, but the group was so continually breaking up and reshaping itself, with the addition of new elements, and the departing scattered in so many different directions, and toward destinations so unguessable, that once out of sight they seemed to have no more substance or permanence than figures twitching by on a film.

This sense of unsubstantiality had eased Kate Clephane's taut nerves, and helped her to sink back almost unaware into her old way of life. Enough was known of her own existence in the interval—a shadowy glimpse of New York opulence, an Opera box, a massive and important family, a beautiful daughter married to a War Hero—to add considerably to her standing in the group; but her Riviera friends were all pleasantly incurious as to details. In most of their lives there were episodes to be bridged over by verbal acrobatics, and they were all accustomed to taking each other's fibs at their face-value. Of Mrs. Clephane they did not even ask any: she came back handsomer, better dressed—yes, my dear, actually *sables!*—and she offered them cock-tails and Mah-Jongg in her own sitting-room (with a view of the sea thrown in). They were glad of so useful a recruit, and the distance between her social state and theirs was not wide enough to awaken acrimony or envy.

"Aline!"

The maid's door was just across the passage now; she appeared almost at once, bearing a breakfast-tray on which were several letters.

"Violets!" she announced with a smile; Aline's severity had of late been tempered by an occasional smile. But Mrs. Clephane did not turn her head; her colour did not change. These violets were not from the little lame boy whose bouquet had flushed her with mysterious hopes on the day when her daughter's cable had called her home; the boy she had set up for life (it had been her first thought after landing) because of that happy coincidence. Today's violets embodied neither hope nor mystery. She knew from whom they came, and what stage in what game they represented; and lifting them from the tray after a brief sniff, she poured out her chocolate with a steady hand. Aline, perceptibly rebuffed, but not defeated, put the flowers into a glass on her mistress's dressing-table. "There," the gesture said, "she can't help seeing them."

Mrs. Clephane leaned back against her pink-lined pillows,

and sipped her chocolate with deliberation. She had not yet opened the letters, or done more than briefly muster their superscriptions. None from her daughter: Anne, at the moment, was halfway across the Red Sea, on her way to India, and there would be no news of her for several weeks to come. None of the letters was interesting enough to be worth a glance. Mrs. Clephane went over them once or twice, as if looking for one that was missing; then she pushed them aside and took up the local newspaper.

She had got back into her old habit of lingering on every little daily act, making the most of it, spreading it out over as many minutes as possible, in the effort to cram her hours so full that there should be no time for introspection or remembrance; and she read the paper carefully, from the grandiloquent leading article on the wonders of the approaching Carnival to the column in which the doings of the local and foreign society were glowingly recorded.

"The flower of the American colony and the most distinguished French and foreign notabilities of the Riviera will meet this afternoon at the brilliant reception which Mrs. Parley Plush has organized at her magnificent Villa Mimosa in honour of the Bishop of the American Episcopal churches in Europe."

Ah—to be sure; it was today! Kate Clephane laid down the newspaper with a smile. She was recalling Mrs. Minity's wrath when it had been announced that the reception for the new Bishop was to be given by Mrs. Parley Plush—Mrs. Plush, of all people! Mrs. Minity was not an active member of the Reverend Mr. Merriman's parochial committees; her bodily inertia, and the haunting fear of what might happen if her coachman tried to turn the horses in the narrow street in which the Rectory stood, debarred her from such participation; but she was nevertheless a pillar of the church, by

reason of a small but regular donation to its fund and a large
and equally regular commentary on its affairs. Mr. Merriman
gave her opinions almost the importance she thought they
deserved; and a dozen times in the season Mrs. Merriman
was expected to bear the brunt of her criticisms, and persuade her not to give up her pew and stop her subscription.
"That woman," Mrs. Minity would cry, "whom I have taken
regularly for a drive once a fortnight all winter, and supplied
with brandy-peaches when I had to go without myself!"

Mrs. Minity, on the occasion of the last drive, had not
failed to tell Mrs. Merriman what she thought of the idea—
put forward, of course, by Mrs. Plush herself—of that lady's
being chosen to entertain the new Bishop on his first tour of
his diocese. The scandal was bad enough: did Mrs.
Merriman want Mrs. Minity to tell her what the woman had
been, what her reputation was? No; Mrs. Merriman would
rather not. She probably knew well enough herself, if she had
chosen to admit it . . . but for Mrs. Minity the real bitterness
of the situation lay in the fact that she herself could not
eclipse Mrs. Plush by giving the reception because she lived
in a small flat instead of a large—a vulgarly large—villa.

"No; don't try to explain it away, my dear" (this to Kate
Clephane, the day after Mrs. Merriman had been taken on
the latest of her penitential drives); "don't try to put me off
with that Rectory humbug. Everybody at home knows that
Mrs. Parley Plush came from Anaconda, Georgia, and everybody in Anaconda knows *what* she came from. And now,
because she has a big showy villa (at least, so they tell me—
for naturally I've never set foot in it, and never shall); now
that she's been whitewashed by those poor simple-minded
Merrimans, who have lived in this place for twenty years as if
it were a Quaker colony, the woman dares to put herself
forward as the proper person—Mrs. Parley Plush *proper!*—to

welcome our new Bishop in the name of the American Colony! Well," said Mrs. Minity in the voice of Cassandra, "if the Bishop knew a quarter of what I do about her—and what I daresay it is my duty, as a member of this diocese, to tell him . . . But there: what am I to do, my dear, with a doctor who *absolutely forbids* all agitating discussions, and warns me that if anybody should say anything disagreeable to me I might be snuffed out on the spot?"

Kate Clephane had smiled; these little rivalries were beginning to amuse her again. And the amusement of seeing Mrs. Minity appear (as of course she would) at Mrs. Plush's that afternoon made it seem almost worth while to go there. Mrs. Clephane reached out for her engagement-book, scrutinized the day's page, and found—with another smile, this one at herself—that she had already noted down: "Plush". Yes; it was true; she knew it herself: she still had to go on cramming things into her days, things good, bad or indifferent, it hardly mattered which as long as they were crammed tight enough to leave no chinks for backward glances. Her old training in the art of taking things easily—all the narcotic tricks of evasion and ignoring—had come gradually to her help in the struggle to remake her life. Of course she would go to Mrs. Plush's . . . just as surely as Mrs. Minity would.

The day was glorious; exactly the kind of day, all the ladies said, on which one would want the dear Bishop to have his first sight of his new diocese. The whole strength of the Anglo-American colony was assembled on Mrs. Plush's flowery terraces, among the beds of cineraria and cyclamen, and the giant blue china frogs which, as Mrs. Plush said, made the garden look "more natural". Mrs. Plush herself sailed majestically from group to group, keeping one eye on the loggia through which the Bishop and Mr. Merriman were to arrive.

"Ah, dear Lord Charles—this is kind! You'll find *all* your friends here. Yes, Mrs. Clephane is over there at the other end of the terrace," Mrs. Plush beamed, waving a tall disenchanted-looking man in the direction of a palm-tree emerging from a cushion of pansies.

Mrs. Clephane, from under the palm, had seen the manœuvre, and smiled at that also. She knew she was Lord Charles's pretext for coming to the reception, but she knew, also, that he was glad to have a pretext, because if he hadn't come he wouldn't have known any more than she did what to do with the afternoon. There was nothing, she sometimes felt, that she didn't know about Lord Charles, though they had met only three months ago. He was so exactly what medical men call "a typical case," and she had had such unlimited time and opportunity for the study of his particular type. The only difference was that he was a gentleman—a gentleman still; while the others, most of them, never had been, or else had long since abdicated that with the rest.

As he moved over the sunlit gravel in her direction she asked herself for the hundredth time what she meant to do about it. Marry him? God forbid! Even if she had been sure—and in her heart of hearts she wasn't—that he intended to give her the chance. Fall in love with him? That too she shrugged away. Let him make love to her? Well a little . . . perhaps . . . when one was too lonely . . . and because he was the only man at all "possible" in their set . . . But what she most wanted of him was simply to fill certain empty hours; to know that when she came home at five he would be waiting there, half the days of the week, by her tea-table; that when she dined out, people would be sure to invite him and put him next to her; that when there was no bridge or Mah-Jongg going he would always be ready for a tour of the antiquity shops, and so sharp at picking up bargains for the little flat she had in view.

That was all she wanted of him; perhaps all he wanted of her. But the possibility of his wanting more (at which the violets seemed to hint) produced an uncertainty not wholly disagreeable, especially when he and she met in company, and she guessed the other women's envy. "One has to have something to help one out—" It was the old argument of the drug-takers: well, call Lord Charles her drug! Why not, when she was so visibly his?

She settled herself in a garden-chair and watched his approach. It was a skilful bit of manœuvring: she knew he intended to "eliminate the bores" and join her only when there was no danger of their being disturbed. She could imagine how, in old days, he would have stalked contemptuously through such a company, without a glance to right or left. But not now. He had reached a phase in his decline when it became prudent to pause and admire the view at Mrs. Plush's side, exchange affabilities with the Consul's wife, nod familiarly to Mr. Paly, and even suffer himself to be boisterously hailed by Mrs. Horace Betterly, who came clinking down the loggia steps to shout out a reminder that they counted on him for dinner that evening. It was the fate of those who had to stuff their days full, and could no longer be particular about the quality of the stuffing. Kate could almost see the time when Lord Charles, very lean and wizened, would be collecting china frogs for Mrs. Plush.

He was half-way across the terrace when a sudden expanding and agitating of Mrs. Plush's plumes seemed to forerun the approach of the Bishop. An impressive black figure appeared under the central arch of the loggia. Mrs. Plush surged forward, every fold of her draperies swelling: but the new arrival was not the Bishop—it was only Mrs. Minity who, clothed in black cashmere and majesty, paused and looked about her.

Mrs. Plush, checked in her forward plunge, stood an instant rigid, almost tilted backward; her right hand sketched the gesture of two barely extended fingers; then her just resentment of Mrs. Minity's strictures was swept away in the triumph of having her there at last, and Mrs. Plush swept on full sail, welcoming her unexpected guest as obsequiously as if Mrs. Minity had been the Bishop.

Kate Clephane looked on with lazy amusement. She could enjoy the humours of her little world now that her mind was more at leisure. She hoped the scene between Mrs. Plush and Mrs. Minity would prolong itself, and was getting up to move within ear-shot when the Bishop, supported by Mr. and Mrs. Merriman, at length appeared.

Mrs. Clephane stopped short half-way across the terrace. She had never dreamed of this—never once thought it possible. Yet now she remembered that Dr. Arklow had been spoken of at the Drovers' as one of the candidates for this new diocese; and there he stood, on the steps just above her, benignant and impressive as when she had last seen him, at St. Stephen's, placing Anne's hand in Chris Fenno's . . .

Mrs. Clephane's first impulse was to turn and lose herself in the crowd. The sight of that figure brought with it too many banished scenes and obliterated memories. Back they all rushed on her, fiercely importunate; she felt their cruel fingers at her throat. For a moment she stood irresolute, detached in the middle of the terrace; then, just as she was turning, she heard Mrs. Plush's trumpet-call: "Mrs. Clephane? Yes, of course; there she is! Dear Mrs. Clephane, the Bishop has spied you out already!"

269

He seemed to reach her in a stride, so completely did his approach span distances and wipe out time. She saw herself sitting again in a deep leather armchair, under the photogravure of Salisbury Cathedral, while he paced the worn rug before the hearth, and his preacher's voice broke on the words: "Sterile pain . . ."

"Shall we walk a little way? The garden seems very beautiful," the Bishop suggested.

They stood by a white balustrade under mimosa boughs, and exchanged futilities about the blueness of the sea and the heat of the sun. "A New York February . . . brr . . ." "Yes, don't you envy us? Day after day of this . . . Oh, of course a puff of *mistral* now and then . . . but then that's healthy . . . and the flowers!"

He laid his large hand deliberately on hers. "My dear—when are you coming home to New York?" She felt her face just brushed by the understanding look she had caught twice before in his eyes.

"To New York? Never."

He waited as if to weigh the answer, and then turned his eyes on the Mediterranean.

"Never is a long word. There is some one there who would be very happy if you did."

She answered precipitately: "It would never have been what he imagines . . ."

"Isn't he the best judge of that? He thinks you ought to have given him the chance."

She dropped her voice to say: "I wonder he can ask me to think of ever living in New York again."

"He doesn't ask it of you; I'm charged to say so. He understands fully . . . He would be prepared to begin his life again anywhere . . . It lies with you . . ."

There was a silence. At length she mastered her voice

enough to say: "Yes; I know. I'm very grateful. It's a comfort to me . . ."

"No more?"

She waited again, and then, lifting her eyes, caught once more the understanding look in his.

"I don't know how to tell you—how to explain. It seems to me . . . my refusing . . ." she lowered her voice still more . . . "the one thing that keeps me from being too hopeless, too unhappy."

She saw the first tinge of perplexity in his gaze. "The fact of refusing?"

"The fact of refusing."

Ah, it was useless; he would never understand! How could she have imagined that he would?

"But is this really your last word; the very last?" he questioned mildly.

"Oh, it has to be—it has to be. It's what I live by," she almost sobbed.

No; he would never understand. His face had once more become blank and benedictory. He pressed her hand, said: "My dear child, I must see you again—we must talk of this!" and passed on, urbane and unperceiving.

Her eyes filled; for a moment her loneliness came down on her like a pall. It was always so whenever she tried to explain, not only to others but even to herself. Yet deep down in her, deeper far than her poor understanding could reach, there was something that said "No" whenever that particular temptation stirred in her. Something that told her that, as Fred Landers's pity had been the most precious thing he had to give her, so her refusal to accept it, her precipitate flight from it, was the most precious thing she could give him in return. He had overcome his strongest feelings, his most deep-rooted repugnance; he had held out his hand to her, in the extremity of her need, across the whole width of his traditions and his convictions; and she had blessed him for it, and stood fast on her own side. And this afternoon, when she returned home and found his weekly letter—as she was sure she would, since it had not come with that morning's post— she would bless him again, bless him both for writing the letter, and for giving her the strength to hold out against its pleadings.

Perhaps no one else would ever understand; assuredly he would never understand himself. But there it was. Nothing on earth would ever again help her—help to blot out the old horrors and the new loneliness—as much as the fact of being able to take her stand on that resolve, of being able to say to herself, whenever she began to drift toward new uncertainties and fresh concessions, that once at least she had stood fast, shutting away in a little space of peace and light the best thing that had ever happened to her.